THE TEMPLE

THE TEMPLE

by

Tom Grundner

Fireship Press
www.FireshipPress.com

The Temple - Copyright © 2009 by Tom Grundner

ISBN-13: 978-1-934757-79-6
ISBN-10: 1-934757-79-9

BISAC Subject Heading:
FIC014000   FICTION / Historical
FIC032000   FICTION / War & Military

Address all correspondence to:
Fireship Press, LLC
P.O. Box 68412
Tucson, AZ 85737

Or visit our website at:
www.FireshipPress.com

1.0

To my cousin Bill Parish
(the REAL William Parish),
and the entire Lecznar clan.

CHAPTER ONE

Sidney Smith bent over and half-heartedly poked at the logs in the fireplace. A brief shower of sparks flew upward and a wave of comforting heat blossomed outward to take a bit of the winter chill out of the room. For a brief moment, the smell of burning pine overcame the musty odor of damp stone walls. But it was all too brief. After a few seconds the chill returned along with the cloying, stale, moldy, odor of a prison.

But the worst part, he thought, wasn't the cold or the odors; it was the doors. There was a door to get onto the prison property, a door to get into the prison itself, a door to get up the staircase, a door to get into his room, an oak door here, a steel door there. And every one of them... locked!

He stared into the diminishing fire for a moment. No matter how comfortable his surroundings might be, Sidney had learned there is something endlessly unnerving about a door—any door— that you *can't* go through. It touches something deep in your being, something fundamental—an urge, perhaps even an instinct—to be free.

He gave an audible sigh, placed the poker back in its holder, and walked around the large table that dominated the center of the room. Against the opposite wall was a small rosewood desk where he sat down and started reading the letter he had begun several days earlier.

Tom Grundner

At the Temple Tower
Paris, 4 February 1798

My dear Mother, I hope the French gazettes, copied into the English papers, will have kept you abreast of my captivity, and consequently relieved your mind from the anxiety you must be under, lest you learn that something worse has befallen me. I am well in health, and all the better for having nothing to do or to worry about all day. The only pain I experience is the knowledge of what those must suffer who interest themselves in my fate. Hopefully, some of these fears will be diminished by the indulgence that is granted me of writing these letters. It will be no small consolation for you to know that humanity is as much the characteristic of the present rulers in France, as cruelty was that of those they have supplanted.

Robespierre's system ended with him, and it is no longer a crime to be kind to the unfortunate. Urbanity of manners is by no means extinguished in Paris. This we daily experience, as far as our confined situation allows.

At this point, Smith had stopped writing to tend the fire. He was uneasy because he had just written his mother a lie and, as a result, he felt the need to walk around a bit. Oh, it was pretty much true up until a few weeks ago. His jailers both at the Abbaye Prison and later here at the Temple were decent enough in their treatment of him. He was a gentleman; they were gentlemen; and that was all that was needed for the rules of civility to be applied.

But a few weeks ago all that changed, and he didn't know why. Previously he had been allowed all the indulgences that could be offered under inherently restrictive circumstances. He was allowed unlimited visitors, and unlimited writing and reading materials, including newspapers. His servant, John Bromley, was allowed to go out to the Marché des Enfants Rouges—a small open-air market across the street—to buy fresh vegetables, fruits and meats. Even Sir Sidney was allowed out on occasion, as long as he gave his parole—his word of honor—that he would not try to escape. All that was needed was his word that he would come back, and they knew he would do so.

But suddenly, it ended. There was a tension in the air that wasn't there before. He could see it in worry lines on the faces of

2

the prison workers and in the abrupt way in which the guards now spoke to him. He could no longer borrow books from the prison superintendent. No more newspapers. No more visitors except the prison physician once a week. And most demeaning of all, his letters—both outgoing and incoming—were being opened and read.

Something had happened, but he had no idea what. A shiver of fear crept into the edge of his consciousness. As unbelievable as it might sound, for the past two years, he had been coordinating the *Agence de Paris*—Britain's primary spy ring in France—from his cell. The irony of that fact was not lost on Sidney. The reason he was not being treated as a routine prisoner of war was because, when they captured him, they said he was a spy—which he wasn't. So they locked him up in the Temple Prison where they assumed he could never be involved in espionage—which he was.

It wouldn't do to dwell on what would happen to him if his role were discovered, so he picked up his quill to continue his letter. Maybe in reassuring his mother, he could somehow reassure himself.

Indeed, I realize now how remiss I have been all these months in not adequately describing to you my surroundings. I earnestly hope you will recognize the caliber of my accommodations and circumstances, and that this will put your mind even more at rest.

You know, of course, that I am being held in Paris in a prison they call "The Temple." That is an odd name, I know, but it is because it is located at a fortress that was built by the Knights Templar in the 12th century. It seems the "Temple" name carried over when, in a later day, it was converted into a prison. But, as you shall see, it is not just any sort of prison. Indeed, I am almost honored that they have chosen to put me here.

One enters the grounds through an ornamented gate that must have once been a lovely affair. This opens up on to a courtyard, which leads to what was once the mansion of the Grand Prior of the Knights Templar. Passing through the rather run-down old mansion, you travel along a similarly run-down brick pathway to where the actual prison begins.

A high wall surrounds the grounds, and entrance can only be gained through one of two large stone guard-houses. Once through the walls, however, your vision is immediately drawn to the massive structure that dominates the center of the yard.

To visualize this structure, imagine a large, square, stone building rising five stories high. On each corner place a circular tower that runs the full height of the building, plus an additional story, with a conical red tile roof on top. This is the Grosse Tour, the main part of the prison. Attached to one wall of the Grosse Tour is a smaller rectangular stone structure, called the Petite Tour, which only goes up to the third floor. It also has circular towers on it's two outward corners; and serves as a kind of porch for the first three floors.

When I said that I was almost honored to be put in this place, I do not speak in jest. Those who have gone before in these accommodations include the entire royal family—King Louis XVI, Marie Antoinette, Madame Élisabeth, and Princess Marie-Thérèse. It is true that this was the last abode of all except Princess Marie-Thérèse, but I confidently expect no similar fate to befall me. It is said that the child Louis XVII—the dauphin—also died here about a year before my arrival.

At this point, Sidney put down his pen and reflected on one of the stranger episodes of his imprisonment. He was walking in the prison yard one day when he came upon a gardener working in one of the prison's many vegetable patches. Seeking someone new with whom to speak, he engaged him in conversation. Sidney had spoken French fluently since he was a child and had no trouble asking the old man about the weather, the prospects for the garden, how long he been working here, and so forth.

At one point he asked him if he had been here when the royal family was in "residence," and if he had ever seen them. He said he had, which pushed the conversation in a new direction. That's when things got strange.

At one point Sir Sidney said, "Is it not a tragedy that the king's son, the dauphin, should die here also?"

The man said, "Do you think so, monsieur?"

"Do I think it was a tragedy? Of course I do. He was only... what? Ten years old?"

"No, monsieur. Do you really think he died here?"

Smith was not quite sure how to reply to this unexpected question. "Well, that's what I've been told. Do you *not* think so?"

But the man would say no more. He just turned away and continued working—the conversation at an end.

What made things even more unusual was that from time to time he would have similar conversations with other prison workers. Whenever he brought up the death of the dauphin, he almost always got the same type of response. It got to the point where, if he got anything other than an enigmatic reply, he could be sure the person was a relatively new hire.

Sidney picked up his pen and continued.

In fact, you might be pleased to know that I am occupying the very same apartments as did Louis XVI, so perhaps I should describe those next.

I am on the third floor of the prison. Access is gained by coming up a stone spiral staircase in one of the corner towers. Upon reaching the third floor you go through a solid oak door, down a short hallway and through a sold steel door into an antechamber. This is rather a plain room with a tiny decorative table against one wall, a small stove for keeping food warm, a writing table, and five crimson velvet chairs. In a rather ironic touch, above the writing desk is a framed copy of the Statement of Human Rights.

From this room there are three doorways. One leads to a small informal dining room with a mahogany table about four feet long and two feet wide, with a china cabinet, a serving table, and of course chairs. The other door leads to a bedroom, which is where my servant John Bromley slept before he was exchanged and sent back to England. I dare say, never has a servant lived in better surroundings. This includes a four-poster bed, with a canopy embroidered with a colorful green, red, and yellow oriental pattern, and a bed consisting of a horsehair base, two mattresses, a bolster, a feather mattress, and two wool covers.

The third door leads to my room. The centerpiece is a beautiful large oak table, with a top covered in green Moroccan leather. My bed is also a four-poster, but much larger than Bromley's. It has four white columns with a canopy of green Damascus. The bed has a base, three mattresses covered in white fustian cloth, and a bolster of white taffeta with several feather pillows. Along one wall is a mahogany chest of drawers with a white marble top.

Along another is a rosewood secretary with four drawers and ample room for writing. And dominating the fourth wall is a fireplace with a long mantle carved from a single piece of white marble. On it there is a charming clock that I must tell you about. It sits in a gold framework on a gray marble base. On the hour a figurine that looks astonishingly like Louis-François Dutertre rides forth and circles the base as the hours are chiming. I suspect this clock was placed there to torment Louis XVI, as Dutertre was once Minister of Justice—until he was guillotined for "conspiracy against the constitution."

In the corner is the entrance to a room in one of the circular towers. I call it my "chapel," which it apparently was back when the King lived here; but I have converted it into a very comfortable reading room. It has a small stove to keep the chill at bay, a cane chair with a horsehair cushion, a footstool, and even drapes on the windows.

To finish off my main room, there is a bergére upholstered in green damascus silk, two armchairs, also in green damascus, two small straw footstools, several silver candelabra, and not one, but two, gold barometers.

Make no mistake, my ma-ma, I am indeed in prison; but it is a prison that is literally fit for a king.

As relatively comfortable as my surroundings may be, I must tell you that were it not for John Bromley, and my fellow captive John Wesley Wright, I think I should have gone mad long ago.

Bromley served me well and I miss him very much. He was given the opportunity of release in a prisoner exchange and, despite his protests, I ordered him to go. His last words to me were that he would visit you as soon as he got back to England to give you a full report of my circumstances. I don't know if he has done so yet; but if he should turn up, I beg you to treat him with the utmost consideration. In addition to being my body-servant these many years, he has also been a true friend.

Sidney paused for a moment and smiled. Actually, the devoted Bromley's last words were: "Smith, when I get back to England I'll find a way to get your carcass out of here." Indeed, John Bromley's name wasn't John Bromley at all. It was Jacques-Jean-Marie-François Boudin, otherwise known as the Comte de Tromelin. He was a resistance fighter, operating under General Louis de Frotté with the *Armée Catholique et Royale*, otherwise known as the Chouans. He was serving with Sidney Smith as a liaison officer to the various resistance groups along the coast of France when they were both captured. If his true identity had become known, it would have meant instant death. So it was agreed he would adopt the name "John Bromley" and pose as Smith's servant. It was a role he would maintain for over a year.

But the man who has truly maintained my sanity has been Midshipman Wright. He is a person of high intelligence and excellent breeding; and our many hours of conversation have been a delight. Why the French have chosen to maintain him here with me, instead of moving him to Verdun with the other captured British officers, is beyond me.

It wasn't beyond Smith at all. Of the group, the only true professional spy was John Wesley Wright. Fortunately, the French didn't know that. But they might have suspected that something wasn't quite right about a midshipman who was 26 years old, and they probably retained him on those grounds alone. What they didn't know was that he was one of the brightest lights in the master spy, William Wickham's, stable of talent.

He was originally from a family of proud Romney Marsh smugglers. He served briefly as an army ensign, transferred to the navy where he took part in the Siege of Gibraltar, then left the navy to return to school. While working for a London shipping company he met William Wickham, who recruited him into what would later become known as the British Secret Service. He was of average height, average weight, and, in every other respect, of average appearance. In short, he was just what you wanted a spy to be—someone who could instantly blend into any crowd. What wasn't average about him, however, was the fierce intelligence that blazed behind his penetrating black eyes. He was quiet, soft-spoken, self-effacing and infallibly polite; but he was also a person you definitely did *not* want to cross.

So, as you can see, I am doing as well as could possibly be expected under the circumstances. Indeed, I should say that I am being treated rather better than I probably have any right to expect. Nevertheless, I yearn for the time when I can again walk freely on the soil of my native land, and take comfort within the bosom of my loving family.

Please express my love to father, and to my faithful brothers,

Believe me, my dear mother, I am
Your affectionate and dutiful son,
W. SIDNEY SMITH

Mrs. Smith, Catherine Place, Bath.

P. S. Oct. 12. A delay in the departure of my letter enables me to add, that I have experienced some further relaxation of the strictness of my confinement. Wood fires make the air of Paris clear and good: and white bread has been granted me today.

Smith leaned back in his chair and dusted the pages with black sand to dry the ink. After pouring the excess back into the cherrywood sander, he folded up the pages into an envelope and was about to retire to "the chapel" for some reading. He had no sooner stood up when he heard the sound of a struggle coming from the circular staircase, followed by a series of exclamations in the worst French he had ever heard.

"Trouver votre la poignée de main tourné myself, vous fripouille! [Literally: Find your handshake off me, you knave!]

"Vous appelez cet imbécile un chef? Je vous dis qu'il est un assassin. Il était sur le point de servir des pommes de terre de Monsieur Sidney avec les peaux dessus ! Pouvez-vous imaginer cela? [You call that imbecile a chef? I say to you that he is an assassin. He was on the point of serving potatoes to Sir Sidney with skins on! Can you imagine it?]

"Alors il bat le rumsteak comme des femmes de ménage nettoyant une couverture, met en assez d'ail pour obstruer un Turc, et pense que vous pouvez faire un prune-pudding dans une heure. [Then he beats the rump steak like a cleaning women dusting a rug, puts in enough garlic to obstruct a Turk, and thinks that you can make a plum-pudding fruit sponge in one hour.]

"Je vous ai dit que... obtenez vos mains outre de moi!" [I said to you... that acquire your hands besides from me!]

At this point the door to the antechamber burst open and Lucas Walker was brought in struggling. A prison guard firmly held each of his arms and bringing up the rear was the prison superintendent, Citizen Mutius Lasne.

Once through the narrow doorway, Lasne pushed to the front.

"Pardon the interruption, Sir Sidney," he began in passably good English. "But it seems a little while ago this man snuck into our kitchens posing as a delivery man. Then, for some reason, when he saw the chef preparing your dinner, he went *aliéné*... er... insane. He claims to know you."

Smith looked from Lasne to Walker and back, not sure what was happening or what to say. He, of course, knew Lucas Walker. He, along with Susan Whitney, had been Smith's two closest friends ever since he was a was first lieutenant aboard the old *Richmond*. Together they survived the Battle of the Capes, the Battle of the Saints, the burning of Toulon, and a dozen other adventures.

But, Walker didn't suddenly materialize in a Parisian prison cell because he happened to be in the neighborhood. The question was: how to play this situation. Fortunately Walker intervened to give Smith time to think.

"Of course he knows me, you bumpkin. I told you I've been his personal chef since he took command of the *Diamond*; and I demand to be allowed to resume that role."

"You will keep a civil tongue in your head, Monsieur Walker, and demand nothing!" Lasne snapped. "One more outburst and you will find yourself in a cell—and, trust me, it won't be anything like this one."

"He is who he says he is," came a voice from the other end of the room. The group swiveled around and there was John Wesley Wright leaning against the wall. He had heard the noise, come from his room on the Petite Tour porch, and had taken in the situation and it's implications at a glance.

"Hello, Walker," he continued smoothly, nodding at Lucas as he walked over to the group. "He was most recently Captain Smith's personal chef. Before that... before Bromley took over the job... he was Sir Sidney's servant; and before that he was my valet."

Lasne looked to Sir Sidney. "Is that so, Captain?"

Smith thought quickly. "Indeed, I have known Lucas Walker for many years," he replied without lying.

Lasne looked from Smith, to Walker, to Wright, and finally shrugged his shoulders and sighed. "I have never heard of anyone trying to break *in* to the Temple; but then again, all you *Anglais* are mad as hens anyway.

"In that you have lost your previous man, Monsieur Walker may stay as your servant and chef. But I want no trouble from him, Captain. I will hold you personally responsible for his conduct. And you, Citizen Walker, will apologize to our prison chef the very next time you see him, *and* you will pay for the damages."

"But he threw that pan at *me!*"

"Ah... I will personally guarantee payment for any and all damages," Sidney said. Then under his breath to Walker, "whatever that might mean.

"But thank you for your generosity, Citizen Lasne. I have truly missed the services of Monsieur Bromley and I am sure Walker will fill in nicely."

Lasne finally decided that the glass of Madera he had been drinking before he was so rudely interrupted was more important than the present company. Shaking his head and muttering something about the sanity of Englishmen, he and the guards departed down the staircase, locking the door behind them.

"Walker, it's good to see you. There is much for you to do here." Smith continued the charade in case there was anyone listening at the door. "Let's start with my room and I'll show you your duties."

As soon as they were safe from eavesdropping, Smith turned to Walker. "Lucas, what in God's name are you doing here?"

"Well, Susan and I were doing a little vacationing in Paris and thought we'd stop in."

"Susan? Where is she?"

Walker went over to a barred window that faced the Rue de la Corderie, took a white kerchief from around his neck and briefly waived it out the window. A few moments later Susan Whitney appeared on the top floor balcony of a house across the street and, beaming, waved back. If that were not astonishing enough to Smith, the house was an *Agence de Paris* safe house and the one he had been using as a communications relay station ever since he had been transferred to the Temple.

"I think an explanation is in order," Smith said quietly.

The three sat down at the large leather-covered table. Wright filled brandy snifters for Smith and himself, and poured Walker a cup of water cut with a bit of wine—just enough to give the water a

10

little flavor. Walker was a former alcoholic and would take nothing stronger.

"I must apologize for not having your customary lemonade drink at hand," Wright said as he sat down, "but as Sidney pointed out, your arrival was a bit unexpected. I too would like to know why you're here."

Walker took a sip of his drink and began. "Let me start by getting you caught up on things since your transfer here.

"When last I saw you I was being taken back to La Havre and you were being packed off to... well, at the time I didn't know where. About a week later, I was exchanged and learned, via the French newspapers no less, that the dangerous incendiary Sidney Smith was being held in the Temple.

"That began one very crazy period. I was in London with Susan, so the first thing I had to do was to talk her out of single-handedly storming the Board of Admiralty, St. James Palace, and if necessary, the Directorate in Paris to get you released. I told her about our meeting in the woods with William Wickham and your new role as the coordinator of the Paris *Agence*."

"You did what?!" Wright interjected.

"I know, I wasn't supposed to; but believe me, there was a need for her to know. Using some of her unofficial back-channels she had already made a proposal to the French to make the exchange." Walker shook his head in resignation. "You don't know that woman like I do John."

"What happened to the exchange?" asked Sidney.

"Well, officially the admiralty tried to exchange you for a Captain Jacques Bergeret. In fact, he even made it as far as French soil when he had to turn around and go back because the French scuttled the deal. I think the admiralty knew that would happen or they wouldn't have allowed the negotiations to take place.

"Then Susan made her attempt, but that failed because the French wanted too much in exchange."

"What did they want?" Sidney asked.

"Twelve thousand French prisoners!"

"What?" Wright and Smith exclaimed simultaneously.

"That's right. Twelve thousand prime seamen for one British sea captain—and a junior one at that. I can tell you a lot of people were mighty impressed at your perceived value."

"Anyway, fortunately, all that fell through; and, ever since, the Admiralty has been very pleased with your productivity here in Paris."

"But that still doesn't explain why you're now here," observed Wright.

"I am getting to that."

"Everything changed on September 4th of last year... well, no... actually it was more like last May."

"Lucas, will you get to the point?"

"All right. All right. Last May there was an election in France. To the horror of the Directory the revolutionaries were voted out in the majority of the councils and more moderate, some even openly royalist, deputies were voted in. Pichegru became President of the Five Hundred; a Royalist, Barthélémy, was elected to be one of the five Directors; and a conservative, Carnot, was re-elected.

"This became too much for the Directory. What they had hoped and assumed was that the elections would cement the gains of the revolution. What they got was a legislative body that was more moderate and conservative then they ever dreamed. So, they decided to annul the election, but they didn't know how. The answer was handed to them on a silver platter.

"The royalists began attacking one of the better French generals, someone named Bonaparte..."

"Yes, I remember him from Toulon," said Sidney. "Napoleon Bonaparte. Only he was a colonel than, as I recall."

"I remember him also," replied Walker. "I watched him open fire on a crowd of defenseless civilians with grapeshot-loaded cannons. Then, as if that weren't enough, he had those who had dropped to the ground for safety stand up—and fired again.

"In any event, the royalists began attacking Bonaparte for his open looting of Italy, for overstepping his authority in dealing with the Austrians, and a host of other things. So, the Directory asked for his help in quashing the elections, which they called a royalist plot to overthrow the "republican institutions." Bonaparte was only too glad to oblige.

"Bonaparte sent one of his generals, Augereau I believe, to Paris to implement a *coup d'état* of Bonaparte's design. Elections in forty-nine departments were annulled, the councils were purged, and Augereau's troops arrested conservative deputies all over Paris. The lucky ones were thrown into prison. Those less fortunate, which included Barthélemy, Pichegru, Barbé-Marbois and

Ladebat were deported to that hell-hole the French operate in Cayenne.

"So, the Jacobins are back in charge of the government again," observed Wright.

"Yes and no. The revolutionaries now control the Directory, but Bonaparte controls the revolutionaries. There is no way that they can stay in power without his on-going military support. They know it; and, more importantly, he knows it."

"Then that explains why things have been so tense around here these past few months," Sidney said.

"Precisely. Everyone in France is holding their breath waiting for the Reign of Terror to start again. But it has also created problems for us."

"In what way?"

Before Walker could answer, Wright interrupted. "If Augereau swept up all those royalists and conservatives, he must have gotten a good many—maybe even most—of the people we depend on for information." Wright paused for a moment, lost in thought. Then it all became clear to him.

"Sidney, you're in trouble."

"What? How?"

"If those intelligence sources are now languishing in prison, it's only a matter of time before one or more of them decide to see if what they know about our intelligence network might get them freed. It will be a gamble on their part. They might win their freedom, or they might be immediately transported to the guillotine. There's no way of knowing which way it will go, and that will give them pause for a while. But only for a while.

"Sooner or later someone is going to try it. If he's successful, it will lead the authorities to others, which will lead to others, and eventually back to you."

"Exactly." Walker resumed. "And that's why I am here. An escape is being planned for you, and I am here to facilitate it. Even as we speak, someone by the name of Etches is trying to arrange it; or at least he was given £1200 last month to get things going."

"Who is Etches?"

"I have no idea; but it's supposed to be Etches and someone named Viscovitch who are making the arrangements."

"I know Etches and I know of Viscovitch." All eyes turned to Wright.

"Etches is Richard Cadman Etches, alias Andrew Smith, alias Richard Ellis, and God knows how many other aliases. He's had so many; even he probably doesn't know his real name any more. He is a Dane by birth and learned his craft as an international agent in the court of Empress Catherine of Russia. In fact, he was Catherine's Commissioner of Marine when you were fighting for the Swedes against the Russians a few years ago.

"Anyway, he eventually found his way to London where he wrote First Lord Spencer and offered to spy for him."

"Doing what?"

"Actually, he's been quite effective. It seems he is an accredited purchaser of prize vessels. That, along with his neutral Danish citizenship, allows him to visit any French seaport, anytime he wants. And with every visit, he never fails to come back with useful intelligence. In addition, because of his ability to throw money around, he has many friends in the French Ministry of Marine. That has proved useful on more than one occasion."

"What about Viscovitch?"

"That one I know less about. His name is Count Antoine Viscovitch; but he's not a French count. He's either a Dalmatian or a Pole; I forget which. Anyway, near as I can tell, his primary job is to collect bribes to line the pockets of one of the five Directors—Paul Barras. I had heard he was working for us from time to time, but I've never met him personally.

"That only leaves me with three questions," said Sidney. Turning to Walker, "The first is: why you?"

"Who would you trust more than me?"

Smith shrugged. "That's certainly true, but why as a chef? You are a trained physician."

"Because, as your personal chef, I will be required to leave the prison on a regular basis to buy food and supplies. It's part of the job. And whenever I do, I can meet with people and get information back to you. Remember, I am not the prisoner here; you are. So, I can come and go pretty much as I please."

"Lucas... can you cook?"

"Can I cook?" Walker said with forced outrage in his voice. Turning to Wright. "Did you hear that? He asked if I can cook? Can a bird fly? Can a fish swim? Can a bear..."

"Lucas!"

"Well, no, not really. But Lord Spencer doesn't know that; and Susan showed me two or three dishes before we left."

"So our lives are hanging on your being able to convince people your two or three dishes qualifies you as a chef?"

"Yes, indeed. What was your second question?"

"Did Bromley—or I should say de Tromelin now... Did he make it back to England all right?"

"Yes, and as soon as he landed, he turned around and went back to France. I don't know where he is now, but I understand he has reconnected with his wife and last I heard he was living in Normandy. But that was some time ago.

"Your third question?"

"What the devil is Susan doing in that house across the street?"

"She's there... well... because she's Susan."

*****

The old man hobbled back from his third trip to the window, and sat down heavily behind his desk. He was Georges René Le Peley de Pléville, and he was the French Minister of Marine.

As a young naval officer, his feats of courage were nearly legendary. In 1770, for example, he was the harbor-captain of the Port of Marseilles. Then, on the night of May 1st, the British frigate *Alarm* ran aground in a storm off the coast of Provence. It was lodged in among some boulders and was being dashed to pieces. When he found out about it, de Pléville gathered all the available harbor pilots and seamen and went to the scene. Sliding along the slippery boulders, he got to the ship, took command, ordered a maneuver that managed to get it refloated, and sailed it back to safety. What made it all the more remarkable was that he did it on one leg, having lost the other in a six-hour battle with two privateers some years before. Ironically, the privateers were British.

In a further irony, the captain of the imperiled frigate was none other than John Jervis, who was later to defeat the French at the Battle of Cape St Vincent. As a result of that battle he became the 1st Earl of St Vincent, then First Lord of the Admiralty, then commander of the Channel Fleet, and eventually became Admiral of the Fleet—the highest possible rank in the British Navy. In repayment, however, in 1780 de Pléville's son was captured and taken to England. When the British authorities found out who he was, they not only released him without asking for an exchange from the French, but they allowed him to pick three other French naval officers to go with him.

But the operative words here are: "In his youth..." He was now over 70 years old, a frail, sickly old man who wanted nothing more than to resign his post and go into quiet retirement. That, however, was not to be.

"You must pardon me if I seem a bit distracted, Monsieur Etches. I am supposed to depart soon for the Peace Conference in Lille with Letourneur and Maret. They were supposed to be here a half-hour ago, and I can't imagine what is keeping them."

"Then my gratitude is doubled for your seeing me on such short notice, Admiral. It seems that their delay has become my good fortune, however, because it gives me a chance to bring to your attention..."

Richard Etches droned on about the outrageous prices that were being asked for captured British ships, the near total lack of cooperation he was getting from the repair dockyards, and on, and on. But Etches was an unusual man. Among other gifts, he had the amazing ability to talk about one thing, while thinking about another, and not have either process compromised. He was doing that now.

"So, the old fox is going to Lille, huh? And he's going with Étienne Letourneur and Hugues-Bernard Maret. But, why just the three of them? And why Letourneur? I thought he was leaving office soon. London will need to know about this quickly," he thought.

Etches continued talking and thinking about de Pléville; while de Pléville continued half-listening and thinking about the maddening itch he had at the end of his amputated leg.

After several minutes de Pléville's secretary came in carrying a small stack of papers.

"I am sorry to interrupt, Admiral, but your carriage has arrived and they are loading your trunks on now. Before you leave, however, there are a few small matters that need your attention."

Etches assumed an air of nonchalant indifference as he looked about the room. After all, that was the real reason he was there. In a later age it would be called "casing the joint." He knew that soon he must break into this very room and he wanted to memorize it's layout and any locks or other security that might be in place. His plan was to return in a few nights to steal..."

"And finally, Admiral, if you would be so good as to sign of a few of these blank sheets of paper at the bottom."

Etches' head shot around to stare at the two men. Fortunately, neither noticed.

"What for?" the admiral asked.

"This is in case any orders need to be issued in your absence. If I have some signed blanks, all you need to do is inform me by messenger what you want done. I can then write the order over your signature and it will have the same force and effect as if you were here."

"I suppose that makes sense." Turning to Etches, "You see, monsieur, how the wheels of bureaucracy continue to grind no matter what."

Etches gave his best sympathetic smile, while his mind raced. He was there to examine the office so that in a few days he could come back to steal some blank stationary. Now, right in front of him was a growing pile of papers containing both the Ministry of Marine logo *and* the Minister of Marine's signature. He had to get one of those sheets. But how?

His tasks at an end, de Pléville stood, which was Etches' cue to do the same. The three men walked out of the office and through the waiting room. They had almost gotten to the door when Etches said, "Ah, *mon Dieu*. I've forgotten my cane. I will be right back."

Before anyone could say anything, Etches shot back through the waiting room and into the office. He grabbed his cane with one hand while grabbing a sheet of signed paper with the other. Doing a one-handed fold, another trick he had learned during his years as a spy, he stuck the sheet inside his waistcoat, and emerged from the office as quickly as he had entered.

Waving his cane in the air like a trophy, he hurried to rejoin the Admiral who was about to exit through the door.

*****

The hard days of February and March had given way to a tantalizing, coquettish, April. At the Temple Sir Sidney Smith continued his work of rebuilding and restructuring the *Agence de Paris*. When he entered the Temple on July 3, 1796, the *Agence* was in shambles. By April 1798 he had it running with well-ordered efficiency.

In those years Paris was a hotbed of espionage activity. In addition to the Royalist contingent, the city swarmed with secret service operatives from every country in Europe. Sometimes they were known as *accapareurs*, sometimes as *agents de l'étranger*, but to the average French citizen they were simply known as *Pitt-et-Coburgs* after the British Prime Minister and the German royal family.

There were agents from London, Berlin, St Petersburg, Copenhagen, and Stockholm. They occupied high positions in the army, navy, and government service, as well as lowly positions in everyday occupations. The one thing they had in common, however, was that they were all well supplied with money. It was this money, judiciously applied, that allowed them to get the information their governments desired, as well as foment counter-revolution, undermine various government projects, hinder the production of military supplies, and free the odd political prisoner.

Smith was simultaneously coordinating a half-dozen of these agents. There was Weber, who specialized in obtaining plans to French fortifications; Greenwood, who specialized in giving dinners for, and thereby recruiting, down-on-their-luck Royalists; Mrs. Knox, who specialized in compromising government officials; and the dynamic duo of Dickson and Winters who were Smith's freelance wildcards, as they could and would do just about anything, any time it was needed. Tying it all together was one of the most ingenious communication schemes in prison history.

One afternoon, shortly after his arrival at the Temple, Smith was looking out the barred window that faced the Rue de la Corderie. He noticed that the balcony entrance to a third floor apartment across the street was wide open; and his attention was drawn to a light that shown from within. After observing a few shadowy figures passing back and forth, he soon saw a sheet being stretched across the far wall of the room. To his astonishment, in a few minutes a magic lantern was turned on, throwing a bright beam of light against the sheet and projecting the letters of the alphabet one at a time. Soon there was a pause and a message began: WHAT DO YOU NEED?

At first he was at a loss as to how to communicate back; then he had an inspiration. He tore some pages out of an old prayer book that he found in the cell, grabbed a burnt stick from the fireplace and wrote out the alphabet, one large letter per page. Then he went to the window, held up the letter "A", and grabbed the first bar on his window at the very top. He then held up the letter "B", grabbed the second bar at the top, and so on. Every letter had a specific location on a specific bar, and he could communicate with the outside world. To be sure, the messages had to be short, and infrequent enough to avoid detection; but the system worked.

That afternoon he signaled back: MONEY

Two days later Smith received his weekly visit from the prison physician. Because he was considered a high-value prisoner, the French wanted to make sure that he remained in good health. What they didn't know was that the prison physician had, for many years, been a British employee.

At the end of the examination the physician grabbed Smith's hand and pulled it toward him. While one hand was feeling for a pulse, the other was slipping Smith a roll of gold coins. Without a word or a gesture of any kind, the physician then completed his examination and silently left the room. Smith knew that the biggest barrier to running his spy network had just been removed.

*****

Walker strolled into Smith's "King's Chamber" one afternoon and found him standing at the window alternately grabbing various bars. He paused for a minute, grabbed a few more bars and walked away.

"What was that all about?" Walker asked as he sat down on the green armchair with little white *fleur de lis* embroidered on the back. It was his favorite chair.

"It was for you, actually. It just said: SEND WALKER TO MARKET."

A few hours later Walker returned from his errand and, grim faced, walked Smith out into the "King's Chapel" where there was no possible way they could be overheard.

"I wasn't told much," Walker began, "but the escape has been planned. Within the next week you'll have to find a way to get free of the prison long enough for them to explain the details to you. Once you've figured out how to do that, send them a message via the window-telegraph telling them where you'll be and when you'll be there. That's all I know."

What they were requesting wasn't impossible, but it was risky. On several occasions Smith had been let out of the prison for a few hours to "take the air." He would give his word of honor that he wouldn't escape and the previous prison superintendent, Mutius Lasne, would let him go. But Citizen Antoine Boniface had recently replaced Lasne, and Smith had no idea whether Boniface would be nearly as agreeable.

Smith thought for a few moments. "Chef, you're going to cook me a birthday dinner."

"Birthday? Your birthday isn't until July, and it's only April 10th."

"Yes, but Boniface doesn't know that. My new birthday is... shall we say... April 13th? No, let's make it April 14th. That will be a Saturday and there will be more people out on the streets for me to get lost in—if I can get there."

"The 14th also has one other advantage," Smith added.

"What's that?"

"It will give you an extra day to learn how to cook."

*****

Citizen Boniface was a large man with a small balding head. Some might call him fat, but those who knew him knew that there was also considerable muscle underneath his flabby exterior.

Generally speaking, there is no middle ground with fat men. They are either good-natured and soft-hearted, or they are ruthless and cruel. I say "generally speaking" because Boniface was an example of a very real compromise. One moment he could be seen giving and spending freely. He could be seen weeping at a sentimental song or, without hesitation, releasing a fly from captivity. The next moment, however, his eyes could turn dark and fierce, and his ferocious mustache would start quivering. At that point, he was fully capable of being as ruthless as any man on the planet. The problem was that one never knew which Boniface they would meet.

Boniface was not a particularly bright man; but he compensated for his lack of intelligence by clinging to certain fixed beliefs and rigid routines. Among those beliefs was one that held that there was a special relationship between the prisoners and him. More specifically, he firmly believed that if the Temple should someday find itself missing a prisoner; he might, the following day, find himself missing his head.

For that reason, he was a fanatic about security. He slept with the prison keys under his pillow. He would appear at the most unexpected times to make sure the guards were alert. And he knew exactly who was locked-up in the secret dungeon cells, why they were there, and which ones might be desperate enough to try an escape.

But, while he was paranoid about *les malheureux*, he was far more trusting of Sidney Smith. After all, Sir Sidney was a gentleman—a man of honor—a man of accomplishment—a man of learning—a man of refinement. Deep down that was what he wanted to be too; but he also knew that would never happen. He knew that, under more normal circumstances, a man like Sir Sidney would have had little or nothing to do with a man of his station. But these were not normal circumstances. Thus it was with some satisfaction that he found himself this evening sitting at Sir Sidney's table, even if that table was in the middle of a glorified prison cell.

Walker had pulled out all the stops for tonight's meal and did, he thought, surprisingly well considering all the limitations that were inherent in prison cooking. The first course consisted of a fish soup, some sliced turkey, and a variety of cooked vegetables. The second course included a Ragout a la Français, a large Sirloin of Beef, and several rather delicate pastries. After those dishes were cleared away, he brought out a dessert course that was a lively selection of nuts, raisins, apples, oranges, and small cakes. It wasn't exactly fit for a king, and not as extensive as a formal dinner usually was in England; but it would have to do.

Following dessert, the dishes were again cleared away and a decanter of highly fortified port wine was set in front of Sir Sidney. As a good host, he immediately pushed it over to Boniface, who was seated in the guest of honor position to his right. He took some and pushed it over to John Wesley Wright, who was at the end of the table. Wright poured himself a glass, and Walker, who had served the meal, brought it back around to Sir Sidney. Around and around the decanter went as small talk continued.

Boniface didn't really notice that he was drinking out of a large tumbler, while Smith and Wright were drinking out of small wine glasses. If he did notice, he would have assumed it to be a British tradition accorded to any "guest of honor." Before long, however, the wine began to have an effect. Bonifaces' head occasionally drooped, his eyelids seemed heavy, and his speech was occasionally a bit slurred.

"Ah, it is my turn already?" Boniface asked. "Then I propose the following toast:

> Here's to a country better than France;
> A city finer than Paris;
> And a wine sweeter than this;
> But where can you possibly find them?

With a chuckle at his own wit, he quaffed the remainder of his wine. Walker immediately appeared at his side, grabbed the decanter, and re-filled his glass.

Boniface took several more drinks, then looked hard at his host. "Sir Sidney, for a person who is at his birthday celebration you are looking rather pre-occupied."

"Forgive me, Citizen Boniface. It's just... your last toast has put me in a pensive mood."

"Oh, and why is that?"

"You mentioned a country better than France and a city finer than Paris. Please do not misunderstand me. France is a lovely country, and Paris is a delightful city; but I am sure you will forgive me if my thoughts travel to my beloved England, and the City of London."

"I have no problem with your thoughts traveling there as often as you wish—as long as your body remains here in the Temple."

Smith had to laugh at the comment.

"You know..." Boniface stared off into the distance as if trying to decide whether to complete the sentence. "You know, I have something with me, and I've been debating all night whether to show it to you."

"What's that?"

Boniface reached inside his jacket. "It's a note that arrived today from the Minister of Marine. A friend within the Paris Police sent me a copy. Let me read it to you.

The Minister of Marine
*   To the Minister of Police*
> *I have been informed by a private person, that Commodore Sidney Smith, imprisoned at the Temple, will escape in ten days, and that he is allowed to go out to supper in the city. I must request that you order that an officer should be set to guard him, and another to watch the jailer and prevent him granting leave of absence until I have been able to obtain more ample and more certain information respecting this prisoner and his secretary."*

Walker, who fortunately was standing behind Boniface, looked stricken. Smith had a spasm of alarm, but covered it well. Wright was the only person who seemed unaffected by the note.

This was a disaster. The whole purpose of the dinner was to get Boniface to allow Smith to go outside the prison that night. He only needed a few minutes, but he had to have them. The rendez-vous had been all set up.

"Citizen Boniface," Smith stammered. "I have no idea what to say to such... such..."

"Well, I do!" Wright intervened. "I have never heard anything as outrageous as that. I do not know how you can bear the insult, Citizen Boniface! Why, in England, I've seen men called onto the field of honor and shot dead for less than that."

When sober, Boniface was not an exceptionally bright man and the copious wine had done nothing to sharpen his intellect, so he was confused by Wrights' comments. "Did he just ask: how can *I* bear the insult?" he thought. "I thought this was about Smith trying to escape."

The confusion showed on his face, and that was all Wright needed to drive home the point.

"How dare that dog... Who was he? Minister of Marine? How dare that dog suggest that a police watch be kept on the superintendent of the most famous prison in all France—maybe even the whole world? And then he has the gall to suggest how *your* prisoner should be guarded. Monsieur, I don't know about you, but I could not live with such a humiliation."

"Really?" Boniface thought. "Is that how a gentleman would react... how a gentleman *should* react? I am a gentleman. Well, almost a gentleman. Should I challenge the minister to a duel or something?"

Wright did theme and variation for another minute. "I must emphasize again, monsieur, what right does the Minister of Marine have to interfere with the workings of the Temple prison?"

"That's true," thought Boniface.

"What right does he have to second guess one of the world's great prison wardens?"

"Yes, that's true too," Boniface said, now speaking his thoughts aloud. "Why... I should go over there right now, and shoot the *cochon!*" The wine was now gleefully participating in his deliberations.

"That's why I say: you should allow Sir Sidney Smith out on parole this very evening! There is not a moment to lose."

"What?"

"Absolutely, even if it's only for a few minutes. This over-reaching bureaucrat must be taught a lesson. He must learn that he can not interfere with the professional judgment of the *Directeur de prison*, the world renowned Antoine Boniface."

"Oh, I am not sure about that. Give him parole this very evening, you say?"

"I tell you, this minister must be taught a lesson! If you do not, every petty bureaucrat in Paris will hear of it within a fortnight, and you will be treated like dirt for the rest of your career."

"That's not good," Boniface dimly concluded.

Smith now saw where all this was going. "Monsieur, today is my birthday. Let me have this one special treat."

Boniface still hesitated.

"If you are worried about Sir Sidney doing anything dishonorable, why don't you go with him? You can both go out for a bit of night air. How much more secure could a prisoner be than if guarded by the *legendary* Antoine Boniface?"

Smith looked at Wright as if to say: Are you crazy? Wright just shrugged back as if to say: Hey, it's the best I could do.

But Boniface was weakening.

"Sir Sidney, if we go out, do you promise on the word of an honest man that you will not attempt to escape?"

"Better than that. I promise on the word of an English gentleman. I will make no attempt whatsoever to escape until... midnight tonight. Until that time, you and I will be friends and colleagues. After that, we will again be prisoner and warden."

Boniface thought for a moment. Tonight he would be the personal friend of a knight—a real English knight—and what would they say about *that* back at his home village?

"No good," he suddenly replied. "You must give your parole until noon tomorrow. I will want to get a good night's sleep tonight."

"Can Walker accompany us?"

"I see no reason why not. He is not a prisoner, at least not officially."

"Then you have my word as an English officer and gentleman. Neither Walker nor I will attempt to escape between now and noon tomorrow. We two gentlemen shall go out on the town. May I call you Antoine?"

"You certainly may, Sidney."

And the three men—two of whom were arm-in-arm—descended the long winding stone staircase that lead to the prison courtyard and eventually the street.

*****

Although Boniface had seemed quite inebriated when in Smiths' suite of cells, the evening air was rapidly clearing his head. He slapped at his right leg as if punishing it for its unsteadiness as they passed through a side gate of the prison. But he was still enough under the influence that the *bon homme* had not left him.

"*Liberté, Equalité, Fraternité,*" Boniface said jovially as he slapped Sir Sidney on the back. "May my head tumble in the sawdust if I thought you would play me false. We are simply two friends... old and dear friends... who are out for a night on the town. *Au Boulevard!*"

And with that the three men passed on to the Rue de la Corderie, past Smith's communication house, which he managed to avoid looking up at, and on to the Rue de Bretagne. From there it was a short walk to the Rue des Filles, and from there to the Boulevard des Calvaire, their ultimate destination.

Boniface was still in an effusive mood. He chatted. He laughed. At one point he did a little dance, and then told a story about a homeless duckling on a farm, which made him tear up. But the more they walked, the more his head was clearing. And the more his head cleared, the more he was having second thoughts about this whole venture. He went from eager anticipation, to lingering doubt, to the conclusion that he had been a total fool for allowing this to happen—especially after having been warned by no less than a full Minister.

He was quickly sliding into paranoia mode. He started looking around more. Every passerby was being carefully scrutinized. He frequently looked over at Sir Sidney to make sure he was there, and occasionally even looked back at Walker. His concentration on the obvious was so great that he failed to hear the more subtle sound of footsteps approaching from the rear. But the sound was not lost on both Smith and Walker.

Trailing behind the three was a female, heavily cloaked and veiled. Before long she had caught up with Walker who had intentionally lagged behind. It was Susan Whitney.

"Are you and Sidney ready?" She whispered as she pulled along side of him.

"Yes. When?"

"When? Right now! We have people positioned both ahead of you and behind you, and there is only that latch-key to stop us."

"I thought we were just going to get some information tonight."

"You were. But why not take advantage of this opportunity? We have no idea if our original plan will work; but we *know* this one will. Sidney could be free in two minutes."

Walker said nothing for a long moment, lost in agonized thought. Then he finally said, "We can't."

Susan couldn't believe her ears. "You *can't*? And why, may I ask, can you not?"

"Because Sidney gave his word that he would not escape tonight."

Susan stopped walking for a moment, stunned by these words. She quickly caught up again.

"Lucas, Sidney's life is hanging by a thread. There is a rejuvenated collection of madmen now running the Directory; and at any moment they could decide that Sidney... and you... need to disappear. And you're telling me that he can not walk away from all that—right now—this instant—because he gave a promise to a half-drunk jailer?"

"Yes. That's exactly what I am telling you."

Susan paused while she digested Walker's statement. "Well, then what about you? Let's get you out tonight anyway."

"I can't go either."

"Because?"

"Because Sidney also gave his word that I would not try to escape."

Susan's frustration with the male wing of the species now reached an all-time high—and that's saying quite a bit. She started to lay one of her patented diatribes on Walker's head when he stopped, took her by the arm, and spun her around.

"Look, Susan, Sidney gave his word of honor that he would not try to escape. It doesn't matter if that were given to the King of England, or to a hod-carrier lounging around an opium den. It was his word, and it *must* stand. Our whole world, everything we know and love, runs on that system of honor. If the day ever comes when a gentleman's word is no longer his sacred bond, then it all... then everything... comes apart."

"What about you? Did you give your word?"

"No. Sidney gave it for me. And I will not allow him to compromise his honor either for me, or for himself."

Susan said nothing for several minutes. Then, "All right. The rendezvous takes place tonight as planned. You'll get the final details then." She slowed her pace, fell well behind the group, and disappeared into the night.

A few minutes later the group emerged on to the Boulevard des Calvaire. A few blocks to their left that same street was known as Boulevard du Temple, and a few blocks to the right it was called the Boulevard Saint Antoine. But here it was the Calvaire district, and it was the hub of the entertainment they were seeking.

They passed theaters, restaurants and hotels. They saw jugglers, dancers, and trained dogs. They paused to marvel at Madam Brochard's wax museum, then walked past innumerable patent medicine salesmen, prostitutes, and card-sharps. And all of it was pressed together into a whole by the sheer mass of people. There were men and women, the wealthy and the poor, the promenaders and the idlers—all going nowhere in particular, but enjoying every step.

By the time they had gotten to the menagerie, just past the start of the Rue du Temple, Boniface was feeling better about things. At least he was feeling better until he turned around and saw that Walker was no longer with them.

"*Morbleu*, Walker is gone!" Exclaimed Boniface.

Smith turned, looked around briefly, and said, "Don't worry, Antoine. He's probably just lost in the crowd."

"Lost in the crowd? Lost in the crowd?" Boniface's voice was rising. "He is probably half-way to being lost in the crowd of London!"

"Antoine, my friend..."

"Do not tell me 'my friend.' Is this the way an English officer—an English gentleman—keeps his word?"

"But Walker's not a prisoner. Surely, he can come and go."

"Not when you gave your word that there would be no 'going.' If you lied about Walker not attempting escape, perhaps you lied about yourself as well, eh?"

"Antoine, calm down. I give you my word..."

"Your word?" Boniface was now almost shrieking. "I know what your word is worth. Come with me, monsieur. We are going back to the Temple as fast as we can get there."

Boniface took Smith by the arm and hustled him down the closest side street, hoping to take a shortcut back to the prison. He had not gone far before three men appeared from a darkened doorway and stood in front of him.

"And where might you be going with this honest-looking citizen, monsieur jailer?" said the middle of the three men. "Don't look surprised. We know who you are."

The man on the left joined in. "Don't you think you could get back to your prison much faster if you didn't have to lug this man around?"

"Make way, damn you! I am on official business of the Directory. I am a representative of the Republic..."

"Ah, yes, The Republic... 'One and Indivisible' or should I say on these streets, 'One and Invisible.'"

"Let me through, you *canaille!*"

The three men closed in around him, and talk gave way to fists and kicks. A few minutes later Boniface found himself laying face down on the street with Sidney Smith no where to be seen.

Bleeding from the nose and from a cut over his eye, Antoine Boniface dejectedly walked back to the prison. All he could think about was what would happen to him and his family. He knew there was no excuse for what he had done, and there would be no mercy shown. If he lived until Monday, it would only be because the magistrates would not wish to bestir themselves on a Sunday. He could envision the executioner's herald intoning: "Citizens, behold what happens to the enemies of the Republic. Behold the fate of Citizen Antoine Boniface—agent of *Pitt-et-Coburg.*"

As he rang the bell for the guards to admit him to the Temple grounds, he was wondering if a head still retained consciousness after it was cut off; and, if so, for how long. His thoughts were interrupted by the voice of Sir Sidney Smith.

"May I have your permission to enter also, Monsieur Boniface?"

Boniface whirled around, saw Smith, and nearly collapsed. His mouth opened to speak, but nothing came out.

"You know you really must do something about the crime in this city. Those thieves got little from me, for I had little with me. But did they steal much from you?"

"No. No, I am fine." he stammered.

About this time the heavy oak door swung open, and Boniface whisked Smith inside. No sooner had the door shut than he could hear someone pounding on the other side.

A guard opened the door again and Walker slipped through. He was visibly upset.

"I don't know what France is coming to when a man is abandoned by his jailer, has to walk all the way back to the prison, and then pound on the door to demand to be let in!" And he disappeared in a huff toward the entrance to the staircase that would take him back to his jailhouse home.

CHAPTER TWO

It was close to midnight when Walker wandered into Sidney's "King's Chamber." The outward reason for the visit was to see if he could borrow something—anything—to read. But, if he were honest, he would have admitted that there was more to it than that. In fact, he wanted to talk. Just that. Talk.

They knew that the escape attempt would occur any day now, but they didn't know exactly when. Walker was no coward, but only a fool would not be a bit nervous about an impending event that could result in his death. Walker knew that and sought out the kind of comfort that can only be found in human communication. He didn't necessarily need to talk about the escape; but, consciously or unconsciously, he needed to talk.

He entered the chamber and was surprised to find it empty and dark. Off in the corner, however, he could see light coming from the "King's Chapel," the room that was a part of the circular tower that ran up that corner of the building. It was Sidney's favorite room. It was the place where he could go to be by himself—to look out the window and dream the universal dreams of the imprisoned.

This evening, however, he was not at the window; he was next to it. He had a lit candelabrum on either side of him, and he was writing something on the window's white wooden shutter.

Walker watched in amazement for a moment, and then interrupted.

"Sidney, what are you doing?"

"I am writing a message to that fellow, Bonaparte."

"I see." Walker was frantically searching his memory for every medical school lecture he had ever attended on mental instability. "May I ask why?"

"Certainly. You said that he is now the power in France, and likely to be in control for some time."

"So?"

"So, I want to write him a message."

Walker paused to digest this statement then, trying to be as tactful as possible, said gently. "Are you... ah... planning to mail him that shutter?"

Smith turned around with a surprised look. "No, of course not; but he'll read it. I know he will... sooner or later."

He stepped back, admired his handiwork for a moment, put down his quill and said: "There it's done," and he gestured at Walker to take a look.

Walker held up a candelabrum and started to read:

One has to admit that Fortune's wheel makes strange revolutions, but before it can truly be called a revolution the turn of the wheel must be complete. Today you are as high as you can be, but I do not envy you your happiness because I have a still greater happiness, and that is to be as low on Fortune's wheel as I can go, so that as soon as that capricious lady turns her wheel again, I shall rise for the same reason that you will fall.

I do not write this to distress you, but to bring you the same consolation that I have when you reach the point where I am. You will occupy this same prison—why not you as well as I? I did not expect to be shut up here any more than you do now.

In a partisan war it is a crime in the eyes of one's opponents to do one's duty honorably as you do today, and in consequence you embitter your enemies against you. No doubt you will reply, "I do not fear the hatred I arouse in them. Has not the voice of the people declared for me?" That is well spoken. Sleep in peace. But before six months have passed, if not today, you will learn what the reward is for serving such masters, the reward for all the good you have done them. Pausanias wrote long ago, "He who has placed all his hopes on the friendship of the public has never come to a happy end."

But of course I don't have to convince you that you will come here, because to read these lines you must be here. I assume that you will have this room also because the jailer is a good man: he gave me the best room and will do as much for you.

Walker turned and looked at Smith, but there was no emotion to be read on his face. He was as matter-of-fact as if he had just written out a laundry list.

Walker blew out the candles on the second candelabrum and started to walk out to the main chamber holding his light a little higher.

"Come, Sidney. It's time we got some sleep."

*****

About the time Sir Sidney started writing his message, across town, on the other side of the Seine, a hooded figure was hurrying down the Rue du Bac, past the Rue de Bourbon and Rue de Verneuit, to Rue de l'Université. There she paused for a moment to get her bearings. A block away, to her right, she could see the Hotel d'Auvergne. Now she knew where she was. The place she was looking for was right across the street from the hotel.

Her destination was a small rooming house. It was a bit run down and seedy looking, but that was fine. That made it look pretty much like every other building in the area, and that was just what they wanted.

She rapped twice at the side door. A peephole opened up, an eye materialized in its center, and she was admitted. The doorkeeper immediately disappeared into the back of the house.

Throwing off her hood, she found herself in a large downstairs common room. Four men were seated at a dining table, all of whom stood up when she entered, and one of which came over to greet her.

"Susan. How good it is to see you again!" The speaker was Jacques Tromelin. "Come in. Please, take off that damp cloak and sit down." Tromelin, who only a few years ago had been the Count de Tromelin, had not forgotten his court manners.

"Can I get you something to drink... something to take the night chill out of your bones?"

"If you had some brandy, that would be wonderful, Jacques."

As Tromelin proceeded to a sideboard to pour her drink, she noticed how thin he looked. His face had the kind of pallor that can only be found on someone who has spent significant time in prison.

The last time Susan Whitney had seen him it was aboard the *HMS Diamond*, Sir Sidney's last command. He was getting into a boat with Sidney, Wright, Walker and 10 or 12 crewmen. They were about to board and capture a ship that had been plaguing British merchantmen, and capturing vital governmental gold shipments, for months. It was in that boarding attempt that the three were themselves taken.

That single night, just over two years ago, had broken up the team of Smith, Walker and Whitney. It was a trio that had been together for most of the last 17 years and they knew each other like family—even better, they loved each other like family. They had been together in battles and in peacetime, in terror and happiness, in wealth and in poverty. They functioned together like a complex machine, each with strengths and weaknesses that complimented the other two. But, at the moment, one of the parts was missing—and Susan Whitney was all about getting that piece back in place.

Tromelin gave Susan her brandy and sat down.

"Susan, let me introduce you to the other gentlemen. On your right is Louis Boisgirard. If you've been to the Paris Opera lately, you might have seen him, as he is one of their principal dancers. He is also one of our best agents here in Paris.

"To his right is Le Grand de Palluau. You may not remember him, but he remembers you. He was a young lieutenant with General Frotté when Sir Sidney met with him and his Chouans a few years ago.

"Joining us soon will be Picard de Phélippeaux, who has planned the details of the escape and will be briefing us tonight.

"Gentlemen, may I introduce Susan Whitney who..."

"Who is also known as Lady Susan Whitney."

Susan looked toward the doorway of the room and saw a tall thin man about 30 years old. Moving with an athlete's grace, he casually took his place at the table, talking the whole time.

"Lady Susan Whitney, who was named a 'Maiden in Waiting to the Court of St. James' for her efforts in the heroic rescue of Prince William from that disaster at Yorktown. She has seen duty—as a combatant, gentlemen—at the Battle of the Capes, the Battle of the Saints, and the Siege of Toulon. She is rated, unofficially of course, as an Able Surgeon's Mate; but she could easily fill-in as a fully qualified Gunner's Mate if need be.

"Shall I go into your humble origins at Portsmouth; how you nevertheless became quite well educated, how you found yourself aboard the *HMS Richmond* where you met Sidney Smith and Lucas Walker, how..."

"I think these gentlemen have learned quite enough about me for the moment, sir. Indeed, I rather fear what you might reveal next." The man smiled at this reply and Susan continued. "But you have the advantage of me..."

Tromelin jumped back in. "Lady Whitney, may I introduce Picard de Phélippeaux. He was a Colonel in General Conde's army on the Rhine frontier. For the last three years, however, he has been William Wickham's primary intelligence officer in western France and has worked extensively with John Wesley Wright. More recently, he himself was in a French prison and rescued by Louis Boisgirard here, and Monsieur Hyde de Neuville, who could not be here tonight as he had other duties.

"This is the group that has been put together by Richard Etches to rescue Sir Sidney and Lieutenant Wright."

"I must say, I am impressed," Susan truthfully observed.

"Then let us begin," Phélippeaux resumed.

"Everyone here is going to have a role in the escape. Jacques already knows most of the plan; but Boisgirard, Le Grand, and Lady Whitney..."

"Could we just use Susan?" Whitney interjected.

"But this will be the first that Boisgirard, Le Grand, and Susan will have heard about it. Here's how it will work."

Phélippeaux continued for the next 15 minutes, producing a map of Paris and moving a small snuffbox on it to illustrate his plan.

"And that's the essence of it," he concluded. "Any questions? Comments?"

The room was eerily silent. Susan, looking down at the table muttered, "It's madness."

"Yes. Quite." Phélippeaux nonchalantly replied. "But it will work."

Susan looked up at Phélippeaux with a new respect. "There are a million things that could go wrong; but, yes, I believe it *will* work."

*****

There was no sun shining on Paris that morning, or anywhere else in northern France. A chilly weather front had moved in the previous night and it had been raining off and on for the past several hours.

About 8:00 AM the rain stopped and an enclosed four-wheeled fiacre drawn by four horses pulled up to the main gate of the Temple prison. Below the black top, and in contrast to the gloom of the day, the body was painted a bright yellow. It was huge—big enough to accommodate a very large family with room to spare.

On top was the hired driver. Seated next to him was a man with the floppy brim of his hat pulled down over his eyes, looking every inch like a police inspector. Inside were four people: a staff officer, a captain of Voltigeurs, a gentleman in a heavy dark cloak, and a Lady. Hanging around the carriage were several disreputable-looking characters who could only be police spies.

The scene was such a common one at the Temple that it excited no particular interest from either passers-by or the off-duty guards who were hanging around the entranceway. What they could not know was that the man next to the driver was Jacques Tromelin, the staff officer was Boisgirard, the captain was Le Grand, the man in the cloak was Phélippeaux, and the lady was, of course, Susan. In case anything went wrong, the "disreputable-looking" police spies were Hyde de Neuville, the espionage operative Viscovitch, and two experienced Chouan fighters named Laban and Sourdat.

The two officers got out, proceeded to the administration building of the prison, and presented themselves to Boniface.

"Monsieur, I am Citizen Auger, adjutant-general of the Army of Paris," said Boisgirard. "I am here to see to the transfer of..." he glanced down at a piece of paper "...of a Commodore Sidney Smith and a Captain John Wright, to the prison at Fontainebleau."

"I see," said Boniface. "And this is?"

"This is Captaine de Voltigeur Corriveau who will be in charge of security."

"And your authority for this transfer?

Boisgirard reached into an inner uniform pocket, withdrew a letter, and handed it to the jailer. Boniface sent a guard to fetch down Smith, Wright and Walker while he studied it over.

Paris, the 5th of Floreal, Year VI

The Minister of Marine and the Colonies
To Citizen Boniface, head-jailer of the Temple.

The Executive Directory having ordered in its decree of the 28th of Ventôse, sent herewith, that all English prisoners of war, without distinction of rank, should be collected into one prison, I charge you, citizen, to consign forthwith to the bearer of the present order, Citizen Etienne Armand Auger, Commodore Sidney Smith, and Captain Wright, prisoners of war, to be transferred to the general prison of the Department of Seine-et-Marne, at Fontainebleau.

You are enjoined, citizen, to observe the greatest secrecy in the execution of the present order, of which I have informed the Minister of Police, in order to prevent any attempt to rescue the prisoners whilst on their journey.

The Minister of Marine and Colonies
Pléville-Lepeley

Boniface signaled to his clerk. "Aubrey, get me that directive we got from Minister de Pléville last month." Boniface compared the two signatures and they were exact matches.

"Forgive me, citizen; but one cannot be too careful. Indeed, a few days ago Citizen de Pléville himself sent out a warning to be on guard for the escape of those two."

"To the contrary. You are to be congratulated on your diligence, monsieur. I believe that is why they, along with all the others, are being concentrated at one prison. The Temple is a very secure place, but let them try to escape from Fontainebleau, eh?"

"To be sure, citizen. To be sure."

The door to the jailer's office opened and two guards escorted Smith, Wright and Walker in.

"Commodore, this is adjutant-general Auger. You and Captain Wright will be leaving us this morning.

Smith looked around and showed concern. He asked, "Citizen Boniface, prisoners are rarely removed from the Temple in order to improve their health. May I ask where we are going?"

"Have no fear, Commodore. You are simply being transferred to the prison at Fontainebleau."

Smith nodded his head, but still showed concern. That was not hard for him to do because he *was* concerned. He knew from the rendezvous meeting 10 days ago that the royalists were going to try to arrange a transfer and would spring the escape plan as a part of that. However, he had never seen these two men before. Was this part of the escape plan, or was he really being transferred? If the latter, then any hope of liberation in the near future would vanish.

The adjutant added. "Commodore, the government has no wish to aggravate your misfortunes. You will be very comfortable at the place to which I am taking you."

Smith caught the vagueness of that last sentence and decided to play it as if this were the real escape. As the clerk copied the order into the prison books, he expressed his gratitude to Boniface and all the personnel at the prison, and concluded with, "And Fontainebleau is not very far. You will come see me, won't you citizen? As for my clothes and books... perhaps it would be best if you were to send them to me. I don't think it's worth taking them with me tonight."

"I shall be honored to do so, Commodore. It is the least one gentleman can do for another."

"I thank you, citizen. You are indeed a true gentleman."

Boniface beamed.

By this time, work on the prison log had been completed and, with a flourish, the adjutant signed the receipt for the prisoners. He started to gather up his charges when Boniface stopped him.

"Citizen, these are uncertain times on the streets of Paris. Let me provide you with an escort of... say, six men... to go with you to Fontainebleau."

"That is most generous of you, citizen. Thank you very much."

Smith's heart sank. This was *not* the escape! They really *were* transferring him and Wright. This ruins everything!

Auger paused for a long moment then said, "Monsieur Boniface, as I think about it, that might not be necessary."

Turning to Smith, "Commodore, I am an officer and you are an officer. Give me your word that you will not attempt to escape and there will be no need for an escort."

Smith quickly decided to roll the dice; but he had to choose his words carefully.

"Sir, if that is sufficient then... I give you my word as an officer and as a gentleman that... that I will accompany you wherever you choose to take me."

Boniface clapped his hands. "Bravo, Commodore! Monsieur, I can assure you from personal experience that this man's word is his bond."

The six men walked from the administration building to the gate leading to the old mansion of the Grand Prior. Smith, Wright, and Walker shook hands with the jailer one last time, said their farewells, passed through the interior gate, through the mansion, and out the main gate onto the street.

As they approached the carriage, Smith looked up at the man sitting next to the driver. The man lifted the wide brim of his cap and he saw it was Tromelin. With a wide grin, he entered the carriage.

"Allez, driver! Go!" Tromelin said. "Time is of the essence and speed will bring you a handsome tip."

Tromelin had the right idea, but the wrong vehicle. The words "speed" and "fiacre" are not normally found in the same sentence. The carriage hadn't gone 100 yards before it started fishtailing on the wet street. The horses, feeling the carriage breaking lose, became uncontrollable and plowed off the street and into a fruit cart. Standing next to it was a little girl who was knocked to the ground and started crying loudly.

A crowd quickly gathered, outraged at the carelessness of the driver.

"Who are these bâtards?"

"Why were they going so fast?"

"We should take them to the police!"

"Forget the police. We should teach them a lesson of our own."

Apples and oranges were strewn everywhere. The crowd was getting angrier. The cart owner was screaming obscenities. The little girl was shrieking.

And Phélippeaux took charge.

"Everyone out! Scatter in different directions. We'll meet at the safe house."

"But we don't know where the safe house is!" replied Walker.

"You and Sidney stick with Susan. She knows where it's at.

"Everyone, out! Now!"

The doors on both sides were flung open and the occupants tumbled out. Susan immediately headed for the child, who appeared more frightened than hurt, but Walker grabbed her by the arm and swung her around. In doing so she bumped in to a man with a strange red birthmark on the left side of his neck. She looked back at him. Had she seen him before?

"No, Susan. This way." Walker shouted.

They broke through the crowd and both Walker and Smith looked to Susan.

"Down the Rue du Temple!"

They started running like people who thought they had an irate mob on their heels. About 200 yards later they arrived at the corner of the Rue des Gravilliers and Smith looked back.

"All right. That's enough. They're not chasing, and we can't go running through the streets of Paris all morning like we just robbed someone."

They slowed to a fast walk and tried to catch their breath.

"Well, that was certainly refreshing," Susan finally said. "It's always nice when something goes exactly as planned."

Smith smiled. Walker did not. He was not at all amused.

It was only about a half-mile to where the Rue du Temple ends. They then followed the Rue de la Tisseranderie and cut past the Hotel de Ville to the Quay de Peltier, which runs along the Seine. Walking past the Chateau du Louvre they arrived at what used to be called the Pont Royal Bridge, crossed over, and continued on the Rue de Poitiers to the Rue de l'Universite and the safe house. It was a walk of only about two miles, but all three were more than glad to see the door of the safe house swing open.

*****

Two hundred miles away another journey was also ending. Two men, one a civilian and the other a full admiral, got out of a coach and walked through the doors of a large government office building just off Abchurch Street in London. The building was rather run-down, but it was decided not to put any money into its restoration because it was to be only a temporary clerical facility. That decision had been made 132 years earlier.

The admiral and the civilian walked down a long, well worn, oak-floored hallway to a room at the very back of the building. The closer they got to their destination, the more clearly they could hear the sound of slow, sad, flute music being played. The admiral gave the civilian a quizzical look, but the civilian said nothing.

They entered the room. It was surprisingly large but it contained no furniture other than a desk, a chair, a music stand, and a man. No papers. No books. Just the man, seated at the desk, playing his instrument. As the two officials came in, the musician neither acknowledged their presence nor stopped his mournful dirge.

The civilian spoke, "Mr. Parish, we have some work for you."

The flutist ignored him.

"I say, Mr. Parish..." Parish kept playing.

The two men looked at each other, then back at the man who continued to ignore their presence. Finally, the admiral leaned over the desk and, with his finger, moved the mouthpiece away from Parish's lips.

"Young man, the First Lord of the Admiralty, the Earl Spencer, is speaking to you," he said sternly.

"I know who he is," Parish replied testily. "And you are Admiral of the Fleet Gambier. And, if you don't mind, I am not finished playing this song." With that, he raised the instrument back to his lips and continued.

Gambier looked outraged, but Spencer only dropped a sheet on paper on his desk.

Parish took no notice of it.

Spencer picked up the sheet and placed it over the music, causing Parish to finally stop playing.

"Mr. Parish, we need this to be decoded. It was intercepted last week by one of our privateers; and we think it might be important. Our best cryptographers have been unable to break it."

"My Lord," Parish began resignedly, "what you call 'cryptographers' are a collection of idiots. They are a group of officers who are too incompetent to be trusted on a ship, and too well connected to be cashiered from the service. Is it any wonder that they have been unable to break the...

Parish studied the sheet of paper for a long moment. "To begin with, Lord Spencer, it's not a code, it's a cypher." He then turned back to the music stand and lifted his flute. The admiral pushed it down again.

"But can you decipher it?" Spencer asked with some exasperation.

"My God, a child could decipher it." Without looking at the paper he continued. "It's a complaint from the officer-in-charge of the French garrison on Alderney Island, to the commanding officer at Le Havre. He's complaining because they are running low on water, the last wheat shipment was contaminated with mold, and the men have not been paid in..." He finally glanced back at the paper. "...in six months. *That* is your important message."

Gambier picked up the sheet and all he saw was a page full of nonsensical letters. "How can you be so sure?" He asked.

Parish saw that any hope of continuing to play his flute had vanished. He sighed and continued.

"I shall explain it to you, admiral." He produced a pencil from the desk drawer and turned the sheet over.

"This message was probably written by a bored clerk who was too lazy to use a more creative encryption method. It's simply an Atbash with a Caesar-6 shift. Look."

Parish wrote down the letters of the alphabet on one line, skipped a space, and wrote it again in reverse order. When he was done it looked like this.

A B C D E F G H I J K L M N O P Q R S T U V W X Y Z

Z Y X W V U T S R Q P O N M L K J I H G F E D C B A

"All right. That's an Atbash cipher. It was a code used by the ancient Israelites; in fact you can find reference to it in the Old Testament in the Book of Jeremiah. If you want to use the letter A, you would write "Z." If you wanted to use "S" you would use "H." "K" would be "P," and so on.

"But what our ever-so-clever French friends did was to insert a Caesar-6 shift between the two lines. It's the cipher that Julius Caesar used to use. He would just shift the letters of the alphabet over by a certain number of characters and then write his message.

"Let me show you..."

Parish then inserted a line in between the two he had previously written, so that it now looked like this:

A B C D E F G H I J K L M N O P Q R S T U V W X Y Z

T S R Q P O N M L K J I H G F E D C B A Z Y X W V U

Z Y X W V U T S R Q P O N M L K J I H G F E D C B A

"There. In the middle, I've taken the third line and shifted it by six characters. So now, if I want to encode a message I use the first two lines, as before, only now "A" becomes "T," "S" becomes "B," "K" becomes "J," and so forth.

"As I said, a child could decipher that message."

"But how are you able to read it so fast?" Gambier asked.

"I don't know." Parish shrugged "I just am." And with that, he reached for his flute.

"What an amazing gift!" Gambier remarked with a touch of awe in his voice.

Parish put down the flute. "A gift? You call this a *gift*? Once upon a time, I was a contented, successful, musician. An *artiste*! My wife and I used to travel all over Europe giving concerts before royalty."

Lord Spencer looked askance at that comment and Parish caught his look.

"Well, all right. But some of them were *almost* royalty.

"Anyway, we had a good life. Then one day I had a few too many at a tavern and I started playing word games with some naval officers—some of Lord Spencer's aides it turns out. The games got more and more intricate and next thing I new I was pressed into the Royal Navy. Not to serve aboard a ship. Oh, no. At least there I'd be on the great oceans of the world. I could travel. I could have some adventure. My spirit could *soar!* No, instead I am condemned to sit in this... this crumbling brick pile every day like I was a prisoner.

"And that's not the worst of it. Do you know what would happen if I didn't show up here every day? I would be hung as a deserter. A deserter, mind you! Hung!"

"Some gift, huh, admiral?" And Parish began playing his flute again. He got about eight bars into the piece when Lord Spencer placed another document on the music stand. Parish stopped playing instantly.

He stared at the sheet. Looked up at Spencer and then back at the sheet.

"Where did you get this?" He said in awe, as if he were looking at the Régent diamond.

"Where and how we got it is no concern of yours. However, I can tell you this. We know that Napoleon is massing ships, troops, and supplies at Toulon and a number of other ports. He is clearly planning an invasion; but an invasion of who, where and when... we have no idea. We think this document will tell us."

Spencer paused and then continued, "Can you read it?"

Parish stared at the paper in silence for a full minute.

"No," he finally whispered.

*****

The second phase of the escape began early the following day.

A hired carriage pulled up to the l'Universite safe house and four people got in: Smith, Walker, Whitney and Phélippeaux. They had already said their good-byes and expressed their thanks to the members of the escape team. Tromelin was going back to Caen where his wife was giving birth to their first child. Le Grand was going home to Valençay; and Boisgirard was going to continue to dance in the Paris Opera. The group assumed that John Wesley Wright was going with them, but he declined. He said he had "other business" to attend to and everyone knew enough by this time not to ask what that business might be.

The plan was to exit Paris and travel north to the town of St. Denis, and then head west on the road that runs from there all the way to Rouen. Because they had no idea when the French would discover that they had been duped, Phélippeaux had arranged with sympathizers to have safe hiding places spotted along the route. There were locations in St. Denis, Pontoise, Magny, St. Clair, Ecouis, Bourgbaudoin, La Fosse and, of course, a final safe house in Rouen. From Rouen it would be a short journey to Le Havre, and an even shorter boat ride to one of the British ships that was blockading Le Havre Harbor.

Everything had been carefully planned. Every eventuality had been considered—except one.

The carriage followed the Seine eastward to the Pont Neuf Bridge, where they crossed the river and connected with the Rue St. Denis. It was an especially enjoyable ride for Smith. During the two years he was in the Temple, he had acquired a profound long-ing—one that he had told no one about. He literally dreamed of one day experiencing the simple joy of traveling down a broad boulevard, teeming with people, including himself, who were free to come and go as they pleased. The few times he was allowed out of prison for a few hours of parole did nothing to satisfy that urge. On the contrary, it intensified it; and now all of Paris was before him. He was not safe yet—not by a long shot—but even if he were re-captured that very day, this ride would have made the escape attempt worthwhile.

As they approached the St. Denis Gate, Phélippeaux glanced out the window and said, "We're almost there. Now, remember, the objective is to be as inconspicuous as possible. We don't want the guards to remember even seeing us. Just stay calm and...

As if on cue, the right front wheel of the carriage came off, and rolled toward the two guards who were sunning themselves in front of the guard house. The carriage did not topple over onto the right front corner, but it was now leaning heavily in that direction.

As they were getting out, Susan felt the need to make several poignant observations about the quality of French carriages, the incompetence of all carriage drivers, and the caliber of Parisian roads.

The two guards assigned to the St. Denis gate were suffering from the universal malady of all guards, in all times, at all places—boredom. But here was something that offered to break that mo-notony. It wasn't much, a carriage with a broken wheel, but it was something. They left their post and came over to inspect the acci-dent.

The driver had come down and was bemoaning the shoddy workmanship of the blacksmith who had "just last week repaired that very same wheel." The guards, of course, felt duty-bound to offer their suggestions as to the best way of reattaching it without, of course, themselves being involved in actually doing it. Smith, Walker and Whitney we're doing their best to fade into the back-ground and not be noticed.

In the process of willing herself invisible, Susan looked around and noticed that there was now no one guarding the gate.

"Sidney," she whispered.

He looked over and she nodded toward the unguarded exit. Touching Walker on the arm, Smith looked meaningfully at that same gate and then over at Phélippeaux. He nodded back, and everyone was on the same page.

Phélippeaux now decided to raise the confusion level a bit and started loudly cursing the driver for hiring out a faulty carriage, how they could have been killed by his incompetence, and so forth. This amused the soldiers no end, and they were now hoping a fight would break out. Meanwhile the three fugitives slipped through the gate. They walked for a few hundred yards, and then crept into a small grove of trees and brush where they could remain unseen, but still have a view of the road.

About a half-hour later the carriage came by, they stopped it, and started to get in. When the driver began to ask questions about what was going on, Walker just smiled and flipped a gold coin up to the driver. This guaranteed an uneventful ride the rest of the way to St. Denis, with a completely disinterested chauffeur.

At St. Denis they paid off the Parisian driver, had lunch, switched to a different carriage and continued. It was a two-day journey, but not an unpleasant one. They stopped overnight in Magnay and again about five miles outside of Rouen in a little town called Saint Pierre. The purpose of the last stop was for Phélippeaux to go into Rouen to make sure the alarm was not out and the safe house was still safe.

*****

Boniface was nervous. An official from the Central Bureau was inspecting his prison books; and, even though it happened every week, it still unnerved him.

Moping a small bead of sweat from his brow, he said, "As you can see, Monsieur, our census count is quite correct, and all prisoners are either on premises or are accounted for."

"Yes, yes, citizen. It all seems in order except... This transfer of Commodore Smith confuses me. I understand that he and Captain Wright have been removed, but the census shows the transfer of three people. Why is that?

"Ah, the third is a Mr. Walker. He appeared a few weeks ago as a volunteer chef and personal servant to the Commodore. Because his previous servant had been exchanged, I allowed Walker to serve the Commodore as a supernumerary. He was a part of the prison census, but he was not here under sentence."

"I see." The official looked thoughtful, and a bit suspicious. "May I see the order authorizing the transfer?"

"It has been copied into the Daily Report book. It's right there in front of you."

"No, I want to see the original order... the document that was served to you."

Boniface went to a file drawer, rummaged for a moment, and pulled out a sheet. "Ah, here it is," he said putting it before the official. "I'll get you several other orders from Minister de Pléville so you can compare the signature."

The official studied the sheet for a few seconds and shook his head. "There is no need, citizen. The minister has a very distinctive flourish to his autograph; and I'd recognize it anywhere. But it puzzles me that we were not informed of the decision to concentrate prisoners at Fontainebleau. I'll ask them about it tomorrow when I audit their books.

"In the meantime... this order is undoubtedly authentic," he said slamming the prison logbook shut. "So, your books are approved for another week, Monsieur Boniface, and I will so signify in my report. Now, what about that new shipment of wine you were telling me about?"

*****

Susan was awakened by the sound of a musket butt pounding against the door of the inn. She went down the short hallway to wake the others.

"Sidney! Lucas! Get up! Something's going on."

When the two men were awakened, Susan crept further down the hallway to see if she could hear anything.

"Citizen, we are looking for three people—two men and a woman. Do you have any such guests staying here?

The innkeeper, a royalist partisan, began stalling—but he was so surprised at the intrusion, he really didn't know what to say or do. Susan didn't wait to find out how he would handle it. She shot back to the room.

"It's a military patrol looking for us! We've got to get out of here."

"This way," Sidney said. He threw on his greatcoat and ran across the hall to the kitchen. Dashing past a startled cook and scullery maid, he burst out the back door and almost knocked over a soldier. The soldier recovered first and was about to call out when Walker clubbed him from behind with a pistol.

"Look out!" Susan cried and pushed the two behind a stack of storage boxes. A moment later a squad of horsemen raced past on their way to search every house in the village.

After they had passed, Sidney cautiously looked around the corner, saw the coast was temporarily clear, and the three half-dressed fugitives dashed across the road. On the other side was a wooded ridge that ran in a diagonal line from the Seine toward Saint Pierre—a distance of about two and a half miles. They climbed half way up the ridge and ducked behind some large rocks.

"What the devil went wrong?" Walker asked. "Was Phélippeaux captured? Did he betray us?"

"He might have been captured, but I am sure he didn't betray us." Sidney answered. "The word must be out now that we've escaped. Phélippeaux probably was intercepted coming from this direction, and without papers, he was arrested. They are probably searching every town and village along this road."

"What do we do now?" Walker asked.

Smith thought for a moment then said. "I suggest we follow this ridge west. It will at least give us some cover as we travel; and sooner or later we'll reach the Seine."

"What then?" Susan asked.

"I don't know."

"Then why are we going there?"

Smith smiled. "Because the Seine is a river and I think better on water."

*****

The old fisherman had just finished patching yet another tear in his one and only remaining sail. There was nothing he could do but repair it—or at least try to repair it. The war had consumed every inch of sailcloth, every spar, every mast, and every bit of rope in France. These were hard times for a fisherman, but he looked on the bright side. At least he still *had* a boat; and at least he still *was* a fisherman.

The man looked up and saw two disheveled men and a woman walking toward him. They were coming from the general direction of the village of Belbeuf, but they didn't seem to have come from there. It looked more like they had come from the wooded ridge. Most curious.

48

"Good morning, Citizen," one of the men began. "Is this your boat?"

"It is."

"Good. We would like to engage your services. My friends and I have a particular reason for visiting one of the British ships that are lying off Le Havre. I know that might seem like a somewhat risky venture for you; but the fishing can not be that good in these troubled times. So, I would be willing to pay you well—very well—if you could arrange it."

The old man thought it over. "You will pay in gold? If I do this I will only accept gold coin."

"I will."

The fisherman continued to study the three over. The man spoke French like a native; but this whole thing didn't add up. Still, he thought, receiving payment in gold coin was not something to be trifled with. He might earn a month's pay in a single day. Besides, there was something about the man that seemed oddly familiar to him.

He finally made up his mind. "When do you want to go?"

"Right now. This morning." Smith replied.

He paused for a moment. "Then you'll have to help me bend on this sail." The work was quickly completed and the boat set off.

They started their journey just south of where the Seine begins a large sweeping turn at the city of Rouen. The river was peppered with hidden sand banks; but the fisherman knew their every location, as well as the best side on which to take each island as it came up.

The most dangerous part of the journey, however, lay just ahead. It was the city of Rouen itself. Obviously the authorities knew Smith had escaped. Equally obviously they knew he would try to make it to the coast, and the nearest major port was Rouen, with Le Havre a bit further down river. Those cities would be on high alert.

The boat was approaching St. Paul Island, just south of the Rouen docks. Here the low marshy island occupies most of the river so the boat must pass through a very narrow passageway if it is to get by at all. At exactly that point an inspection boat had been posted.

"All of you," the fisherman said, "get into the hold and cover yourselves with the bags you find there."

The three quickly did as he asked. The boat was a shallow draft smack with an open fish hold; but by scrunching up into the forward overhang and covering themselves up, they were relatively safe from prying eyes. If the soldiers decided to come aboard and look around, however, it would be all over.

The fisherman reduced sail and drifted toward the inspection boat. As the three were finishing covering themselves with burlap, the fisherman said, "By the way, monsieur, I know who you are."

Whitney and Walker looked at each other with alarm. Smith froze; but there was nothing to be done. With a few words the fisherman could now turn them in and probably receive a far greater reward for their capture than anything he could offer for their safety. Walker's grip tightened on his pistol.

"Good afternoon, Citizen. Please tell me where you are from, and where you are going," the officer asked.

"Good afternoon to you, monsieur. I am bound for the fishing grounds off of Le Havre. I am out of Belbeuf and hope to be back tomorrow night."

"I see. I must inform you, we are looking for three fugitives from French justice—two men and a woman. Have you seen any such today?

"Three fugitives, eh? Well..." the fisherman paused and the three stowaways tensed. "No, I haven't. You can see for yourself there is no one on this boat but me; and you can see into my hold from where you are."

The officer had been inspecting boats all morning and was loath to clamber aboard yet another one. So he just glanced in the direction of the fish hold and said, "Have you seen anything suspicious along the shoreline?"

"No, nothing at all."

"All right, citizen, you may go," he said with a wave. Good fishing."

"Thank you, monsieur."

The three stayed hidden until the boat had rounded the Rouen bend and travelled as far as Point Aunay.

"You can come out now," the fisherman said. "I think we're in the clear."

The three climbed out of the hold and looked around. They could see the Forest de Rouvray to their left, and the Forest de Roumares to their right; but no other boats on the water.

Smith looked at the fisherman for a long moment. "Monsieur, just before we came upon that inspector you said you knew who I was. Who am I?"

"You are Captain Sidney Smith."

Smith was stunned. "And how is it you know me?"

The fisherman laughed. "Captain, many years ago I used to sell fish to your ship, the *Diamond*, when you were on duty along this coast. Indeed, many is the time on a cold night you have, with your own hands, given me a cup of British grog to warm me up; and you always paid a fair price for my fish. You never tried to cheat me like some of the other captains.

"Oh yes, I remember you very well. I had heard a long time ago that you had been captured, and then suddenly there you were before me. So I added the tally and figured you had escaped."

"Then on behalf of my friends, may I offer my deepest thanks for not betraying us."

"It is not a problem, Captain. I would be a scoundrel if I had done so. Besides, I want to get to that British ship as much as you do?"

"Why it that?"

"Because I've developed a taste for grog," he laughed.

CHAPTER THREE

In the spring of 1798 England needed a hero; and for several weeks Sir Sidney Smith was it.

The frigate *Argo* picked up their fishing boat and once the captain was convinced that he really *was* Sir Sidney Smith they were whisked into Portsmouth. From there it was a mad coach ride to London to report to the Admiralty. At that point, however, events took on a life of their own.

The newspapers and magazines all carried multiple major articles about the "daring escape of our beloved hero." Each one tried to outdo the others with their breathless reporting. If that meant making up a few "facts" about the audaciousness of his escape, or the rigors of his confinement, well, so be it.

The King received him in a private audience. Smith, Walker and Whitney dined with Prince William, their old friend from Yorktown days. Lord Spencer dragged them to inumerable balls, dinners, concerts and private meetings with politicians—all the while beaming like a proud father whose wayward son had returned covered in glory.

Sidney might have suffered through all that if it were not for the public adulation he was also receiving. He could meet with kings and princes with no problem, but the admiring glances and whispered recognition on the streets made him uncomfortable—very uncomfortable. Unfortunately he had no control over that, and the public worship continued.

Poems were written about him, songs were composed, Astley's Theater even produced a play called: "The Lucky Escape, or the Return to the Native Country" which was playing to sold-out audiences.

He finally called a halt and suggested that the three meet at Lucas Walker's London apartment.

"I have a suggestion," Smith began. "What do you say we adjourn to Bath for a few days. You know, take the waters. Relax a bit."

"Take the waters in Bath?" Susan asked, skeptically.

"Yes, they're quite medicinal you know. People have been swearing by them since Roman times."

"And you want to relax a bit."

"Yes."

"Sidney, you just got out of two years in prison. Were you somehow unable to sleep in while you were there?"

She gave Sidney her "What's going on?" look. Walker just sat there and smiled. He knew Susan, he knew that look, and he knew she had just skewered Sidney in a white lie. He was glad it was Smith's turn for a change.

"All right. I just want to get out of London. If I had known there was going to be all this folderol, I think I would have stayed in the Temple."

"Are you really that uncomfortable with it?" Susan asked.

"Yes, I am. I mean, what am I supposed to do? What do people want from me? I get dragged around from event to event and present myself like a specimen to be inspected. I step forward as if to say: 'All right. Here I am. Here's your hero. Come look... but don't touch, please. You there, sir. Please stay behind the ropes.' I never bargained for all that."

"What would we do in Bath?" Walker asked.

"Lord Camelford has a townhouse there. He's my uncle; you know... my mother's sister is married to him. In fact my mother has recently gone to visit her; so I am sure we can stay at their place.

"Plus, we really can take the waters, you know. They have magnificent hot baths; and I can show you where I went to school. Bath Grammar School. It's just... I need to get away from all this for a while, and they've probably never even heard of me there."

Sidney was wrong. Very wrong.

They arrived in the late afternoon and the carriage driver was directed to Lord Camelford's magnificent house on the Grand Parade, overlooking the river. Within a few minutes he was hugging his mother, within an hour the news of his arrival had spread from one end of town to the other, and within two hours the local volunteer regiment was drawn up in front of Camelford's house—complete with regimental band.

By then it was dark, but the people who were filling the street brought their own torches. The town's mayor, not wishing to miss being associated with the occasion, was standing in Lady Camelford's flower garden addressing the crowd. As he was doing so, however, three schoolboys snuck through the horde and presented themselves at the mansion's door.

After knocking several times, a servant finally answered.

"Good evening, sir," the oldest boy nervously began. "We are here representing the students of Bath Grammar School. We would like to pay our respects to our most illustrious alumnus, Sir Sidney Smith."

The servant was about to summarily dismiss the children, when Susan Whitney happened to pass by and overheard the exchange. She intervened.

She led the boys down a hall to the drawing room, slid open the doors slightly, and walked through. There she found Sidney sitting by the fireplace looking miserable.

"Sidney, there is a delegation here in the hall that wishes to see you."

Smith looked up irritably. "Susan, you know that I..."

But Susan had already opened up the doors wider to reveal the three boys standing there with hats in hand. Smith stopped in mid-sentence.

The boys timidly entered the room, quickly gazed around at the expensive furnishings, then at the object of their quest.

Smith looked at the boys, then at Susan, then back at the boys. "And you are?"

"Good evening, sir," began the spokesman. "I am Thomas De Quincey. This is Michael Haley and to my left is Gary... er... Gerald Spade. We are here representing the boys of the Bath Grammar School, and wish to officially welcome you home, sir."

This was too much for Sidney, even in his blackened mood. He welcomed them warmly, had them sit, caused fresh lemonade to be made, and pumped them for news of the school. Was old Mr.

Morgan still the headmaster? Have the upperclassmen invented any new and creative ways of harassing incoming students? Was the food still as bad? Did the roof on the dormitory still leak over in the northwest corner?

He was truly enjoying himself for one of the few times since his return. Then Susan re-entered.

"Sidney," she began, "I am sorry to interrupt, but you're really going to have to do something for that crowd outside. At least go out and wave to them."

"Yes, yes... just one moment, if you please. I'll go out and see them shortly."

"No, Sidney. The mayor is hinting at the possibility of a riot."

Sidney resigned himself to his fate, until a thought hit him.

"Boys, would you like to help out an old schoolmate?"

A few minutes later the door to the Camelford mansion swung open and out walked the three boys, followed by Sir Sidney. The four of them stood on the veranda smiling and waving at the crowd, as if the *four* of them were each conquering heros.

That was what made Sidney's public appearance possible. The public's gaze could now be spread among several people, not just himself. The crowd might not know who these boys were, or what their connection was to Sir Sidney, but they cheered them all the same—and thereby diluted their attention.

After several minutes Sidney quieted the crowd, said a few words of thanks, and said how glad he was to be back in his "second home," Bath. The crowd roared with approval and pride. But Sidney went on to point out that he was still rather fatigued from his trip from London, and asked their indulgence. Thanking them again, he and the boys disappeared back behind the security of the door; and the crowd, satisfied, dispersed.

Final relief didn't come until the next day, however, when a courier knocked on the door with a letter for Sir Sidney to report immediately to Portsmouth. Never was he more glad to receive a set of orders.

*****

James Gambier was not a man to be trifled with; and he couldn't help feeling that this insolent, insubordinate, young man before him was doing just that. He was a rear admiral in His Majesty's Navy. He was one of the heroes of the battle of the Glorious

First of June. He was one of the Lords Commissioners of the Admiralty. And he was decidedly *not* accustomed to being brushed aside as if he were a tradesman trying to collect an overdue bill.

Fortunately, Gambier was deeply religious man; because if it were not for that fact he would have had Parish taken out and shot a long time ago. But when it came to breaking codes, he had to admit, the man was a genius; and they desperately needed his skills at the moment. Maybe he could shoot him later.

So Gambier swallowed his pride, took a deep breath to try to keep the anger out of his voice, and continued. "Mr. Parish, it has been nearly a month since you started work on that message. I ask you again, sir, what progress have you made?"

Parish looked up from his work. His physical appearance had visibly altered in the preceding month. Parish was a man in his early 30's and, in normal times, of average—even slightly thin—build. His most distinctive feature was probably the impish smile that would break out at odd intervals from beneath his perpetually twinkling eyes and balding head. That, however, was not the way he looked now. After nearly a month of constant brain-wracking work, he had a drawn, emaciated, look. His eyes had lost their luster, the smile rarely appeared, and his face—normally sporting a healthy reddish blush—looked pale and haggard.

"It's coming along, admiral. It's coming along."

"But you've been saying that for weeks. Can you read to me what you have so far?"

Parish made no effort to keep the frustration out of his voice. "It doesn't work that way, admiral. Let me explain it this way.

"Every language has it's own characteristics—peculiarities in the way the letters are used or arranged. In the English language, for example, the most frequently occurring letter is "e." The most frequent word is "the." If a word has two letters, "o" is probably one of them; and if you find an "o" in a word of more than two letters, it's often followed by a "u." If a word has more than one syllable, you look first to see if it ends in "-ing," and so forth.

"The trick of deciphering is to identify those language patterns, then try different possibilities until you can build up a kind of dictionary of reliably deciphered code-groups and the words they represent. Every time you add a word or letter to the dictionary, the next one becomes that much easier."

"And you say French has these patterns?"

"Absolutely. The most frequent letters in French are "e" and "i." The vowel "e" is often found at the end of words; and if the word ends in a double letter, it's probably "ee." The most common two-letter word is "et." If a word ends in "m," there is almost always a vowel immediately before it.

"I could go on, but I think you get the point. Deciphering is a matter of slowly building up that dictionary until you can read the whole."

"Then why is it taking so long? After all, the message is a short one."

"That's exactly the problem. The longer the message is, the easier it is to find and attack the repetitive patterns. I have almost nothing to work with here. That's why I've been sending letters to Lord Spencer practically every other day asking... no, *begging*... him to get me more messages like this one to work with."

Parish knew he was blowing smoke up the admiral's stern sheets. It was true that the message was only one sentence; but it was long enough. He had found the patterns; but none of them made any sense. Every time he thought he had a word or letter pinned down, it would not pan-out elsewhere in the document. It was as if every letter was encrypted using a different code table, and *that* was clearly impossible. He didn't need more messages; he needed time—more *time!*

"Yes, well, that's one of the reasons for my visit today." Gambier replied. "We have no other messages like that one here in London; but we do in Gibraltar. At least we think we do. The message you hold was on its way to Napoleon when it was intercepted. As you might imagine, we have agents who occasionally are able to obtain copies of coded traffic. When they do, they are forwarded to our base in Gibraltar."

"What good does that do me? I need them here."

"Lord Spencer understands that, so we've decided to send you there."

"Send me where?

"To Gibraltar."

"On a ship?"

Gambier tried to keep the sarcasm out of his voice, but failed. "We decided not to have you walk."

"But I mean... on a Royal *Navy* ship?"

"Yes, of course. When you break the code... notice I said 'when' and not 'if,' young man... we're going to have to get the intelligence to our fleet in the Mediterranean. So, why not have the information go forth directly from Gibraltar and save some time?"

Parish was more excited by this news than he had been by anything in years; but he tried to maintain the outward appearance of calm.

"If I go, admiral, I must be allowed to take my flute."

"That's fine. You can take your flute."

"And if I go, my wife must be allowed to go with me."

Gambier paused for a moment. Personally he didn't agree with the policy many captains had of allowing women on board their ships; but transporting civilian officials—including their wives— was not all that unusual, so he said, "Yes, fine. You can take your wife."

"But if I take my wife, she must have her harpsichord with her."

This was too much. The man was impossible. Gambier felt a flush of anger welling up in him again, but he quickly got it under control and in a strained voice said, "Fine! You can take your flute, and your wife, and your wife's harpsichord, and your grandmother's whalebone corset for all I care; but you're leaving in two days."

Parish looked off at some distant point with his mind's eye and murmured. "Admiral, I've always wanted to go to..."

*****

"Gibraltar?" Walker asked. "What's in Gibraltar?"

The three were in a hackney coach on their way to the Navy Pier at Priddy's Hard in Portsmouth. With the pier in sight, Smith was finally at liberty to disclose more information.

They had been in town for several days and Susan was in her element. The previous day she had taken the two men on a coach tour of her old neighborhood in Portsmouth Common, north of town. Walker was intrigued and asked questions about everything. Smith was more subdued. He was appalled by the filth and squalor he saw all around him. He looked at the dirty street children, boys and girls, and tried to imagine a pre-adolescent Susan as one of them. He said nothing, but he quietly acquired a new appreciation for who she was, how far she had come, and the barriers she had overcome to get there.

Shortly after arriving in Portsmouth, Sidney had met with Lord Spencer who had come all the way from London to brief him. After his meeting, Smith announced only that they were going to sea again, but couldn't tell them where they were going. Walker and Whitney knew better than to press him; so Walker spent the afternoon getting his medicinal chest re-stocked, and Susan put her expensive dresses into a storage trunk and got out what she called her "sea-goin' duds."

The three were now on their way to their ship when Smith revealed their destination.

"Why Gibraltar?" Smith replied. "I am not sure exactly. It's all very strange."

"It seems that Napoleon is mustering his army at Toulon and several other ports, and is obviously planning to sail off with them. Everyone knows that, but no one knows where he's planning to go.

"About a month ago the admiralty obtained a message that supposedly contains the information they need to intercept Bonaparte. If we can catch him at sea with a significant enough fleet, it could end the war. The problem is that it was encoded; so they put their best code breaker on it."

"What did it say?" Walker asked.

"They don't know. He hasn't been able to break it yet. Apparently, he needs more messages like it in order to complete his work. Anyway, that's our mission. They have a small pile of coded French traffic collecting at Gibraltar, so I am supposed to take Mohammed to the mountain, so to speak. I... I should say we... are to escort this code-breaker to Gibraltar then, when he cracks the code, get the information to Nelson who is wandering around the Mediterranean somewhere."

"If it's still not decrypted, how does the Admiralty know that the message contains the information they need?" Susan asked.

"They don't; but two men died getting it into British hands, and *they* seemed to think it did."

During this exchange, Walker was staring intently at something outside the window of the coach.

"Sidney, I don't think we're going anywhere very soon.

"Why not?"

"Because our ship is currently lying on it's side with its hull being re-coppered."

Smith, who was facing Walker and Whitney, slid across the seat to look for himself. "No, that's the *Bellona*, a 74-gun frigate. She's been here in Portsmouth for refitting since last April. Our ship is the one beyond it."

Susan leaned over Walker, looked for a moment, and said. "There *is* no ship beyond it."

"Sure there is. Right there. To the left of the *Bellona* and about a quarter-mile out.

Susan looked out at the ship, looked at Sidney, then back at the ship, and said, "It's a brig-sloop!"

"So, what's wrong with that?"

"Sidney, I own bathtubs that are larger than that ship."

"Now, Susan, it's an excellent vessel. It's called the *Mutine*. We captured her from the French about a year ago. The French are good ship-builders, you know. They're terrible at fighting them, but their ships are very well built."

"Before Susan could get her sails up and rigged, Smith continued. "A young lieutenant captains her by the name of Hardy... Thomas Hardy, I believe... who was also the one who captured her at Santa Cruz last May. He's supposed to be a real up-and-comer, this Hardy fellow."

Susan looked at him with more than a bit of skepticism on her face, and was about to say something when Walker piped up.

"She might be a good ship, but what I am trying to understand is why there's a harpsichord dangling from her rigging."

The carriage pulled up to the pier, the three got out and, sure enough, there was a harpsichord, 15 feet above deck, hanging like a bizarre Christmas tree ornament from the main yard. They spent a few moments gazing at it in amazement before hiring a boatman to take them out.

As they approached the ship they got a chance to look at her more carefully. She was a two masted, 16-gun brig-sloop—a hybrid of two ship-types. She had the hull lines of a sloop, but her stern was squared-off like a brig. She had two masts—a main-mast and a mizzen—like a sloop; but her sails were square-rigged like a brig. Under staysails and jib, she was as nimble as a sloop; and under square sails she could fly before the wind like a brig. All in all she was a nice compromise.

Her length was only 106 feet, her beam 28 feet; and, at 349 tons, she was little more than a glorified yacht. This fact was underscored by her armament, which consisted of fourteen 16-pound guns, augmented by two 36-pound carronades. To be sure, the carronades had some bite if she could get in close enough to use them; but with whom would she get in close? Even a half-hearted broadside from a frigate would reduce her to matchsticks in an instant. But still, her captain was very proud of her—as are all first-time captains, of all first ships, in all eras, everywhere.

They found the captain at the breast rail of the quarterdeck, megaphone in hand, heaping abuse on his first lieutenant, who was heaping it on the boatswain. The boatswain, in turn, was displaying a masterful selection of obscene words and gestures in the direction of a seaman who was up in the rigging. And the latter was frantically sidestepping out on the main yard while swearing at a fouled block that was causing all the commotion.

On the main deck, at the base of the mast was a civilian who was looking up and offering suggestions that everyone was ignoring, and beside him was a lovely young lady who was wringing her hands with anxiety.

Smith said, "I see you got the latest admiralty directive. The new signal for getting under way is now: "Harpsichord from the mainmast (starboard side)."

Thomas Masterman Hardy turned toward the source of this impertinent remark and saw Commodore Smith in full uniform. Technically Smith was only a senior captain. He had held the temporary rank of commodore prior to his imprisonment when he commanded a small squadron off the French coast. Lord Spencer decided he should keep the rank for the time being. This would make sure he would be senior to any ship's captain he might meet, and only one step below Rear-Admiral Nelson. Hardy was still a lieutenant and only called "captain" because he was the commander of a ship. It's a courtesy afforded the commander of any ship—however small.

"Commodore Smith," Hardy said with some surprise. "We weren't expecting you until later this afternoon."

Smith shrugged. "I didn't see any reason to delay my arrival." Then gesturing to his companions. "May I introduce my companions: Dr. Lucas Walker, who is a warranted naval physician, and Lady Susan Whitney, who is an Able Surgeon's Mate."

Hardy quickly looked at Smith as if to say, "Wha-a-a-t?" but Smith continued. "Don't let the 'Lady Whitney' part fool you, Captain. She really does carry an 'Able' rating, unofficially of course, and has probably eaten more gun smoke than all of us put together."

Hardy bowed formally to Lady Whitney and shook hands with Walker. "We are indeed privileged to have a physician on board, doctor. That's extremely rare for a ship of our size. In fact, even having a qualified surgeon's mate is very rare. And Lady Whitney... I..."

"We're aboard ship now, captain. I am no longer Lady Whitney. It's 'Whitney,' or 'Susan,' or even 'Hey, you.' I wish to be treated like a member of your ship's compliment just like any other; and I neither seek, nor do I desire, special status." Hardy was more than glad to hear those words. Having a titled lady on board was one thing; he could handle that. Having her functioning as a crew member was quite another, and would pose impossible quandaries of etiquette.

"Well, we're certainly glad to have all the medical assistance we can get, ah... Whitney. Of course, we won't be able to carry you officially on the ship's books."

"Yes, I quite understand that."

"Don't worry captain," Walker interjected. "Whitney here will serve as my assistant. She will be under my direct supervision and control at all times, and I will be responsible for her every action." Susan softly muttered, "In a pigs eye," but no one heard it.

"Yes, quite." Hardy replied. "But I am not sure I understand how Lady Whitney came to be rated as..."

"It's a long story, captain," Smith interrupted, "which I am sure we'll get to during the course of our voyage. In the meantime, if you would be so good as to..." He was about to say "sway our luggage on board" when he realized that the stalled harpsichord was still occupying the tackle on the main yard.

"I am terribly sorry, Commodore, but we've had a slight malfunction while getting that... that *thing*... on board. I am sure it will be cleared up soon and we'll have your baggage in hand shortly."

At just that moment, the snarl in the line that was running through the main yard block released itself. The harpsichord went into a 12-foot free-fall, catching up just before it hit the deck. The civilian female let out a soprano screech, which was matched by a similar sound in the tenor range coming from her husband.

"And those people would be..." Sidney asked.

"That is your code-breaker and his wife." Hardy paused for a moment then added, "And good luck to you, sir."

Smith was about to ask what he meant by that, but Captain Hardy had already focused his attention on the next task of the hundreds that needed to be done to get the ship ready for sea.

*****

All was chaos at the waterfront.

Toulon harbor is shaped like an out of proportion hourglass. The inner harbor, the Petite Rade with the city of Toulon in the northeast corner, had the better anchorage; but it was small and confined. The outer harbor, the Grande Rade, had fewer good anchorage areas; but it was large and expansive. Between the two, at the waist of the hourglass, was an opening only 500 yards wide, guarded by forts on either side.

For weeks, soldiers had been pouring into the port city from all over France, more than doubling the size of the town. Finally, orders came for the troops to go to their assigned ships, and the embarkation had begun.

The basic uniform of the French soldier was a blue cut-away coat, with red collar and cuffs, white vest and pants, and long black spats running halfway up their shins. Those uniforms were simply everywhere. But, as with many armies of the day, there were often exceptions to the basic uniform, and those exceptions were on magnificent display. In one section of the boarding area, lined all the way up a side street, were the green coats and red fronts of the 3rd dragoons. In another area were the red striped pants of the grenadiers of the 18th Demi-Brigade. Off to the side were the powder blue uniforms of a group of carabineers from the 21st Light Demi, and behind them the red coats of the 7th Hussars.

At long last Captain Joseph-Marie Moiret was able to set foot into a longboat that would take him to his transport ship. Looking around for a seat that approximated being clean, he finally gave up and sat down next to his friend Captain Horace Say.

"Joseph, if you're looking for a way to keep those white trousers of yours clean, you can forget it. This is not going to be an excursion down the Seine, you know."

"More's the pity," Moiret replied. "I could do with a bit of cheese, a fine bottle of wine and an even finer mademoiselle on my arm about now. Instead we're...

"Corporal, watch what you're about!" Moiret exclaimed as a young soldier lost his balance in the bobbing boat and fell into him. Apologizing profusely, the young man regained his balance, clambered over several other soldiers and found a seat.

Moiret then spent several minutes fastidiously restoring several imaginary discrepancies in his uniform. Both Say and he were officers in the 75th Infantry Demi-Brigade under General Kléber, with their bright red coats, sky-blue collars and cuffs, and white piping. Captain Jean-Honoré Horace Say was dressed in the same uniform, except his collar and cuffs were black, denoting that he was an engineer assigned to the 75th.

Their ship was located in the Grande Rade—the outer harbor—so it would be a while before they would reach it. That was fine with both men as it gave them time to get caught up, and there was much to talk about.

A week earlier General Napoleon had reviewed his army; but the highlight was the address he gave to the troops afterward. In it he alternately promised the men adventure, honor, and glory. He reminded them that the Romans fought Carthage by sea as well as by land; and he concluded by promising each man seven acres of land after the campaign was over. The soldiers wildly cheered this, even though Napoleon never said where those acres might be—in France, along the Nile, or for that matter, along the Ganges.

The officers, however, just looked puzzled—wondering how a general could possibly make such a promise. Indeed, a few days later Napoleon had to produce a poster of the text of that speech with the land reference omitted. But the men knew what they so clearly heard. They would get *land*, and they were still buzzing about it.

The key phrase for the officers came at the end of his speech when he said: "The genius of liberty, which has since it's birth rendered the Republic the arbiter of Europe, is now headed toward the most distant lands." That was what had the officer corps intrigued. What "distant lands" was he talking about?

"So, what do you think he meant, Horace?"

"I don't know, nor does anyone else. No one knows where we're going."

"Yes, but where do you *think* we're going?"

Say paused for a moment. "I think we're going to England."

"Why?"

"I think the general has a two stage plan. The first stage requires the navy to seize control of the Mediterranean. To do that they need bases, and that's where we come in. I think we're headed off to take Sardinia, Malta, and probably even Sicily."

"Then what?"

"Once we have control of those islands the fleet can operate out of their ports and block all traffic going east-west. That will give us a stranglehold on every country bordering the Mediterranean, and the British will have to respond. Once the British fleet commits to the Med, we then break out through Gibraltar and attack England."

"But why couldn't the British then move their fleet back to their home waters?"

"I am sure they'll try; but it'll be too late. Once we've landed in England, we have them. At that point it doesn't matter what their precious fleet does, because we won't need ships any more. We'll be on the beaches of *les rosbifs*, and they don't have the military strength at home to stop us."

Moiret thought about Say's analysis all the way out to the transport ship and decided it made sense—or at least as much sense as anything else he had heard. What else could it be? They had already conquered Italy. They could be going to Greece, but why move troops by ship all the way from France, when the Army of Italy was only 50 miles away across the Adriatic Sea. No, Horace is right. It has to be an island-hopping expedition. Why else have all these ships?

*****

"Sit down, Horace. Sit down."

His formal name was Horatio, but he detested it; so all his friends called him Horace. Horace Nelson. And the man on the other side of the table, Admiral John Jervis, 1st Earl of St. Vincent, was indeed his friend.

Lord St. Vincent owed Nelson a lot. At the Battle of Cape St. Vincent in February of the previous year, Jervis was commanding a fleet of 15 British ships of the line and attacked a Spanish fleet of 28 ships. The Spaniards broke for their port in Cadez, so Jervis placed his fleet into a giant U-turn to chase them. Nelson's ship, the *Captain*, was at the end of the long British line and thus much closer to the fleeing Spanish. Reasoning that they would never catch them by chasing; he decided to disobey orders. He pulled the

Captain out of the British line, cut in front of several other ships, and threw his 74-gun vessel in front of the 136-gun *Santisima Trinidad*. The ensuing havoc delayed the Spaniards long enough for the British to catch up.

As battles go, it wasn't much as only four of the 28 Spanish ships were captured. But, for this victory Jervis was made Earl St. Vincent, and Nelson was knighted. In effect, as Sidney Smith well knew, Jervis was made an Earl because he won a battle that he was miles away from, when a hot-headed underling decided to disobey his explicit orders. Since that time, however, Nelson became Jervis' protege, and Jervis was not exactly a man without influence.

"Horace, I've recently received a letter from Lord Spencer and I'd like to read you part of it." He laboriously took out a pair of spectacles from inside his coat, adjusted them, and read.

The circumstances in which we now find ourselves oblige us to take a measure of a more decided and hazardous complexion than we should otherwise have thought ourselves justified in taking; but when you are apprized that the appearance of a British squadron in the Mediterranean is a condition on which the fate of Europe may at this moment be stated to depend, you will not be surprised that we are disposed to strain every nerve, and incur considerable hazard in effecting it.

If you determine to send a detachment into the Mediterranean [instead of going in person with the fleet], I think it almost unnecessary to suggest to you the propriety of putting it under the command of Sir Horatio Nelson, whose acquaintance with that part of the world, as well as his activity and disposition, seem to qualify him in a peculiar manner for that service.

I am as strongly impressed, as I have no doubt your Lordship will be, with the hazardous nature of the measure which we now have in contemplation; but I cannot at the same time help feeling how much depends upon its success, and how absolutely necessary it is at this time to run some risk, in order, if possible, to bring about a new system of affairs in Europe, which shall save us all from being overrun by the exorbitant power of France. In this view of the subject, it is impossible not to perceive how much depends on the exertions of the great Continental powers; and, without entering further into what relates more particularly to them, I can venture to assure you that no good will be obtained from them if some such measure as that now in contemplation is not immediately adopted. On the other hand, if, by our appearance in the Mediterranean, we can encourage Austria to come forward again, it is in the highest degree probable that the other powers will seize the opportunity of acting at the same time, and such a general concert be established as shall soon bring this great contest to a termination, on grounds less unfavorable by many degrees to the parties concerned than appeared likely a short time since.

"There you have it young man," Jervis said with a wry smile. "Lord Spencer wants to place the fate of the empire in your hands."

"I take it you don't agree with his assessment," Nelson replied.

"His assessment of you? No, I quite agree with him. About the rest, I don't know what to think. One part of me is convinced that Bonaparte is going to launch a direct invasion of England. I mean, it only makes sense that he should do so. On the other hand, he is clearly massing troops and ships at Toulon, as well as at Genoa, Ajaccio, and Civita Vecchia. I have no idea why he's doing it; but I also have no doubt there is mischief afoot, and Bonaparte is behind it."

"So, what then would you like me to do, Admiral?"

Jervis leaned back in his chair and thought for a moment. "Lord Spencer would have me send everything that can float into the Mediterranean. But, you'll notice, in his letter he does not remove the responsibility of my keeping the Spanish fleet blockaded here at Cadiz. So..." Jervis thought for another moment.

"All right, young man, here's what we'll do. I am not going to send a battle fleet. I simply can't afford to draw down our current strength either here at Cadiz or at Gibraltar. Instead, I am going to send a 'squadron of observation,' and you're going to command it.

"I want you to proceed to Gibraltar. There you'll be assigned, let's say... three 74's and three or four frigates. I want you to take them to Toulon and keep an eye on Boney. If he gets underway, you are not to challenge him—you won't have the ships to do that anyway. But I want you to get word back to me via the fastest means available, and then follow him. I want to know where he's going and what he is up to. If I think the time is ripe, I'll send you additional ships so that you can take more forceful measures."

"What ships will I have, sir?"

"I think I can get you the *Vanguard*, the *Orion* and the *Alexander*. I am not sure about the frigates yet. Come by in a couple of hours and I'll have your orders drawn up.

"Yes, sir. Thank you, sir."

"Oh yes, one more thing..."

"Sir?"

Jervis' voice softened, "Good luck, Horace. I mean that. When Lord Spencer writes..." Jervis re-applied his glasses and glanced down at the letter. "When he says '...the appearance of a British squadron in the Mediterranean is a condition on which the fate of Europe may at this moment be stated to depend...' I don't think he's joking."

Nelson left the ship and Jervis wondered for a minute about whether he had chosen the right man—no matter how much he owed him. He was not alone with those doubts. The appointment sent a shock wave through the Royal Navy. A host of officers, notably Sir William Parker and Sir John Orde, were indignant that such a junior officer should be given so important a command over them.

Parker publicly read to the officers aboard his ship, the *Prince George*, a letter in which Lord St. Vincent was denounced for having sent so young a flag officer as Nelson to seek the French fleet. Orde went so far as to challenge Jervis to a duel, although it was never fought. Jervis eventually had to issue a statement saying that "Those who were responsible for measures had a right to choose their men."

Jervis hoped that statement would quell the unrest; but still, in private moments, even he had some doubts.

*****

On May 18th the last officer to board a long boat in Toulon was the most important. He was General Napoleon Bonaparte.

The preceding days of embarkation had almost a carnival atmosphere to them. The troops boarded in high spirits, as if they were going to a party. Along the piers of Toulon were tearful wives and sweethearts, but the men had an almost supernatural joy at beginning their adventure. Who knew what rewards awaited them? Who know what glories they might achieve? And, looking back at their wives and sweethearts, who knew what other enticing young ladies they might meet along the way?

Yes, they were going to war, and in war people are killed. They knew that; but not one of them thought for an instant that death would be *his* fate. No soldier ever did. They couldn't, for if they really and truly believed they were going to die, you would never get them to the battlefield.

As soon as Napoleon's boat pushed off, guns started erupting and bells started pealing throughout the city. As he made has way out onto the bay, ships along his path would add their gunfire tributes, which was eventually picked up by every ship in the fleet, large or small.

His destination was the *Orient* which was one of the largest warships of it's day. It was an Océan Class, 120-gun, ship of the line. She was 214 feet long, 53 feet wide and carried over 32,000 square feet of sail.

The *Orient* was big and fast, to be sure; but her real threat came from her firepower. She had thirty-four 12-pounders on her upper deck, thirty-four 24-pounders on her middle deck, and thirty-two 36-pounders on her lower deck. Add to that twenty 8-pounders on her quarterdeck and forecastle, and you had a fearsome weapon. A single broadside could hurl over 1200 pounds of shot into an enemy, which meant she was capable of dissolving a ship the size of a frigate like a sugar cube.

When Napoleon reached the *Orient*, they thought that it might be somewhat undignified for the General to have to scramble up the side like a common seaman. So, they swayed over a chair-lift to bring him on board; but Napoleon would have none of it. To the raucous cheers of the ship's company, he came up the small footholds that were built into the side of the ship.

With this arrival, however, all analogies to the common seaman ceased. Napoleon's quarters on board the *Orient* were spectacular—literally fit for a king. His quarters were lavishly furnished with the finest rugs and furniture, in his receiving room there was a gold playing table on which he and his officers could play cards, and in his stateroom his bed was mounted on casters to help reduce any feeling of seasickness he might experience. All in all, it was the kind of accommodation you might expect to see on an expedition heading to Peru, not an expedition heading to fight the enemies of the Republic, whoever and wherever *they* might be.

*****

On May 9th 1798 Rear-Admiral Horatio Nelson got underway from Gibraltar with three 74-gun ships of the line, one 32- and three 36-gun frigates, and one 20-gun corvette. He headed directly to Toulon to take station as Jervis' "squadron of observation."

On May 20th, General Napoleon Bonaparte put into motion 13 ships of the line, seven 40-gun frigates, 24 smaller frigates and sloops, and nearly 200 transports carrying 36,000 troops. No one—not the troops, not the officers, not even the ship's captains—knew where they were going.

And on May 21st a tiny brig-sloop left Portsmouth Harbor bound for Gibraltar with one of the few men in the world who could decode the message that would answer the question of Napoleon's destination.

CHAPTER FOUR

When Parish first heard the sound, he couldn't quite believe his ears. They were a day out of Portsmouth and the weather had turned mean. Within the span of an hour, the seas had gone from a gentle rolling blue, to a foam-flecked gray under an overcast sky. With the rising seas the ship's timbers began to bend and work more strenuously. As a result, with every pitch, roll or yaw the seams between the timbers would work open slightly, admitting a small quantity of water. That water eventually would find its way to the bilge and had to be pumped out.

The *Mutine* had four elm tree pumps. Two were located on either side of the mizzenmast. These were sea suction pumps and were used to draw water from the ocean to clean the decks. Two other pumps were located on either side of the main mast. These connected to the bilges, and were the pumps that were at work when Parish heard the song.

He drifted up to the main deck like a moth looking for a briefly glimpsed source of light. He found it in the form of three men, a work party that was pumping out the bilges. One man was on each of the long-handled pumps, working them up and down to a regular rhythm. The third man, seated on a nearby hatch cover and singing the verses to a song, provided the rhythm. The pump men joined in on the chorus, and kept time by working their respective handles.

Verse
  We'll haul the bow-lin,
    so early in the morn-in.
Chorus:
  We'll haul the bow-lin,
    the bow-lin, haul!

We'll haul the bow-lin,
  for Kitty is my darlin
We'll haul the bow-lin,
  the bow-lin, haul!

We'll haul the bow-lin,
  the skipper is a growlin'
We'll haul the bow-lin,
  the bow-lin, haul!

And on it went across seemingly limitless verses, none re-peated, and all under the direction of one of the most valuable men on board—Jack Gerard, the ship's "shantyman."

Shanties, whether called that or not, have been sung for as long as there has been manual labor. Whether you're aboard ship hauling on a line, or in a field swinging a scythe, the work is simply easier if you do it to a rhythm. What better way to establish and maintain a rhythm than to do it to a song?

Not every ship, especially small ships, had a shantyman. He was a sailor who took it upon himself to learn dozens of verses to scores of songs; and, if he ran out of verses, have the ability to make up new ones on the spot. No verse could be repeated, if he wanted to maintain his reputation. The shantyman sung the verses, the men sung the choruses, and work—sometimes brutally hard work—got done. It was serious business, which is why no shanty was ever sung unless there was manual labor going on; and sea shanties were almost never sung on shore.

Basically there were two kinds of songs: capstan shanties and hauling shanties. Capstan shanties were used when the work was of a continuous nature, such as when the men would walk around a capstan, pushing the bars in front of them, to haul in the anchor. The verses for these songs tended to be longer, and the tune tended to be slower and have a much greater variety in rhythm.

The second type, hauling shanties, were of two kinds. There were songs used for the "long hoist" such as when the men were just beginning to raise a sail and the gear would be slack and easy to pull. The second were songs required for the "short pull" or "sweating up." The shantyman would switch to one of those when the sail was fully raised and the gear taut. At that point much stronger pulls were needed to make everything fast.

In some ways the shantyman was akin to, but the reverse of, an orchestra conductor. The orchestra conductor uses work to produce music; the shantyman uses music to produce work. But both must be highly attuned to those he is conducting and to making the right changes of pace, at just the right time, to accomplish his ends.

Parish, the musician, was entranced.

During the course of that voyage Parish and Lucas Walker became fast friends, almost inseparable. When Walker had ship's duties to attend to, Parish would gravitate to the sailors, watch them work, and plague them with innumerable questions. When the men were off duty or on Sunday, which was "make and mend" day, he could invariably be found among them requesting to be shown how to tie a certain knot, or splice a line, or for the names of the different parts of the ship. The men, however, didn't mind. Parish was a naturally good humored person, pleasing to be around, and they respected him because he was a person with "book learnin'" who didn't hold it over them. Parish responded by being available at all hours to write letters for them and read the ones they had received.

A similar friendship was forming between Terry Parish and Susan Whitney, but it had its origins in a very different set of circumstances.

Terry's harpsichord was placed in a corner of the lower deck near the men's mess area. It was braced so it wouldn't move when the ship pitched or rolled. She still had to tend it carefully almost every day as the salt air was continuously acting on the strings knocking them out of tune.

The morning of the first day, Susan heard a scream from the vicinity of what was already being called the "pi-aner room" by the crew; and Terry Parish came racing around the corner of the sick-bay.

"Susan, please... help me!"

Susan, assuming the worst, grabbed her emergency kit and followed Terry as she ran aft.

"There! That man! He's destroying my harpsichord!"

Susan peered through the gloom of the lower deck and relaxed.

"No, dear. That man is the ship's carpenter and he's sawing the legs off."

"Yes, that's what I said. He's destroying my beautiful instrument."

"No, he's not. He's making the legs removable. Don't worry. I am sure he's quite capable of doing that."

"But why would he want them to be removable?"

"Terry, this is a man of war. It's not a big one; but still, it's a warship. At any point we could run into another warship and have to engage her. If and when that happens, everything—and I mean *everything*—that is not essential to fighting must be moved below to the hold."

"But why?"

"Two reasons, actually. First, your harpsichord would be in the way. And second, if we engage a French ship and they send a shot through our hull, it could very well hit that instrument. If it did, it would disintegrate into hundreds of wood splinters that could easily maim or blind any seaman who was in the vicinity."

Terry looked at Susan in shocked amazement. At some abstract level she knew she was aboard a navy ship, but the reality of exactly what that meant had not hit her until that moment. She was riding on a machine that was specifically designed to kill; and in the process they might well meet other machines that were specifically designed to kill them.

Susan could see the light of understanding growing in the girl's eyes and decided it might be a good idea if she didn't think about it too much just then. So she said something that had been on her mind since she first saw the instrument flapping in the breeze back at Portsmouth.

"Terry, would you teach me how to play the harpsichord?"

*****

The first sign of trouble came late Monday afternoon when the barometer in Captain Berry's stateroom began to drop. The sky, which had been clear most of the day, was transformed into a lead colored canopy. The wind, which had been consistent and moderate for the past day, now began coming in fits and starts. One moment the sails would be full and pulling hard. The next, the wind would die and an eerie silence would descend on the ship, punctuated by the slap of the sails against the masts, the creak of spars, and the swish of water along the hull as the ship lost way. A few minutes later, it would freshen again and the sails would begin to pull; only to go slack in the next lull.

A few hours later, a strange low moaning sound could be heard coming from a particularly dark patch of sky off to the northwest. The moaning became louder and more melancholy with each passing hour. The sea was alive with spindrifts—ribbons of foam—that were flying in all directions. The waves became large and unpredictable; coming in an orderly fashion from a single direction one moment, and breaking into chaos the next without any apparent reason. The water became black as ink.

The men and officers in the *Vanguard* did not need a barometer to tell them they were in for a serious storm. From Rear-Admiral Nelson down to the youngest cabin boy, all hands aboard the 74-gun ship were engaged in readying for the coming assault.

The large sails were furled and the yards were sent down on deck and lashed tight. In their place were mere scraps of canvas—a small storm jib forward to keep the bow of the ship pointed down wind, a main storm staysail, and a triangular "leg-of-mutton" sail on the mizzen to keep the stern steady.

The gunner was passionately directing seamen at the task of securing the guns with extra breechings. Nothing was more dangerous than a 3000 lb gun that has broken loose in a storm. It will uncontrollably rattle around the interior of the ship smashing everything and everyone in its path until, finally, it crashes through the hull of the ship, possibly sinking her.

The bosun had some of the men battening down everything that could possibly work loose in a storm, including extra lashings on the boats. Other groups of men were applying "preventers" to the backstays, braces, shrouds and stays. These were additional lines to help support masts, spars, and other key elements of the ship.

Rear-Admiral Nelson ordered that word be passed to the other ships in his squadron to rig storm lanterns at the top of their masts. This would, at least theoretically, allow each captain to know where the other ships were located; and thus, hopefully, avoid crashing into each other. In practice, there was very little a captain could do to control his ship in a serious storm, let alone deftly avoid another ship; but it was good practice to send the lanterns aloft anyway.

Finally, when all was ready, Captain Berry ordered the *Vanguard* to come about and run before the growing wind. Then, they waited.

The wind had been steadily increasing for several hours and, with it, the seas. With each wave the stern of the *Vanguard* would rise up and place the ship at a heart-stopping angle. It would then career down the wave face like a surfboard, the gunwales almost even with the water as the ship laid over. The only thing that kept the vessel from broaching and rolling over like a turtle was a brilliant helmsman and the hand of God.

About 2:00 AM the main topmast went over the side. To make matters worse, at just that moment the topsail yard was full of men trying to make a repair. One of them, a landsman by the name of Arthur Barker, landed headfirst on the quarterdeck not two yards from where Captain Berry and Admiral Nelson were conferring.

At 3:15 the topmast fell in two pieces across the forecastle, slid over the side and, because it was still connected by lines to the ship, began beating on the ship's bottom. This knocked the best bower anchor out of place, and it too began thumping the side of the ship. What remained of the main topmast began swinging violently against the main rigging; so that with every roll of the ship, the mainmast threatened to break and fall.

Captain Berry gave orders to wear ship—to swing it around in a circle in order to bring it to a different course. He knew they were not far from shore and the danger of running aground was becoming very real. The storm jib was in tatters, but there was enough left to accomplish the maneuver. Men worked frantically to cut away the wreckage of the main topmast and secure the anchor that had come loose.

And still the storm continued.

The main yard was brought down to ease the pressure on the mainmast stays; but because, in effect, the ship had no functioning masts, it began to take terrible rolls. So much water was pouring into the ship that the crew had to cut holes in the lower deck, to let it run down to the bilge where it could be pumped out.

The ship had four Coles chain pumps arranged in pairs of two, side by side, fore and aft of the main mast. A lot of ships had gone to the new suction pump because they were better for fighting fires. But the Coles produced a greater volume of water, and those four old-fashioned pumps were now the only things keeping the ship afloat.

The water that made it into the bilge would eventually find its way to the pump well, amidship in the hold. There the bottom of a V-shaped tube dipped into the water. Inside the tube were a series of saucers with leather washers around the edges that were connected to what was, in effect, a very large bicycle chain. Around and around went the chain, the saucers scooping water from the well, carrying it up the tube and into a cistern, where it drained overboard through tubes called dales. It was men who provided the motive power for that chain—exhausted, terrified, men.

The storm did not slacken until the following afternoon, but by that time the *Vanguard* was a wreck. Her foremast was gone, her bowsprit was sprung, and her main and mizzen topmasts had long since gone overboard. The *Alexander*, another 74, came along side and offered the *Vanguard* a tow. She was four years older than the flagship and built in the same shipyard, but had somehow weathered the storm in much better shape. The tow was accepted, but tow to where?

Nelson huddled with Captain Berry and Captain Ball of the *Alexander*; and it was decided to make for St. Pierre, an island off the southwest coast of Sardinia. At one point along the way they were becalmed and, fearing that the *Alexander* was being placed in jeopardy by the tow, Nelson signaled to Ball to cast loose. Ball ignored the order and eventually they made it to St. Pierre.

The tranquil waters of Carloforte harbor seemed like heaven to the exhausted crews, but Nelson nevertheless called a meeting of the equally exhausted captains—Berry, Ball and Sir James Saumarez of the *Orion*.

The four men collapsed into chairs in Nelson's stateroom, not saying much, mostly just staring off into some vague personal space. Except for catnaps they had been up for almost 48 hours. A servant poured glasses of sherry for each of them and quietly departed. Nelson was the first to break the silence.

"Gentlemen, I can not tell you how pleased and appreciative I am for your efforts over the past few days." The three captains nodded or grunted their thanks.

"But I am afraid I must ask: do any of you know what happened to the rest of my squadron?"

Saumarez finished taking a sip from his drink and said, "The last time I saw our four frigates was Tuesday afternoon. They were about 10 miles out and scattered, but I could see them quite well through my glass, and I am sure they could see us. I have no idea where the little *Bonne Citoyenne* went. She might have gone down."

"What was the condition of the ships you saw?"

"They had obviously suffered some damage, but still seemed seaworthy. I suspect the smaller, lighter, frigates just rode the storm out like so many corks on a mill pond."

"Then where the devil *are* they?" Nelson's fist came down on the table.

No answer from the captains.

"And you there, Captain Ball. "Did you not see my signal yesterday to cast loose the tow? You could have wrecked your ship, and then where would we be?"

"Yes, sir. I saw it."

"And?"

"And I decided to ignore it."

Nelson managed to control his rage long enough to ask through clenched teeth, "May I ask why?"

"Because, sir, you were in trouble. I meant to save the *Vanguard*, no matter what, or go down trying."

Nelson was quite taken aback by his reply and didn't know what to say, so Ball continued. "Sir you just asked me where we would be if the *Alexander* had been wrecked. At that time, I was more concerned with where we would be—where all of us would be—if *Nelson* got wrecked. As you know, sir, sometimes the best way to follow orders is to ignore them."

Ball was referring to Nelson's ignoring Jervis' orders at the Battle of Cape St. Vincent, and winning the battle because of it. Ball and Nelson had never been particularly close, but from that moment on a sincere friendship existed between the two that would last until Nelson's death.

Nelson's head dropped. When he lifted it, he took a large drink from his glass and said, "You know, sometimes I am such a fool."

The captains murmured their objections.

"No, gentlemen. It's true, quite true! Do any of you think that storm was an accident?"

No one said anything, trying to figure out what he was getting at.

"I tell you, it was not! It was sent by God to check my consummate vanity. I hope it has made me a better officer; because I *know* it has made me a better man.

Saumarez, the most senior of the group, ventured to speak for all of them. "Sir, we had a storm. It was a severe storm, to be sure; but I hardly think God had singled you out for it."

"You don't? Mr. Saumarez, on Sunday evening at sunset, there was a vain man seated in this cabin. He had a squadron around him, and his ships were the finest in the world. He had men who looked up to their chief to lead them, and in whom their chief had the firmest confidence.

"Then consider... on Monday morning, when the sun rose, this proud man found his ship dismasted, his fleet dispersed, and he was in such distress that the smallest frigate out of France could have torn him to shreds.

"Do you not think there was a message in that?"

Again the room was silent. Nelson sighed and finished his drink.

"All right, gentlemen. I want each of you to get a good night's sleep, and I want you to rest your crews. Tomorrow we have to start putting these ships back together."

The refitting effort was nothing short of Herculean. In four days the carpenter aboard the *Vanguard*, James Morrison, surpassed all records for repair. He managed to substitute a maintop for a foremast and get it seated, topgallants were used for spars, and the bowsprit, which had been sprung in three places, had been ingeniously fished and was ready for use again.

On May 21st they had limped into St. Pierre. On May 31st they were back at Toulon.

But the French were not there.

*****

The *Mutine* was sailing easy under reefed topsails as she passed between Pigeon Island and the Pearl, around Cabreta Point, and across Gibraltar Bay to Point Europa on the far side. She was rated for a crew of sixty men but, like most Royal Navy ships, she was undermanned and only had forty-eight. They were all busy, however, getting ready to bring the ship to anchor before "The King's Bastion," the British naval base at Gibraltar.

Sir Sidney was on deck, along with everyone else who did not have specific duties, to watch the emerging majesty of "The Rock" as they swept into the bay. It slid into view looking like a lion—a rock lion—a British lion—crouching with his head up, alert, staring off into Spain. Captain Hardy, however, was walking back and forth on the quarterdeck, scanning the bay with his telescope.

"You look as if you've lost something," Sidney remarked.

"No, I am just confused, that's all."

"Confused about what?"

He handed his glass to Smith. "Look over there at that group of frigates."

Smith studied them for a moment. "What about them?"

"Those three 36's are the *Caroline*, the *Emerald*, and the *Flora*. That 32 is the *Terpsichore*. I'd know those ships anywhere. In fact, I know their captains very well. And..." Hardy looked again through his glass, "Yes, over there—that 20-gun—that's the *Bonne Citoyenne*."

"Captain, this is a British naval base. Why are you amazed to find British ships here?"

"It's not the ships I find that worries me, Commodore; it's the ships I don't find. Those frigates and the *Citoyenne* were assigned to Nelson's squadron; but I don't see the rest of his ships. Where are the *Orion* and the *Alexander*? And where is Nelson's flagship, the *Vanguard*?"

He had a point. Battle groups did not go anywhere without frigate scouts. To have one, or even two, of their frigates in port would be unusual but might be understandable. To have all of them here, however, was unheard of unless... unless something truly dreadful had happened.

If it is possible for a geographical location to have had greatness thrust upon it, Gibraltar would be that place. The Rock is a landmark that has been astonishing sailors since the time of the Phoenicians; and it has been fought over for almost as long.

A huge limestone monolith, nearly 1400 feet high, it occupies almost all of a peninsula that juts into the Strait of Gibraltar. One of the reasons that, from a military standpoint, it is so impregnable is that there is almost nowhere to land troops. Except for a tiny strip of beach that runs along the west side, the rock formation drops almost straight down into the water. The largest exception to this is on the northwest side where, on a relatively flat strip of land about three-quarters of a mile long and a quarter-mile deep, the British had co-mingled a naval base with the town of Gibraltar.

The *Mutine* anchored in five fathoms of water just off a jetty the navy had built at the midpoint of the base. It was fortified, and mounted a half dozen cannon that had a clear field of fire up and down the beach in front of the base. With the *Mutine* secured, Hardy cleaned up and went ashore to make the obligatory call on the port admiral, and to find out if there were any orders for him and his ship. He returned in about an hour and Smith immediately wanted to know what he had learned.

"Well, I have to admit," Hardy began, "I didn't learn much.

"Those frigates *were* a part of Nelson's squadron as I thought; but it seems they ran into a storm. The *Vanguard* was heavily damaged and the frigate captains assumed they would be heading back here to Gibraltar, so they decided to run ahead and meet them here. The problem is that none of the 74's have shown up."

"Wait a minute. You said: the 'captains assumed.' Do you mean to say the frigates left the 74's and came back here without orders?"

Hardy, responded with a rueful look, and said, "Yes."

Smith said nothing and just shook his head.

"Well, that's about all that's known. Jervis is on his way here from Cadiz—he should be here in a day or two—and he sent word by packet that if you arrive you should await his arrival. That's all I know—at least for now."

*****

The French soldiers and sailors might not have known where they were going, but they knew they were making good progress in getting there.

The fleet had headed southeast from Toulon. The day after departure they had rendezvoused with ships carrying 7100 infantry, cavalry and horses from Genoa. Two days later, about 20 miles off the coast of Corsica, they rendezvoused with additional ships from Ajaccio adding 4500 more troops. The fleet then cut between Corsica and Sardinia and met even more ships awaiting them from the Italian port of Civitavecchia, and 8,200 more troops were added.

The French fleet was now at full strength. Almost 250 ships were spread across miles of water; all heading generally south, and speculation over their destination was at a fever pitch.

"Atout! Atout! Atout!" The man cried as he stood and dramatically slammed the cards down one at a time on the makeshift table. The other players groaned as he scooped up his winnings. There really wasn't all that much for the men to do. They could play cards, talk to each other, read, or lean over the ship's side and vomit from seasickness. That was about it; and it seemed like everyone had already done all four things, multiple times.

Horace Say and Joseph Moiret, as officers, didn't have anything more to do than the men. They sat in the open air, enjoying the sun, while leaning against a 6-pounder gun carriage, one of the few pieces of armament aboard the old transport.

"Well, Horace, what do you say now about your theory? Are we still going to England via your island hopping campaign?"

"La Patron has done nothing to convince me otherwise. The general still has us headed south."

"But we're almost past Sardinia. I thought that was one of the islands we were supposed to invade?"

"Ah, but that's part of the General's genius. You see, he's going to start at the bottom and work up. Start with Malta, then Sicily, and then Sardinia. I told you, I had it figured out long ago."

Moiret paused for a moment, "You have no idea where we're going, do you?"

Captain Say shrugged his shoulders and admitted, "No, I don't."

*****

Lucas Walker and Susan Whitney had been to Gibraltar before; but they had never really visited it. Their ship had always made a quick stop to pick up water, food, or orders, so they never really had a chance to explore the place. Now they did.

It was easy for them to think of Gibraltar as simply a large fortress—a military and naval base of operations. It was that, of course, but it was also a very old Spanish town. It was this side-by-side intermingling of cultures, Spanish and English, civilian and military, which gave the town much of its charm.

The small ship's boat dropped them off at the quay where they passed under a massive stone archway, through a set of heavy gates, and on to Waterport Street, Gibraltar's main thoroughfare.

"Well, where do you want to go first?" Walker asked.

Susan didn't hesitate. "Up there," she said with a nod of her head.

Walker peered down a side street that was in the direction of her nod. "I am not sure there's very much down that way."

"No, not down there. UP there," and she pointed to the top of the rock.

"O-o-o-o-h, no! I am not climbing up there! Do I look like a mountain goat, for Pete's sake? Besides, it's dangerous, and even if we got up there..."

An hour later they had secured a guide who was leading the donkey. Susan was perched radiantly on the beast, a requirement because the climb was considered too strenuous for a woman. Trailing behind was Walker, who was grumbling with every step.

Walker had to admit that the hike was not as difficult, and the sights much more beautiful, than he had expected. The climb was a steep one, but the well-used trail zig-zagged back and forth making it a long walk, but not as hard as it looked from sea level.

With every switchback they went higher, and the view unfolded more and more. At each rest stop the two would admire the placid sparkling bay, with several dozen war and merchant ships comfortably resting in their own shadows at anchor. By the New Mole there was a small cloud of boats loading and unloading everything from people to trade goods.

But what surprised Walker the most was the vegetation they found. From ground level, the rock looked barren; but up close, it was anything but that. Every crag had something growing in it. There were dozens of different types of flowers, some he recognized from England and America, and some he had never seen before. There were fig trees, almond trees, and myrtle shrubs. There was a heady fragrance of black locust and orange blossoms. In various places white clematis flowers mixed with red geraniums, assaulting the cold gray stone with acts of gratuitous color.

The most stunning moment came when they finally reached the top.

The guide led the way through a narrow opening between two large rocks. Susan, who had dismounted from her donkey, went next. Shortly after she disappeared through it, Walker heard her gasp. Thinking there might be something wrong, he hurried through, and gasped himself.

It was like you were God.

In one glance you could see two continents and two oceans. To their left was the penetrating azure of the Mediterranean; to their right, was the darker cobalt blue of the Atlantic. They were standing atop one of the two Pillars of Hercules—in Europe; and directly ahead of them, to the south, they could see the other, Mount Abyla, the Mount of God—in Africa. Below them to the right was the crisp red brick of the town of Gibraltar. At the foot of Mount Abyla they could see the glistening white walls of the town of Ceuta. It left them speechless.

After spending nearly a half-hour at the summit, they started back down. Just as they were again going through the narrow opening Walker glanced over and thought he could detect an "I told you so" look on Susan's face, although she was struggling hard to suppress it.

They were back in town by about five o'clock, and Susan wanted to go by the marketplace before heading back to the ship. For Walker, this was as much of an eye-opener as the trip up the mountain.

The bulk of Gibraltar's inhabitants were either Spanish or British; but, in addition, it had a large transient population that made it one of the most cosmopolitan cities in the world. There were colorfully robed moors and long-bearded Jews. There were Turks with their baggy pants, a mixed race from the eastern Mediterranean called "Levantines," very black skinned Africans, and even a few representatives of the original inhabitants of Gibraltar, who were known as "Rock Scorpions."

All of these tended to congregate in and around the marketplace, where one's senses came under overwhelming assault. Your ears heard shrill cries in a dozen languages; your eyes beheld a waterfall of colorful dress; and your nose detected mixtures of sweet and pungent odors that it could not even begin to identify.

Night was now descending so they decided to end their sightseeing, as Gibraltar was about to become a very rough place.

The problem was that there simply wasn't enough do in Gibraltar. As a result, the amount of drunkenness among the soldiers was limited only by their ability to purchase the alcohol. What little money the men had from their pay, after various deductions, went directly to the nearly 100 drinking dens scattered throughout the town.

In general, the men only ate once a day. This was a meal of pease pudding and salt meat called "the King's own." Whenever possible they would hire themselves out as day laborers at four pence a shift, payable immediately; with which they would buy "blackstrap," a heavy, terrible tasting but potent, Catalonian wine. Occasionally someone would have the money to buy a bottle of a sweet, white, fortified wine called Málaga. This they would mix with the blackstrap and produce a drink called "thunder and lightening."

Things weren't any better among the officers, who had a tradition of going to bed in a state of glorious drunkenness every chance they could. One officer had two men who were assigned to fetch him each night between 11:00 and midnight and take him back to the barracks. The only difficulty was that the men would get as drunk as the officer while they were waiting, so that the three of them seldom got back before the morning reveille gun.

This, however, was less of a problem than it sounds. There was no morning business to attend to, other than the day's floggings, so the officers would have a late breakfast of broiled ham and cold punch. Then, in the afternoon, they would wrap themselves in flannel coats and play tennis in the mid-day sun, hoping to sweat out their hangovers. They *did* have a genuine military formation each day at six o'clock. For both officers and men this was probably their most lucid hour of the day because, as soon as it was over, the drinking would start again.

Walker and Whitney had almost made it back to Waterport Street when they heard a loud crash and the sound of wood splintering. Looking toward a nearby building they saw a person suddenly appear in a window like he was about to topple backward through it. He caught his balance and swung himself again into the room. Another crash, and a broken chair was flung through the door. A third crash and a man landed face down in the dusty street. He stood, hitched up his pants, and started back into the building. Susan realized the man was Isaac Pulley. Just as he reached the doorway, another body came flying through, knocking Pulley over and flinging both men back into the street. The second man was Cecil Durbin.

A bar keeper appeared at the door shaking his fist. "And don't neither of you rufflers come back. Ya hear?"

Durbin, who was bleeding from cuts to his jaw and forehead, was helping Pulley up. "'eaven and 'ell, Isaac, ya figure we taught them blackguards enuff of a lesson?"

Pulley, who could barely see out of his puffed-up left eye, said, "I'll say. Why they'll not soon forget the day they tangled wif us, I'll be bound." Just as he said that, they both toppled back to the ground in a tangled heap. Susan couldn't tell if this last fall was the result of drunkenness or injury; but, before she could find out, Walker intervened.

"Pulley! Durbin! What's the meaning of this?"

The two looked up through the cloud of dust they had raised as if they were testing reality. Durbin finally asked, "Dr. Walker? Lydy Whitney? Is that you?"

"Yes, it's us. Now stand up you two, dust yourselves off and try to look like Christians!" Walker was trying to sound stern and officer-like. He wasn't very good at it and, more often than not, Whitney had to keep from laughing; but he was giving it his best.

"I asked you, what's the meaning of this?"

"Well, sir," Durbin began "we was just sittin' there loike a couple of proper gen'lemen, enjoyin' a small refreshment, ya understand..."

"Aye," Pulley interrupted "when this geeza..."

"When *six* men..." corrected Durbin.

"When a dozen soldiers an' a pack'a Marines," Pulley continued, "dared to tarnish the reputation of the Royal Navy, and then attacked us."

"And why did they do that?"

"Nah reason, sir," said Pulley.

"None whatsoever," agreed Durbin, shaking his head.

Susan stepped forward and snapped: "Isaac and Cecil!"

The transformation was immediate. In an instant they went from defiant sailors to looking more like chagrinned schoolboys. They had known Whitney and Walker since the Battle of the Saints when Whitney fished them out of the ocean, saving both of their lives. Durbin had returned the favor with a desperate last-second sword lunge that saved Sidney Smith's life, just before they were captured at La Havre. In between, Lucas Walker had stitched up their wounds and treated their illnesses with all the skill of a high-priced London physician—which he once was. When Durbin had a fever, Susan sat up for two nights applying cold compresses to his head. When Pulley learned that both his parents had died, she was his only source of consolation and compassion. The two men were capable of many things, but lying to Walker and Whitney was not among them.

There was silence for a moment, and then Durbin spoke up. "We're bof on the *Caroline*. A couple'a soldiers in there said ever'one on our ship was cowards 'cause we left the 74's and came in ter Gibraltar."

"So, I threw a jug'a pigs-ear in the one bloke's face," said Pulley.

"And I cracked a chair over the 'ead of the other," added Durbin sheepishly.

Susan tried to sound indignant, something *she* wasn't good at, and which often caused Walker to suppress laughter. "Well, I am *very* disappointed, seeing you two acting like common thugs. What are we to do with you?"

The two were sheepishly looking down at the ground, but at this Durbin raised his head. "I ain't sure, but could you start by gettin' us off the bloody *Caroline*?"

*****

The *Vanguard* was wallowing in choppy seas within sight of the outer harbor at Toulon. The ship was a proud one—only eleven years old and in the prime of her life. Launched in 1787, she was the result of 50 years of British experimentation.

In the 1730's, the French had developed the 170-foot, 74-gun, warship. They were an excellent compromise between speed and firepower, and the British had nothing to match them. This began a long series of experiments. The British built three-deck 90- and 100-gun ships but, in addition to being obscenely expensive, they didn't handle very well. In rough weather their high sides worked better as sails then the sails did. Next came the 80-gun ships, and they were even more of a disaster. They packed plenty of guns, but did not provide a large enough base for their weight. As a result, they heeled over badly in almost any kind of wind, which made it impossible to open the bottom row of gun ports without the water rushing in. It is generally not good to pick a fight with a French 74 and have half your guns—the heaviest ones at that—under water.

Next came the 70-gun ships. They were a good idea but the British built them wrong. They weren't long enough, which crammed the guns too close together. This meant they could not be fired without the gun crews tripping all over each other. They also could only carry 24-pound guns, as compared to the French 36-pounders. Next up, they developed 60- and 50-gun ships, but these were essentially large frigates and could not stand up to the French 74's at all—which was the original problem they were trying to solve.

Into this quandary stepped a brilliant naval architect by the name of Thomas Slade. Slade began his working life as a simple apprentice shipwright. By 1750, he had achieved his masters rating, and in 1755 was appointed "Surveyor of the Navy," which effectively placed him in charge of all ship design and building. The first problem he took up was that of countering the innovative French ships.

He realized that the navy was on the right track with the 70-gun vessels; but he also realized their flaws. So, what he did was to reverse engineer the problem. He started by calculating how much room it would take for the crews to comfortably work 74 guns on two gundecks. That gave him the ship's length. He then calculated how high the lower gundeck would have to be above the water so the gun ports could remain open in almost any weather. That told him where the gundecks needed to be placed and told him where he needed to put the ship's center of gravity. Finally, he calculated how much food, water, and gun-powder the ship would need to carry to remain at sea for extended periods. This gave him the ship's hold requirements and, by extension, the basic hull specifications.

With that information, and some new hull shapes, he built seven ships. These became known as the *Dublin* class 74s. He tinkered with the design somewhat and built three more (the *Hero, Hercules* and *Thunderer*). Finally, in December 1757 he built three final ships, known as the *Bellona* class (*Bellona, Dragon* and *Superb*). These last three set the standard for British shipbuilding for the next 20 years. They had most of the firepower of a First Rate, much of the speed and maneuverability of a frigate, and they were exactly what the fleet needed.

The *Vanguard* was a direct descendent of the *Bellona*. Indeed, except for some slight hull differences, she could be her twin sister. She was 168 feet long, and almost 47 feet wide. The gundeck carried twenty-eight 32-pound guns, the next deck up, the upper deck, carried twenty-eight long 18-pounders, and the quarterdeck and forecastle had fourteen long-nines. A single broadside could convey 718 pounds of metal into the side of any opponent.

The problem at the moment, however, was that there were no opponents into whom that metal might be delivered. She was wallowing because all sails had been taken in; and her sails were in because her commander had no idea what to do next.

The ship was deathly quiet. The officers talked, but their voices were hushed. The men worked, but their work was done quietly, almost gently. Even the sounds of the ship bobbing in the cobalt blue water and the cries of the seagull's overhead seemed muted. It was as if the world had slowed down to allow Nelson to catch-up.

Nelson slowly ascended the starboard ladder leading from the quarterdeck to the poop. It was only seven steps, but he climbed them like a man going to his doom on the gallows. He walked to the stern rail, briefly looked down upon the small balcony that jutted out from his cabin one deck below, then looked for what seemed like the hundredth time at the empty harbor of Toulon.

He turned away from that depressing sight and walked back toward the mizzenmast, briefly tripping over the corner of a hatch-cover in the process. The stump of his right arm ached. The socket of his missing right eye was giving him a blinding headache, and the choppy waves were making him seasick yet again. He was about as miserable as he had ever been.

He stopped at the railing at the fore end of the poop deck, paused, thought for a moment, and called down to Captain Edward Berry on the quarterdeck below.

"Captain Berry, send a signal to the other ships, if you please: CAPTAINS TO REPORT ABOARD IMMEDIATELY."

Where had Napoleon gone? The meeting shed no real light on the problem. Opinions ranged from "He has gone to attack England," to "He has gone to attack Constantinople," to "He has gone to attack Malta or Naples." Every point on the compass was suggested except north. The only reason that wasn't suggested was because the only thing north of them was the French coastline, and Napoleon didn't need ships to get anywhere up there.

Nelson took it all in without saying a word or directing the conversation in any way. After all the views had been expressed, there was silence for a long minute while Nelson thought.

"Naples," he said decisively. "He's gone to Naples; I am sure of it. He wants to seal up Italy once and for all. So, gentlemen, that's where we're going."

*****

Eight hundred miles away, in Gibraltar, another man had a headache. He was John Jervis, Lord St. Vincent, and commander of His Majesty's vessels of war in the Mediterranean. Jervis' headache, however, was not caused by troublesome injuries or missing French ships. They were caused by one man, the man with whom he was about to meet, Sir Sidney Smith.

Jervis stood at the window on the second floor of Government House and watched as a carriage pulled up to the iron-latticed gate. The soldiers standing on either side of the portal snapped to attention as Sir Sidney got out. A few minutes later, he was standing in front of Jervis' desk waiting for an invitation to be seated. It was not given.

Jervis leaned back in his chair and took off his spectacles. He studied Smith over for a long minute, and then said. "Smith, I don't like you."

This took Sidney completely off guard. He controlled his rising sense of indignation and calmly inquired, "In view of the fact that we've never met before, sir, may I ask why?"

"I know we've never met, but your reputation precedes you, young man. I have it on good authority—very good authority—that you are nothing but a vain, arrogant, supercilious fool. Just the sort of man this navy does not need. Now, I know there are some who think you are some kind of rising star. I, and most others, do not." He leaned forward as if to emphasize the points he was about to make.

"First, there's the matter of that silly Swedish knighthood you hold. How many English officers did you kill to get it, sir?"

"I killed none," Smith replied frostily. "If Englishmen died at any of the battles I participated in, it was because they, of their own free will, volunteered to serve in the Russian cause."

"I am not interested in your excuses!" Jervis snapped. "And if I want you to speak, I'll ask for your opinion!

"Then there is that little ship-burning debacle at Toulon. You can't even competently burn a collection of anchored ships. God knows what you would do if any of them were underway. Even your little vacation in that gilded cage in Paris... Don't look surprised, Sir Sidney. I've heard all about the rooms in which you were confined.

"And may I add, the only reason I dignified you just now with the title "Sir Sidney", is because our Sovereign has confirmed your knighthood. Personally, I think you are a self-promoting charlatan, *Sir* Sidney. What do you think of that?

"Yes, sir. Very good. Will that be all?" Smith knew he had to get out of the room quickly or he was going to strike the man.

"No, that's not all!" Jervis said.

It was too much—way too much—for Sidney Smith to handle. "Then may I speak freely, sir? As a commodore to his admiral."

"That's what I mean about your vanity, Smith. You are not a commodore—at least not in my area of command. I will grant you 'captain' because I must; but no more than that."

Smith was trying desperately to control his towering rage. "Then may I speak freely as a captain to his commanding officer?"

"You may."

Legally, it was all the permission Smith needed. In the next few moments he could not be charged with insubordination for anything he said; but that's not the same thing as saying that what he would say would be wise.

"How dare you call me a charlatan? I at least earned my knighthood—Swedish though it may be—in battle. How did you get your earldom, my Lord? By half-winning a battle? By losing control of your own officers? By having a pompous bluejay like Nelson disobey your explicit orders, and *finally do the right thing* at the Battle of Cape St. Vincent? How far away from the battle were you at the time, sir? A mile? Two miles? Three? Could you even see what Nelson was doing through your glass?"

"Enough!" Jervis shouted and pounded his fist on the desk hard enough to knock the quill out of its holder next to the inkwell. Just then, Jervis' clerk came through the door.

"Oh, I am sorry, my Lord. I didn't know you were in conference. Let me just leave these orders here on your desk for your signature, and I'll come back later."

Jervis and Smith maintained an icy silence as the clerk put the papers down. He seemed surprised to see the quill was lying askew on the desk, replaced it, and quietly exited the room. The break was just enough for both men to gain a measure of control.

Jervis, still seething, put his glasses on and picked up the papers the clerk had brought.

"Captain Smith, I did not order you here today to discuss your resume. These are several sets of orders I had drawn up this morning. One set pertains to you; but I thought you might be interested in the others as well.

"This top one is for Hardy to escort some reinforcements to Nelson. I am sending him ten 74's, a frigate and, of course, the *Mutine*. Now, Nelson... there's a real commander for you, Smith!"

Commander? He's your lap dog; or you're his. I haven't figured out which yet. Smith thought to himself. Then it suddenly dawned on him. He knew the "good authority" from whom Jervis had obtained his opinion of him. Nelson!

"This next set is for your friend, Dr. Walker. He will be assigned to the *Bellerophon,* and will be permitted to bring along his... ah... surgeon's mate companion. They have a ship's compliment of about 500 men and, at the moment, only one surgeon."

"And what are your plans for me? I assume I will also be going on board the *Bellerophon* or one of the other 74's."

"By no means, sir! By no means. You, my noble Swedish knight, will remain right here in Gibraltar. I am given to understand that you have some code breaker with you who is trying to decipher a message that might tell us where Napoleon is going. I am holding you personally responsible for making sure that that message is broken as quickly as possible. In addition, should he fail to do so, or should he be too late in doing so, let me underscore the words, 'I am holding you *personally* responsible.'

"That will be all," Jervis concluded with some satisfaction. He knew he had Smith right where he wanted him. If the codebreaker succeeds, Jervis will get the credit. If he fails, Smith will get the blame. Suddenly his headache didn't seem so bad.

Sidney Smith, on the other hand, was crushed. There would be a battle soon—a huge and important one—and he was being held back from it. Almost as bad, the team was being broken up again.

Smith slowly turned to walk out when he remembered something Susan Whitney had asked him to do.

"Sir, as a post-captain I believe I have the right to have a personal servant and a coxswain assigned to me."

"Yes, what of it?"

"There are two men on board the *Caroline* I would like. We've served together several times in the past."

Jervis thought about denying the request for no other reason than Smith had made it; but he was feeling expansive at the moment.

"Yes. Yes, fine." Jervis waived his hand in dismissal. "Give my clerk their names on the way out and he'll cut the orders."

*****

The Grand Master's palace was even more magnificent than usual. Hundreds of torches lined the lane leading up to the residence, as well as every pathway within its spacious gardens. Soldiers in their finest uniforms stood as a guard of honor on the steps leading up to the main entrance. Inside thousands of candles burned in the huge overhead chandeliers and in wall sconces throughout the building. Music could be heard from orchestras playing in each of the two ballrooms.

It was a magical night, a night for laughter and romance. The cream of Maltese society was attending a banquet and ball being given by the Order of the Knights of St. John of Jerusalem—better known as the Knights Hospitaller.

The Hospitallers were a military order whose history went back almost 700 years. Founded just after the First Crusade, they were contemporary with, and rivals of, the powerful and secretive Knights Templar. Their original mission was to establish hospitals for sick or injured pilgrims to the Holy Land, thus the name "Hospitaller"; but they quickly developed a reputation as ferocious warriors as well. The knights, each wearing a black surcoat with a white "Maltese Cross" on the front, distinguished themselves in numerous campaigns against the Muslims.

In 1312 the Knights Templar were brutally dissolved and the Hospitallers were given much of their property. Included in this was the island of Rhodes, which they occupied until 1522. In that year, 7000 knights withstood an assault of 200,000 Muslims under Suleiman the Magnificent; but, after a six-month siege, they were defeated and forced to move to Sicily. In 1530, Charles V of Spain gave them the island of Malta in perpetual fiefdom, in exchange for an annual fee of one Maltese falcon—due each year on All Souls Day.

The hour had grown late. Beautifully gowned ladies and bewigged gentlemen still responded to the call for the minuet, or grand march, but not nearly as many as earlier in the evening. The numerous pots of incense had each contributed to the haze that hung around the chandeliers, softening their light. Older couples had taken their leave hours ago; and younger ones, those that had caught each others eye earlier in the evening, were now in earnest communication—and, in some cases, even holding hands.

Suddenly, there was a loud BOOM from outside the palace, followed by another. The crowd was thrilled. The knights had thought of everything. A grand evening was to end with a display of fireworks. It was perfect!

The crowd bustled out onto the balconies overlooking the harbor, or peered though the opened high-arching windows. A third BOOM filled the night sky, followed a moment later by a fourth; but, oddly, there were no bursts of color in the sky. The military officers figured it out first. That was not the sound of fireworks. It was cannon fire, and it was coming from a ship that had entered Valletta Bay.

Word quickly spread. The ship could now be seen in the moonlight. The shouts of men as they rushed off mixed with demure screams from the ladies. There was panic and confusion everywhere except in one little corner of the main ballroom. In that corner Citizen Matthius Poussielgue, the French agent in Malta, looked over at Grand Master Baron Ferdinand von Hompesch. The two men smiled at one another, for they knew what was going on even if the crowd did not.

The Knights of the Order of St. John were about to lose the island of Malta, and end 700 years of proud military history.

*****

Sidney Smith and William Parish had been holed up in a one-room shack for nearly two weeks. It was formerly a pig farmer's hut, stuck in the foothills on the far end of the peninsula. On the next level down was an abandoned naval hospital, below that were some old watering tanks, and below that was Gibraltar Bay. Jervis put them there, he said, because it would give them "the isolation they need to concentrate." Smith knew better. Jervis' only intent was to humiliate them.

"Let's go through it again," Smith said. "Here, let me look at it."

Parish passed over a sheet, which was a copy of the original message. It read as follows:

4 Floréal An VI

Bonjour,

Wchb êhyj qoe us jiétsac hyous ndhiijgé cjf fv Ewenqnfjfr nléwluws à vshvs à pvnb f'zojnbwie es y'Nusgus nrbmz rir yféplf. Jbdg umfn y'jinfswfjhcfo rr csldjbra zyj qfécjfukjtf nh xv qfrwrlv mo znf mzuôh dds pfvg êgng jiêug.

François de Neufchâteau
Directeur

"It's hopeless," Parish dejectedly said.

"It's not hopeless. Look, we already know part of it. We know it was sent on the fourth day of the month of Floréal, in year six of the revolution—at least according to the French revolutionary calendar. By our calendar, that's April 23rd of this year—the day I escaped from the Temple, in fact. And, we know Neufchâteau, who is one of the five Directors, signed it."

"Sidney, those are the words that are in plain text. We haven't cracked a single ciphered word—assuming it *is* a cipher and not a code."

"You keep using those terms as if they meant something different. I always thought they were the same thing."

"They aren't."

"Then what's the difference?"

"In a code you have letters, numbers, or symbols that stand for complete words or phrases. Usually, it requires a codebook to figure out the message."

Sidney looked blank, so Parish pressed on. "Maybe I can explain it this way. When you send up a flag signal to another ship, what happens at the other end?"

"The signal officer on the other ship will read the flags and look up their meaning in a book."

"Exactly. It's a code. He sees the symbols on the flags, and looks up their meaning in a codebook. A cipher is different. A cipher is a letter for letter substitution. The letter "Q" really means "B", the letter "O" means "R", and so forth."

"Well, how do you know this is a cipher and not a code?"

"I don't."

"You don't?"

"Well, I do and I don't. I think it's a cipher because that's what the French have always used in the past. And..."

"And what?"

"If it's a code we don't have a prayer of breaking it—not without a lot more messages to work with, and a lot more time in which to do it."

A feeling of apprehension starting to descend over Smith, but he hid it well. "All right, so let's assume this is a cipher. Why is it giving you so much trouble?"

"Because nothing fits, Sidney! Here, look at this two-letter word: 'xv'. By all the laws of God, nature, and the French language, it is most likely the word 'et.' All right, so I make that guess. Then I try various alphabetic combinations until I find a sequence that correctly points to the letters "e" and "t". When, and if, that happens, then I apply that same formula to the other words to see if they resolve as well."

"So what's the problem?"

"Nothing works, damn it!

"As soon as I think I have one word figured out, the solution doesn't transfer to anything else. It's like they used a completely different cipher arrangement for each letter of the message—and that can't possibly be. It would be far, *far*, too complicated for anyone to decipher at the other end.

The room was silent for a full minute. Smith got up and stood by the window. Parish stared down at the message, feeling the anger and frustration building up. Finally, he could contain it no longer.

"I am sorry, Sidney." Parish said quietly. "I am so... so... sorry; but I can't do this." Smith looked over and could see the profound sadness in Parish's eyes. "I wanted so badly to be able to break this. I wanted so badly to do something important. I wanted so badly for you, and Lucas, and Susan to... to respect me. But I..."

Parish couldn't complete the word. He rushed out of the house, past Durbin who was sitting in the sunshine outside the door, nodding off. He went over to a large boulder by the cliff edge, sagged against it, and looked out at Gibraltar Bay.

After about five minutes, Sidney Smith came out and joined him.

"You can't quit, William," Smith quietly said. "You think Lucas, Susan, and I are some kind of heroes because we've told you about a few of our adventures. Well, we're not, you know. We're just ordinary people, like you, who somehow find ourselves in unusual—sometimes even impossible—situations. That's just like you as well.

"You didn't ask to be on Lord Spencer's staff; you were forced there. You didn't ask for this assignment; it was forced upon you. But, if Lucas, Susan, and I have a characteristic that's different from others, it's this. We are, each of us, very, very, determined people. That's what you're confusing with courage. When we are confronted by the impossible, we don't ever give up on finding a solution, and we never, *ever*, give up on each other. We just become more resolved, more firm, more dogged. Some day that's likely to get us killed, but that's the way it is.

"You have a gift, William. There probably aren't five people in the world who have your ability to resolve ciphers; and we need you. Your country needs you; Lucas and Susan need you; and I need you. You can't quit now."

Parish thought about Smith's words for a while, then slowly turned and nodded his head. "Yes, I know. You're right. I am sorry." Smith put his hand on Parish's shoulder and the two went back.

As the two approached the hut, Durbin, who was sitting with his chair leaning back against the wall, snapped forward.

"Bone sure, monseers," Durbin said. "That's a French greetin' ya know, 'cept it ain't really a greetin' 'cause I cain't say it right."

Despite his depression, Parish chuckled. "Well, I accept your 'greeting that's not really a greeting'; but I was wondering if you could do me a favor and..."

Parish stopped in mid-sentence, and then went rigid. His mind shifted into overdrive and he grabbed Sidney Smith's arm and squeezed it hard. After a moment he slowly muttered: "Oh... my... God!"

"What's wrong?" Smith asked.

"Wrong? Nothing's wrong. I think I just figured it out."

Parish rushed back into the hut and Smith started to follow him. "No, wait outside" Parish said. "I need to be alone for a while to work this through."

Smith spent the next hour outlining for Durbin, yet again, what it meant to be a captain's servant; but, there was something about the concept of being a "gentleman's gentleman" that could not quite find a home in Durbin's nautical head. Smith sighed in resignation just as Parish flung open the door.

"I have it!" he proclaimed, his face beaming. "I know what they did."

Parish led Smith back to their worktable, and Durbin followed to see what the excitement was about.

"Do you know what a Caesar cipher is?"

"I have no idea," replied Smith.

"It's a long story, but it's the code Julius Caesar used. He just took the Greek alphabet and shifted it a certain number of characters. To use a simple example, if you shifted our alphabet 13 characters, "A" would be "N", "B" would be "O", "C" would be "P", and so forth.

"Is that what the French did?"

"Yes and no. They shifted it, but not in the way you would expect. What they did was to shift the alphabet 26 times and set up, basically, a table of alphabets. Here look at this." Parish lifted a sheet of paper and presented it to Smith.

	A	B	C	D	E	F	G	H	I	J	K	L	M	N	O	P	Q	R	S	T	U	V	W	X	Y	Z
A	A	B	C	D	E	F	G	H	I	J	K	L	M	N	O	P	Q	R	S	T	U	V	W	X	Y	Z
B	B	C	D	E	F	G	H	I	J	K	L	M	N	O	P	Q	R	S	T	U	V	W	X	Y	Z	A
C	C	D	E	F	G	H	I	J	K	L	M	N	O	P	Q	R	S	T	U	V	W	X	Y	Z	A	B
D	D	E	F	G	H	I	J	K	L	M	N	O	P	Q	R	S	T	U	V	W	X	Y	Z	A	B	C
E	E	F	G	H	I	J	K	L	M	N	O	P	Q	R	S	T	U	V	W	X	Y	Z	A	B	C	D
F	F	G	H	I	J	K	L	M	N	O	P	Q	R	S	T	U	V	W	X	Y	Z	A	B	C	D	E
G	G	H	I	J	K	L	M	N	O	P	Q	R	S	T	U	V	W	X	Y	Z	A	B	C	D	E	F
H	H	I	J	K	L	M	N	O	P	Q	R	S	T	U	V	W	X	Y	Z	A	B	C	D	E	F	G
I	I	J	K	L	M	N	O	P	Q	R	S	T	U	V	W	X	Y	Z	A	B	C	D	E	F	G	H
J	J	K	L	M	N	O	P	Q	R	S	T	U	V	W	X	Y	Z	A	B	C	D	E	F	G	H	I
K	K	L	M	N	O	P	Q	R	S	T	U	V	W	X	Y	Z	A	B	C	D	E	F	G	H	I	J
L	L	M	N	O	P	Q	R	S	T	U	V	W	X	Y	Z	A	B	C	D	E	F	G	H	I	J	K
M	M	N	O	P	Q	R	S	T	U	V	W	X	Y	Z	A	B	C	D	E	F	G	H	I	J	K	L
N	N	O	P	Q	R	S	T	U	V	W	X	Y	Z	A	B	C	D	E	F	G	H	I	J	K	L	M
O	O	P	Q	R	S	T	U	V	W	X	Y	Z	A	B	C	D	E	F	G	H	I	J	K	L	M	N
P	P	Q	R	S	T	U	V	W	X	Y	Z	A	B	C	D	E	F	G	H	I	J	K	L	M	N	O
Q	Q	R	S	T	U	V	W	X	Y	Z	A	B	C	D	E	F	G	H	I	J	K	L	M	N	O	P
R	R	S	T	U	V	W	X	Y	Z	A	B	C	D	E	F	G	H	I	J	K	L	M	N	O	P	Q
S	S	T	U	V	W	X	Y	Z	A	B	C	D	E	F	G	H	I	J	K	L	M	N	O	P	Q	R
T	T	U	V	W	X	Y	Z	A	B	C	D	E	F	G	H	I	J	K	L	M	N	O	P	Q	R	S
U	U	V	W	X	Y	Z	A	B	C	D	E	F	G	H	I	J	K	L	M	N	O	P	Q	R	S	T
V	V	W	X	Y	Z	A	B	C	D	E	F	G	H	I	J	K	L	M	N	O	P	Q	R	S	T	U
W	W	X	Y	Z	A	B	C	D	E	F	G	H	I	J	K	L	M	N	O	P	Q	R	S	T	U	V
X	X	Y	Z	A	B	C	D	E	F	G	H	I	J	K	L	M	N	O	P	Q	R	S	T	U	V	W
Y	Y	Z	A	B	C	D	E	F	G	H	I	J	K	L	M	N	O	P	Q	R	S	T	U	V	W	X
Z	Z	A	B	C	D	E	F	G	H	I	J	K	L	M	N	O	P	Q	R	S	T	U	V	W	X	Y

"This is the alphabet written out 26 times, in 26 rows. Each row has the alphabet shifted one character to the left. To encode our message, every time they wrote a letter they would select it from a different row. That's why my solutions wouldn't work. It's essentially the same as having a different encryption system for each letter of the message."

"I still don't understand. If they're selecting each letter from a different row, how does the encoder know which row to choose; or, more importantly, how does the recipient know how to decode it?"

"That's what I couldn't figure out. Early on, I thought they might be doing something like this, but I discarded the notion. I couldn't see how it could possibly work."

"So how did you figure it out?"

"I didn't. He did," and Parish pointed at a startled Durbin. He solved it when he gave me his French 'greeting that's not really a greeting'. That was the tip-off. That word at the beginning of the message, Bonjour—that's not a salutation. It's the key that tells them how to select the substitutions. Here let me show you."

"To encode a message you write the key word, in this case "Bonjour", below the message text. You keep repeating the word over and over until you reach the end of the message. So if I wanted to encode "Attack the enemy", it would look like this:

$$A \ T \ T \ A \ C \ K \quad T \ H \ E \quad E \ N \ E \ M \ Y$$
$$B \ O \ N \ J \ O \ U \quad R \ B \ O \quad N \ J \ O \ U \ R$$

"Then you look up the first letter of the message, "A", in the table using the alphabet in row "B". You look up the second letter of the message using the alphabet in row "O", the third letter in row "N", and so on. So the encrypted message would read:

$$A \ T \ T \ A \ C \ K \quad T \ H \ E \quad E \ N \ E \ M \ Y$$
$$B \ O \ N \ J \ O \ U \quad R \ B \ O \quad N \ J \ O \ U \ R$$
$$B \ H \ G \ J \ Q \ E \quad K \ I \ S \quad R \ W \ S \ G \ P$$

"To decode it, you just reverse the process.

$$B \ H \ G \ J \ Q \ E \quad K \ I \ S \quad R \ W \ S \ G \ P$$
$$B \ O \ N \ J \ O \ U \quad R \ B \ O \quad N \ J \ O \ U \ R$$
$$A \ T \ T \ A \ C \ K \quad T \ H \ E \quad E \ N \ E \ M \ Y$$

"It's brilliant!" Parish exclaimed.

"Yes, that's wonderful; but, William, get to the point! What does our message say?"

Parish didn't reply. He just held up a sheet of paper which had both the original French and the English translation. His smile lit up the room. It read:

4 Floréal An VI

Bonjour,

Vous êtes par le présent texte autorisé par le Directoire exécutif à mener à bien l'invasion de l'Egypte ainsi que prévue. Vous avez l'autorisation de terminer les préparatifs et de prendre la mer sitôt que vous êtes prêts.

François de Neufchâteau
Directeur

4 Floréal An VI

Bonjour,

You are hereby authorized by the Directoire exécutif to proceed with the planned invasion of Egypt. You may complete your preparations and sail as soon as you are ready.

François de Neufchâteau
Directeur

Parish and Smith rushed out of the hut to prepare their horses for a rapid ride back to the main naval base. Durbin lingered a bit longer, looking at the incomprehensible papers on the table. He finally sniffed, "An' thar are blokes what thinks us sailors are stewpid," and proudly walked out the door.

CHAPTER FIVE

While Parish was solving the mystery of the French cipher, another mystery was being played out. Nelson was moving around the Mediterranean like a blind man feeling his way around a strange room. As he continued to chase the French, the French continued to move farther and farther away from him.

Napoleon left Toulon on May 20, 1798. On June 9th, he arrived in Malta, which became the first conquest of his Egyptian Campaign.

In many ways, the capture of Malta began in November of the previous year when Napoleon dispatched an agent by the name of Matthius Poussielgue, previously his finance advisor, to Malta to sew discord. Poussielgue did his work well. He began with a quiet propaganda campaign aimed primarily at the French Hospitaller knights, to convince them of the glorious future of the French Republic, and to sing the praises of the even more glorious victories that Napoleon was winning throughout Europe. However, his primary mission was to compromise the Grand Master of the order, Ferdinand von Hompesch; and at this, he was equally successful.

Hompesch was given his choice of 600,000 francs and a principality in Germany, or a pension for life of 300,000 francs. Each French knight was promised a pension of 700 francs a year for life. All they had to do was do nothing when Napoleon showed up. The bribes had their effect, for that is exactly what happened.

In the weeks prior to his arrival, the forts guarding the harbor, St. Elmo, Ricasoli and Tigné, had their batteries crippled or partially dismantled. This rendered them essentially useless, and allowed Napoleon to walk in through an open door.

He landed 3000 infantry, commanded by General Claude-Henri Vaubois. The knights made a show of resistance—a few cannon shots—just enough so that it could not be said they surrendered without a fight. But, surrender they did. At precisely twelve noon on the 12th, the flag of the Order of the Knights of St. John came down, ending almost 300 years of rule over Malta.

The next week was a busy one for the conquerors. A new system of government had to be created for the island, new laws, new rules, and new rulers. Its forts had to be strengthened and contingency plans drawn up for any kind of counter-invasion by land or by sea. But, most importantly, the place had to be properly looted. The treasure of the Knights of St. John—centuries of gold, silver, and jewels, had to be packed up and taken aboard the ships. This was the money Napoleon needed to finance the second stage of his plan. After leaving behind a garrison of 4000 men, on June 19th he headed for Egypt.

Meanwhile, Nelson spent weeks groping for clues as to where Napoleon had gone. On June 7th, however, his squadron was reinforced by the arrival of ten 74's: the *Audacious, Bellerophon, Culloden, Defence, Goliath, Majestic, Minotaur, Swiftsure, Theseus, and Zealous,* along with a 50-gun frigate (the *Leander*) and the *Mutine*. The captains of these vessels were among the elite of the Royal Navy. They included men such as Thomas Troubridge (*Culloden*), Thomas Foley (*Goliath*), Benjamin Hallowell (*Swiftsure*), Ralph Miller (*Theseus*), and Samuel Hood, cousin of the famous admiral of the same name, on the *Zealous*. They were young, on average under 40, talented, and aggressive.

Nelson became convinced that Napoleon had gone to Italy and was about to attack Naples. Upon arrival there, and discovering no French, he sent Troubridge ashore to confer with Sir William Hamilton, the British ambassador. Hamilton said he thought the French had gone to Malta, which was true; but he failed to inform him that he had also heard they were headed to Alexandria after that. He thought it was merely intentional misinformation so he didn't pass it on.

Initially, on finding Malta occupied, Nelson's hopes soared. He soon realized, however, that the was a subgroup and he had neither the time nor the resources to attack the heavily fortified island. So, once again he was stuck. He had thousands of Frenchmen within range of his guns, but they were not the *right* Frenchmen. He wanted Napoleon.

*****

The tiny, swift-sailing, dispatch boat had been on a chase of its own. It had tracked Nelson from Toulon, to Naples, and finally caught up with him at Malta. In an age when radio was the stuff of fantasy, these "dispatchers" were the lifeblood of naval communications. Unlike their civilian counterparts, these military boats did not carry cargo. They had one function, and one function only—to deliver orders, mail, information and, on rare occasion, people, to the fleet. This was one of those rare occasions.

The HMS *Sting* lay close aboard the *Vanguard*. She remained adrift, bouncing in the choppy seas, as a small boat pulled up to the towering wooden slab of the *Vanguard's* side. Two men clambered up the steps—one gracefully, one awkwardly. The first was a young lieutenant with a large leather satchel of documents for the ships of Nelson's squadron, and the second a slightly balding young civilian.

The marine knocked twice on the admiral's door and waited.

"Come," a voice on the other side said.

The tall marine stepped into the room and automatically bent over slightly because of the low ceiling. "Sir, you have a visitor who just came on board from the dispatch ship."

"Send him in."

Parish stepped past the intricately carved door and paused to let the admiral finish whatever he was working on. Finally, Nelson looked up and said, "And you are?"

"Yes sir, admiral," Parish began. "My name is William Parish and I've come from Gibraltar with some information that I believe will interest you."

"What might that be?"

"I know where Napoleon is going."

Nelson leaned back in his chair wondering if the man was mad or not. Still, he *had* arrived in a Gibraltar dispatch boat, which means that Jervis would have sent him, or at least have approved his departure.

"Needless to say, you have my attention, young man."

"He's going to Egypt."

"How do you know that?"

Parish explained who he was and the work he had done in breaking the French cipher. He concluded by reaching into his waistcoat and producing a copy of his translation of the message. Nelson studied it.

"How do you know this isn't a false message planted by the French?"

"I know it's not."

"I asked you *how* you know, sir, not *whether* you know."

"Because of the technique they used to encipher it, sir. It was masterful—the finest piece of work I seen from them so far—and it was not intended to be broken. If they wanted us to be misled, they would have made it much easier to break."

"But we have only your word on that, correct?"

Parish was taken aback by the question, as it had never occurred to him that he might be doubted. Apparently, though, it had occurred to Smith.

"Sir, I was given a note to present to you if there should be any doubt." He handed it to Nelson, who glanced at it, and then snapped a glare at Parish. The note simply read:

Nelson,

This man is to be trusted.

W. Sidney Smith

"Do you know what's in this note?"

"No, sir, I do not."

"It's from Captain Smith, and he says I should trust what you have to say. I must admit that receiving such a note from Smith is not exactly a ringing endorsement in my ears, but still..."

Nelson studied Parish over for a moment and came to a decision.

"I have no idea whether the French have hoodwinked you or not. On the other hand, I also have no idea where Napoleon is. So, we're going to assume you're correct, and I'll take this squadron to Egypt. But, Parish..."

"Yes, sir?"

"God help you—and Smith—if you're wrong."

The Temple

*****

Smith had a love-hate relationship with London. On one hand, he loved the excitement and the bustle of the town. It had streets that were alive with people, from the fabulously rich to the unfortunate poor, all sharing the same sidewalks in a blur of activity. It stimulated him.

From his coach he could look out and see street peddlers who were selling everything imaginable: cherries, matches, milk, primroses, love potions, mackerels, eels, knives, chairs, eggs, china, and even rat poison. He could hear the singsong of the vendor's calls: "Round and sound, five pence a pound. Buy my cherries-o! Buy my cherries-o!" "Will you buy my sweet primroses. Two bunches a-penny. All a-growin', all a-blowin', who will buy my sweet primroses." "Chairs to mend! Chairs to mend! If I had the money that I could spend, I would never cry old chairs to mend. Chairs to mend!" Their cries mixed with the reedy sounds of wandering flute players, the clatter of horses' hooves, and the shrill cries of children.

On the other hand, London could also be a filthy, disgusting place. On a normal day by 8:00 in the morning, the sky would be blackened from thousands of household coal fires, each sending their tendrils of smoke into the sky. One evening Sidney attended a play wearing a white scarf. By the time he got home, it was gray.

Then there was the sheer odor of the place. Smith was far from being a sensitive dandy, but London suffered from one hundred tons of horse manure being dumped on its streets each day, and no terribly efficient way of getting it up. Add to this the human waste that was dumped directly into the Thames, and then imagine the Thames at low tide, with the mud flats uncovered.

However, in many ways the worst problem was that of crime. London was essentially divided into halves. From the London Bridge westward was the West End. This was where the "better sort" lived. In addition to Westminster Abby, the Parliament Buildings, and St. James Palace, it had the very fashionable residential area called Mayfair. This is where the exclusive men's clubs were located, and the Bond Street stores where the wealthy came to shop. The East End, however, was a different story. It was synonymous with poverty, disease, and despair. It was a breeding ground for crime—crime that spilled over into every corner of the city. Smith knew he could defend himself against any man; but it bothered him that, in London, at almost any time of the day or night, he might have to.

His thoughts were less on social issues, however, then they were on the meeting he was about to have with Lord Spencer.

After Parish and he had broken the French cipher, Parish was dispatched to deliver the message to Nelson. At the same time, Smith was ordered back to London. The strange thing was that the order did not come from Jervis; it came through Jervis, directly from the Board of Admiralty. After a week of cooling his heels waiting for the summons, it finally came and he was on his way to meet with George Spencer, 2nd Earl Spencer, and First Lord of the Admiralty.

Spencer was the one thing that all military men dreaded. He was a politician. Worse than that, he was a Whig; and Smith was very much a Tory. In 1794, William Pitt, the Prime Minister, tapped Spencer to be the First Lord of the Admiralty. This came as a surprise to many; but for several years Pitt had been savaged by the Whig Party, so most people just wrote off Spencer's appointment as a peace offering.

It was not unusual for a civilian to hold the office of First Lord; but in far too many cases, its occupant had viewed it as a sinecure. This was not the case with Spencer. He worked hard to understand the operations of the navy, and had a genuine interest in its welfare. Combine those facts with a keen intellect, and he became very effective at his job, and highly respected by the fleet.

The Admiralty building was a three-story, U-shaped, brick building located between the Mall, the Horse Guards Parade, and Whitehall. Smith arrived early for his appointment, checked in with the clerk, and took a seat in the dreaded Admiralty waiting room. This was the place where officers from lieutenants to admirals waited and sweated, hoping to see someone, anyone, about their promotion, or assignment, or appeal. Sometimes that wait resulted in a new beginning; and sometimes it resulted in an ended career. Smith wasn't sure which would be his fate. He didn't think he was in trouble, but if Admiral Jervis' attitude toward him was any indication, he couldn't be sure.

He expected to wait for several hours beyond his appointed time. That had become something of a tradition at Admiralty House. He expected to eventually be called and escorted up a flight of stairs to either the main boardroom, or Lord Spencer's office. Neither happened. To the shocked surprise of everyone in the waiting room, shortly after the hour, Lord Spencer appeared in person, shook his hand, and led him through a double door out onto a veranda overlooking the parade ground.

"Thank you so much for coming, Sir Sidney. It's such a fine spring day; I thought maybe we could discuss our business out here. You know, being confined in a stuffy building all the time is simply not good for the constitution. I think that's why you naval types seem to live so long. You get that good healthy sea air all the time. It seems to me that..."

Spencer engaged in endless, and largely mindless, small talk while proceeding to the gravel track surrounding the parade field. From there, he strolled toward the side of the quadrangle that bordered St. James Park. When they were well out of the range of any conceivable earshot, Spencer stopped and sat down on a stone bench in a small copse of trees. He invited Sidney to join him and instantly his voice turned serious.

"First of all, let me thank you for the splendid work you did while you were confined in the Temple."

"Thank you for getting me out of there," Sidney replied.

"Well... actually, I have a small confession to make in that regard. You see, we weren't as concerned with getting you out as we were with getting Lieutenant Wright out."

Sidney looked surprised, so Spencer quickly followed up.

"Sorry, old man, but that's the truth of it. Wright is a master spy. He's the best we've seen in a long time—maybe even the best ever—and we had another assignment for him." Spencer paused for a moment and continued. "Indeed, I must say, if it were up to some people, you'd still be in there."

"That bad?"

"In some quarters, yes. On the other hand, there are a lot of people who think you are God's gift to the Royal Navy."

Smith smiled. "What do you think?"

"I agree with the second group, but for different reasons. I think you were sent to us by God... specifically to punish me for some awful sins in a previous life."

Smith couldn't help but laugh.

"But, enough theology. We have some work for you. We know that Napoleon is heading for Egypt, if he's not there already."

"Yes, we decrypted the message."

"Indeed, but we have confirmation now from other sources."

Smith lifted an eyebrow.

"Wright," Spencer simply said, and then continued. "We do not believe that the Egyptian forces can stand against Napoleon's troops; therefore, we believe he will be successful in his invasion. But, Egypt is a vassal state of the Ottoman Empire. If he invades Egypt, the sultan in Constantinople is going to be... to put it mildly... distressed.

"We want to take advantage of that fact. We want you to go to Constantinople and get the sultan to declare war on France, and sign a mutual defense pact with us. If you can get him to throw in a war with Russia, all the better."

"Yes, sir. You know my brother is..."

"Your brother is John Spencer Smith, Minister Plenipotentiary to the Sublime Porte. Yes, I know. That fact, and your previous experience with the Turkish Navy, were the principal reasons I used to get you approved.

"You'll have a ship and a small squadron; but you'll be filling two roles. On one hand, you'll be a commodore with a small squadron. On the other, you'll hold diplomatic status as a Minister Plenipotentiary, with rank second only to your brother."

"That will not make Lord St. Vincent very happy, nor... oh, my... if I am operating in the eastern Mediterranean... that's Nelson's area. Am I under *his* command?"

"You will be for some things, and not for others. Don't worry, I'll send Jervis a letter explaining it all. It won't be a problem."

"But Jervis is..."

"Captain, he will soon be your commanding officer, so watch your tongue. I know you think he is an idiot. Well, he's not. Politically, he is a very, very, savvy man. He didn't get to be commander of our Mediterranean Fleet because he was a military genius, so maybe you'd better start thinking about how he *did* get the post.

Spencer was right, and Smith knew it. Smith continued in a more subdued tone, "And my ship?"

"You'll have the HMS *Tigre*. She's an 80, and a real beauty. We recently captured her from the French."

"Where is the *Tigre* now?"

"She's at Spithead being refitted."

"Personnel?"

"She's rated for 640 sailors and 125 marines. But we also want to send some additional personnel, 76 officers to be exact, to serve as advisors to the Turkish Army—assuming you are successful at getting the sultan to declare war. Lieutenant-Colonel George

Koehler, who will have a temporary rank of general, will head them up."

"Can I take any other personnel?"

"You can take anyone you can get to sign up; but I warn you, getting hands these days will be no easy task.

"Now, unless you have any further questions, I've got to get back."

Spencer stood up and Smith joined him. The two shook hands. "Thank you, sir," Smith said.

"Don't thank me. Just get the job done. That will be thanks enough."

The two men walked back to Admiralty House. As they got near the building, Spencer turned to Smith.

"Captain, I really am among those who believe in you. You have a certain... I don't know how to describe it... you show occasional flashes of a special ability that few others have. Jervis doesn't have it, and never will. Nelson sometimes has it. But both of those men understand something that seems to completely elude you. They understand that there is a political side to all this as well as a military one. If you can ever master that political reality, combined with your military skill, you could become one of the great naval commanders of all time. If you can't, you will still be a man of wondrous ability; you will still be a man of unquestioned courage; but you will be a largely forgotten one."

Spencer proceeded up the steps to the office building. "It's your choice, captain. It's your choice."

*****

The ships bell sounded from somewhere overhead; it's sound muffled by three decks and half a ship's distance away. It rang four times. Ding-ding! Ding-Ding! and Walker knew it was two o'clock in the afternoon without having to look at his pocket watch.

He was in the after cockpit. Above him was the main gundeck with its two rows of fourteen 32-pound guns. Below him was the spirit room where the ship's alcohol supply was kept under tight security. Both rooms could kill; the gundeck in obvious ways, and the spirit room more subtly. As both a naval physician and a former alcoholic, Walker was intimate with both.

The last sailor of the "special sick call" took his leave and climbed up the after ladder. Walker leaned back in his chair and stared vacantly into the murky gloom of the room. Susan Whitney quietly began putting away the vial of mercury that was on the table next to Walker, along with the cup and pitcher of water. Terry Parish, now Susan's volunteer assistant, gingerly folded up the white table cloth and blew out the flame in one of the three overhead lanterns. Neither said anything, as now was not a good time to be talking with the esteemed Dr. Lucas Walker.

It was Walker, however, who finally broke the silence.

"Susan, were you aware that I am a physician?"

"Yes, Lucas."

"No... Really, I am. I hold a Doctor of Medicine degree from Edinburgh University. Did you know that?"

"Yes, Lucas."

Walker paused for a few seconds. "Then why the hell am I not being treated like one!" Lucas slammed his hand down on the table and stood up. "Sidney said this might happen. We were transfered to the *Bellerophon* because they supposedly needed medical assistance. Nobody said anything about the ship already having a surgeon who would be over me."

"George Bellman is..." Susan started to reply; but Walker cut her off.

"Four years ago Bellman was a barber; but, oh yes, he is listed as the ship's surgeon; and I am but a supernumerary. He took a one month training course and a brief apprenticeship; and I took a five year college degree. He has an uncle with Admiralty connections; and I have... we have... Jervis! And that, my dear, summarizes our situation. We have been aboard for weeks, and the only thing I have been *assigned* to do by Surgeon Bellman is treat syphilis cases. Yet, by rights, as a naval physician I should be in charge of the medical affairs for this whole squadron."

"But you've developed a new way of treating those cases."

"I haven't developed a damn thing Susan. I have no idea how to treat it; nor does anyone else. The book says we're supposed to treat them with mercury. Do you remember when we used to inject mercury up their penises—and call *that* treatment?

"Well, I refuse to do it anymore. It doesn't work. Nothing works; and I suspect that's why I was given this as my sole duty."

"But you do use mercury," Terry timidly pointed out. "I just saw you."

"Yes, I put a few drops in a pitcher of water, have them drink some, and tell them it's a new kind of medicine. They don't even get the mercury; it sinks to the bottom. That's my breakthrough treatment."

"But surely you must have *some* idea of how to treat them?" Terry persisted.

Walker paused and gave a rueful smile. "Yes, as a matter of fact I do. All we have to do is give them Malaria."

"Malaria?" Susan asked.

"Yes. Do you remember Hiram Boult, the physician we met on the *Tisiphone* years ago? I got a letter from him when we were back in England. He's in the West Indies again and says that he sees improvements and even cures in syphilitic patients who survive malaria. He thinks maybe the fever sweats the syphilis out of them.

"So, there's your cure ladies. We take patients who are sure to die, later, from one disease; and kill most of them, sooner, with another. Meanwhile, there are a host of things I *can* treat—but I am not allowed to."

Walker slowly arose and proceeded up the ladder to the gundeck, calling over his shoulder. "That's me, ladies. Captain Syphilis—medical savior."

Walker reached the gundeck, and proceeded past the main capstan and the two pumps that were situated on either side of the main mast. He was glad to be on the gundeck because a few of the ports were open, admitting some much needed light and air. He was even more glad to go up two more levels and reach the forecastle where the warm sun and sea breeze could clear his head and hopefully improve his spirits. A few minutes later Susan joined him as he stood near the starboard cathead gazing out at the ocean. She said nothing. She simply slipped her arm around his, and that was all that needed to be said.

Suddenly a call was heard from the foretop, some fifty feet directly above their heads.

"On deck thar! Sail two p'ints off th' starboard bow."

Both Lucas and Susan automatically searched the horizon in that direction, but from their lower vantage point could see nothing. A few moments later a midshipman scurried up the main mast ratlines with a telescope slung over his shoulder. He precariously climbed the outside of the futtock shrouds, gained the maintop, looked through his glass, and made his report.

"Deck there! I see one ship and... yes, there's another just beyond it."

"What type?"

"I can't say, sir. They're both hull-down; but their sails look French cut."

"Very well."

A few minutes later the *Bellerophon* broke out a series of signal flags, which were acknowledged by the flagship, the *Vanguard*. A bit later the *Vanguard* gave a reply that seemed to evoke considerable discussion on the quarterdeck.

Walker found out later that the flag response was to ignore the ships and continue on course. This decision was to have tragic consequences. In his haste to locate the French fleet in Alexandria, Nelson sailed right past them on the open ocean.

*****

When Lord Spencer said the *Tigre* was "a real beauty," he was quite serious. In fact, if anything, it was an understatement. To a landsman, from a distance, she looked like any large British 74. Indeed, the British tended to categorize all *Téméraire* class ships as 74's; but she was much more than that. She was a two decker, and her basic layout was the same as a British third-rate; but that's where the similarities ended. The French tended to build hulls that were longer, lower, and sleeker than the British. This allowed them several advantages. First, they could put more guns aboard, which is why the *Tigre* was an 80-gun ship and not a 74. And second, the low, sleek, hull provided less freeboard—less surface area for the wind to catch—which made the ships more maneuverable.

The *Tigre* had been captured only a few months earlier when a British battle fleet of 14 ships chased a 12 ship French fleet toward the Île de Groix. In a battle lasting almost three hours, three French ships were captured, one of them being the *Tigre*. Another ship, the *Alexander*, taken in the same battle, was already serving with Nelson.

Sidney Smith was being rowed out to the ship by a crew from the *Tigre* headed by his personal coxswain, Issac Pulley. He and Cecil Durban had arrived several days earlier with Smith's personal effects to get his quarters ready for habitation. Smith ordered the boat to take a turn around the ship so he could examine it from the seaward side.

She looked to be in reasonable shape. It was clear that almost all of the rigging had been replaced and the brand new Bridport hemp lines glistened in the sun. He greatly admired the white leaping tiger figurehead in the bow, but he did not fail to notice that the spritsail yard, hanging off the jib-boom, needed to be replaced. A lot of captains did not use spritsails and often had them removed; but Smith was not among them.

Continuing along the larboard side, Smith could see that her trim was off, but that was to be expected as she was still loading supplies and they had not all been properly stowed yet. He could see where shot holes had been repaired. It was obvious not so much by the repairs themselves as by the fresh painting that the area had received.

He didn't really care too much what color the ship was painted, as long as the basic hull was black, and the space between the gun ports was anything *other* than yellow. He knew that Nelson liked his ship, and any ship serving with him, to have their gunports painted black and the space between the gunports, yellow. Thus, when the ports were closed, it gave a black and yellow checkerboard effect that some of his sycophants were already calling the "Nelson Checker." Nelson said he did it so that it would be easier to spot friendly ships during a battle. Smith didn't believe that for one minute and had a simpler explanation. It was simple personal vanity.

He rounded the typically French horseshoe-shaped stern, and gave a quick examination to the underside of the longboat that was housed just outside his stern gallery. They tied on to the starboard side steps that were built into the hull. Smith climbed them with ease, and the instant his head appeared above the deck line two rows of marines crashed their muskets into a salute, a cloud of white pipeclay arose from the immaculate cross-belts the marines were wearing, and a boson's pipe began to wail.

Greeting him was Lieutenant Philip Canes, his first-lieutenant.

"Good morning, Sir. Welcome aboard the *Tigre*."

"Thank you, Lieutenant. It's good to be standing on a deck again.

"Have my belongings arrived?"

"Yes, sir. They arrived two days ago and your servant has been busy stowing them and getting your rooms ready."

"Very good. And what kind of condition is the ship in?"

"We're very nearly ready for sea, sir. There wasn't all that much damage to her to begin with, and that was quickly rectified by Mr. Spuring. He and a number of shipwrights have been added to our complement, although I am not quite sure why."

"The reason will be made known to you in time," Sidney replied, mysteriously. I noticed the rigging has been replaced."

"Yes, sir. The French are apparently suffering quite a bit from our blockades. Without the ability to import good quality hemp, the rope they were using was of the worst possible kind. I, frankly, wouldn't have it on a garbage scow. So, it all had to be replaced along with several other pieces of tackle that were quite worn."

"What about the masts and hull?"

"Excellent. The hull was very well built and the coppering was well done. I believe she had recently been careened and her hull cleaned, so she's in good shape there."

"Very good, lieutenant. Very good. Now, if you please, I would be obliged if you would call all hands. Before I do anything else, I'd best read myself in."

Sidney Smith proceeded up the short ladder that lead from the gangway to the quarterdeck, admiring as he did so the intricate scrollwork on the deck face. He stood on the quarterdeck in front of the aft capstan, looking down on the gangways and, through the hold opening, to the main deck. The bosun and his mates were loudly circulating through the ship calling out: "All hands ahoy! All hands ahoy! which summoned the crew to repair on deck.

As the crew was assembling he was surprised at how many faces he recognized. The *Tigre* had a complement of 640 men and 125 Marines. She was far short of that, of course. No Navy ship was fully manned; but Smith was delighted at how full the ship's complement seemed to be. What surprised him the most, however, were the number of crewmen he could recall from his days on HMS *Diamond*. There had to be at least thirty or forty of them, among them the brothers Hugh and Raymond Hayes. Included in the officer's line was Charles Beecroft, a midshipman who had accompanied Smith on the fateful raid at La Havre. Beecroft had been badly wounded in the hand and leg; and, when last he saw him, Smith wasn't sure he was going to make it. He not only made it, but he was now proudly standing before him, beaming, back in service. Next to him was a young midshipman he did not know. It was Richard Janverin, a 21 year old former master's mate, who had just transfered to the *Tigre*.

He continued to scan the officer line when his reveries were broken by Lieutenant Canes. "The officers and men are assembled, sir."

"Very good lieutenant." Smith reached into a waist-coat pocket, pulled out a piece of parchment paper and unfolded it. They were his orders to assume command of the *Tigre*. Prior to the act of reading them aloud to the crew, he was simply an officer who had come aboard the ship. After reading them, he became like a God, with life and death power over the lives of every man on board.

Smith cleared his throat.

By the Commissioners for Executing the Office of Lord High Admiral of the United Kingdom of Great Britain and Ireland &C and of all His Majesty's Plantations &C

To Sir William Sidney Smith, hereby appointed Captain of His Majesty's Ship Tigre.

Willing and requiring you forthwith to go on board and take upon you the Charge and Command of Captain in her accordingly. Strictly Charging and Commanding all the Officers and Company of the said Ship to behave themselves jointly and severally, in their respective Employments, with all due Respect and Obedience unto you their said Captain. And you likewise to observe and execute the General Printed Instructions and such Orders and Directions as you shall from time to time receive from Us, or any other of your superior Officers for His Majesty's service. Hereof nor you nor any of you may fail as you will answer the Contrary at your Peril. And for so doing this shall be your Warrant.

Given under our hands and the Seal of the Office of Admiralty this Twenty-fifth day of June 1798, in the thirty-eighth Year of His Majesty's Reign.

By Command of their Lordships
Evan Nepean, Secty

Smith knew the power that had just been bestowed upon him; but he also knew about the other side of the coin. It was contained in the phrase: "Hereof nor you nor any of you may fail as you will answer the Contrary at your Peril." He knew what that meant.

He now had absolute authority and control over one of His Majesty's ships. In exchange, he would be placed in unimaginable situations, with inadequate resources, to accomplish impossible tasks. If he succeeded, his superiors would take the lion's share of the credit with, hopefully, a portion trickling down to him. If he failed... they were serious about the part that read "...you will answer the contrary at your peril."

That was simply the way of it—and there were hundreds of officers who would give anything to be standing in his shoes this morning and reading those orders.

Smith turned to his first lieutenant, "That will be all, lieutenant. Dismiss the men."

Canes passed the order to the bosun, but instead of dismissing the crew he said, "All right you men, let's hear it for the Captain! Three cheers and a tiger! At this the men gave a hearty "Huzzah! Huzzah! Huzzah!" and then started chanting "Hi! Hi! Hi" rising in volume and pitch until it ended in a general screeching roar. Smith had heard cheers and a tiger before, but did this one seem especially enthusiastic? He didn't have time just then to think about it, however, and turned to his first officer.

"A bit later I would like to inspect the entire ship, lieutenant. In the meantime, if you would be so good as to show me to my quarters."

Lieutenant Canes suddenly appeared rather nervous. "Well... ah... sir, it seems there are some gentlemen occupying your quarters at the moment."

"Gentlemen? In my quarters? What are they doing?"

Canes paused, unsure how to proceed. "The last time I looked they were playing cards, sir."

Smith wasn't sure he had heard the lieutenant right. "There is a group of men in my quarters playing cards?"

"Yes, sir. And smoking and drinking"

Smith was making every effort to control himself. "And who *are* these gentlemen, lieutenant?"

"I don't know sir. They're civilians."

"Civilians."

"Ah, yes sir. And one midshipman."

"A midshipman? A MIDSHIPMAN who couldn't make it to my reading-in because he was too busy playing cards?

"Well, sir... ah..."

Smith was beyond listening to any more. He knew full well where a captain's quarters were located on a 74 and a French 80 couldn't be too much different. He stormed down the quarterdeck ladder, through the door to the lobby, past the marine guard, barged into his great cabin, and froze in his tracks.

The lieutenant was not lying. There were six men in his quarters. Four of them were playing cards at his chart table, and two others were off to the side conversing. The four playing cards were: John Wesley Wright, Picard de Phélippeaux, François de Tromelin, and Count Antoine Viscovitch. Conversing in a corner were Le Grand de Palluau and a man he didn't recognize but later learned was Charles de Frotté.

John Wesley Wright was the master spy who was imprisoned with Smith in the Temple—and was once again wearing a midshipman's uniform. Charles de Frotté was the half-brother of the Chouan General, Louis Frotté, whose guerrilla campaign Smith had supported when he was aboard the *Diamond*. The other four men had all played key roles in his escape from the Temple.

Smith was literally speechless; but the silence was soon broken by "Midshipman" Wright. "It's about time you got here, Sidney. Have a seat. We'll deal you in on the next hand."

*****

After the greetings were over, after the reminiscences were made, after the toasts were drunk, Smith managed to escort the group to his door under the pretext of wanting to get settled in. But instead of doing that, he walked over to the gallery of windows in the back of his quarters and looked out over the harbor for a moment. He knew how that particular collection of individuals had gotten here, for they had told him. They were ordered here either by the Admiralty, the Foreign Office, or both; but Smith had no clear idea as to why. He suspected the answer lay in his coat pocket. He reached in and pulled out two additional sets of orders, quite different from the ones he had read to the crew. The first was from Lord Spencer:

Sir Wm. S. Smith, Captain of the Tigre

You are to put to sea without a moment's loss of time in the ship you command, and proceed with all possible despatch off Cadiz, and putting yourself under the command of the Earl of St. Vincent, admiral of the Blue and commander-in-chief of his majesty's ships and vessels in the Mediterranean and along the coast of Portugal, follow his lordship's order for your further proceedings.

In case the said admiral should not be off Cadiz when you arrive there, you are to go on to Gibraltar, and, putting yourself under his command, follow his orders, as above desired.

Given, &c, and signed,

SPENCER,

W. Young,

J. Wallace

The second set was from Lord Grenville, the Foreign Secretary. It was a commission, appointing him as joint minister plenipotentiary with his brother, Spencer Smith, to the court of the Ottoman emperor in Constantinople; and it ordered him to proceed there immediately. This commission was separate and distinct from Lord Spencer's admiralty orders.

Sidney Smith just sighed. "I am to proceed to Cadiz... immediately," he thought. "I am to put myself under St. Vincent's command... immediately; as long as he commands me to go to Constantinople... immediately. And what if he doesn't, gentlemen? Do orders from the First Lord trump those of the Foreign Secretary, or is it the other way around? And what about Nelson? When I am in the eastern Mediterranean, am I under his orders via the admiralty's chain of command, or am I on a diplomatic mission and answerable only to the Foreign Office?"

Smith didn't like this situation. He didn't like it one bit. "Lord," he thought. "I hope those people are communicating with each other."

They weren't.

He put the orders back into his pocket, turned around and called out, "Durbin! Durbin, where the hell did you put everything? Durbin!"

*****

It was a few minutes before noon and on the *Vanguard's* poop deck the ship's master was surrounded by a covey of midshipmen. Each was shooting the sun's angle with their sextants—everyone except the master who claimed he could get a far more accurate reading with his old Hadley octant than anyone with one of those new fangled sextant contraptions. At the precise moment that the sun reached the meridian, the master called out "Mark!" This told the quartermaster of the watch that it was exactly noon. The ship

120

was one of the lucky few that had an Earnshaw chronometer on it, which was immediately consulted by the quartermaster and the exact time, to the second, was written down. He also caused the ship's half-hour long hour-glass to be reset, and the bosun to begin the distinctive squealing tone on his pipe that signaled to the crew that it was time for dinner.

While the crew assembled on the gun deck for their meal, each midshipman was hunched over a slate calculating the ship's position. Their solutions would gain them anything from a mumbled "Well done," to a box on the ears, by the master.

The men sat down to tables that had been swung down from the beams between each gun. Each mess had one person selected, on a rotating basis, as the "mess cook" for that day. His job was to serve as a runner to fetch the table's meal from the galley, and to clean up afterwords. Soon the men were contentedly ingesting their food, and gossiping with each other.

At one bell into the Afternoon Watch (12:30), a fifer on the upper deck began playing a spritely tune. Today it was "Nancy Dawson." That was the signal that grog was being served, and it was one of the high points of the sailor's day.

The cook for each mess grabbed a pail and proceeded to a tub where the beverage was being served. Whenever rum was available, they had grog—a mixture of one part rum with four parts water. If they were in the Mediterranean, they often had "Blackstrap" an inexpensive Spanish wine. If they had neither of those, they were given small beer. And if none of those were available—the captain had a very, *very*, unhappy crew.

Over their grog, the men could genuinely relax. Barring an enemy attack or equally serious ship emergency, the officers generally steered clear of the gun deck during this time. The men could laugh, talk, spin yarns, make and settle bets, and generally relax as best they could.

William Parish loved this part of the day. As a civilian supernumerary, he could have taken his meals in the wardroom with the officers. He chose not to. Instead, he applied to one of the crew messes for admittance, which, after some discussion by the men in that mess, was approved.

In the time he had been aboard he had come to cherish the camaraderie he had with the men. They liked his infectious humor; and he liked their simple common sense. They could not respect him as a sailor (they knew he would never be one) but they could admire him for his education and for the fact that he seemed to genuinely respect them in return.

One day Parish had struck a bargain with the ship's purser to buy a set of seaman's clothes from the *Vanguard's* slop chest; but he never told anyone about it. He knew he would never actually wear them aboard ship, that would mark him as a phony, and the men would never, could never, abide a fraud. But he kept them in his chest and he knew he would have them as a treasured possession for as long as he lived.

At three bells (1:30) the "watch on deck" would normally be called back to duty, and the "watch below" was allowed to do pretty much whatever they pleased. Today, however, it was different, for Admiral Nelson, through Captain Berry, had ordered another one of his interminable gun drills. The men groused and moaned, but each man reported to his assigned battle station.

They were going through their third, timed, dry firing of the guns, when the foremast lookout called, "Land, Ho!"

This was a significant event and everyone, including the officers, stopped what they were doing for a moment to see if they could glean any further information. The sighting was soon confirmed by a young lieutenant with a telescope, and hurried conferences were held on the quarterdeck to try to figure out exactly where they had made landfall. With consensus reached, Nelson turned the squadron a few degrees to the east-southeast, hopefully to find Alexandria just over the horizon. He also sent the *Mutine* on ahead to scout Alexandria Harbor and see if the French were there.

The *Mutine* sped off. Parish took up a vigil on the quarterdeck to await the news. Thirty minutes went by... sixty minutes... ninety minutes—minutes that seemed like whole days to Parish. Suddenly another call was heard that the *Mutine* was returning.

A midshipman with a signal book and a glass was dispatched to the maintop. He soon called down.

"The *Mutine* is signaling, sir. She says, The enemy fleet is..." and there was a very long pause. Finally Captain Berry could stand the suspense no longer.

"Blast you, Mr. Thompson! The enemy fleet is... what?"

"I am sorry sir, but her foretopsail is blocking the last flag. Wait! There it is. The enemy fleet is... not in harbor. That's her message sir. The enemy fleet is NOT in harbor."

William Parish was stunned. He felt like he had contracted an instant case of the flu. The color drained from his face, and the bottom fell out of his stomach. The edges of his vision seemed to gray-out and he felt like he was looking at the world through a long narrow tunnel. He turned to Nelson, whose penetrating black eyes were boring into him.

"The French are headed to Alexandria. Is that right, Mr. Parish? You and the Swedish knight have broken some damn code. Is that correct? Well, they are *not* in Alexandria, you fool! They are off doing God knows what, to who knows who, while we twiddle our thumbs on a fool's errand."

"Sir... I don't understand... I..."

"Silence! I want you out of my sight. No, belay that. I want you completely off my ship!" Nelson's voice, which was normally high pitched, raised even higher and crackled with emotion as he screamed. "Off my ship, do you hear? Captain Berry, signal the *Bellerophon* to come along side to receive a passenger. Parish, pack your things. I want you gone within five minutes of the *Bellerophon's* arrival. Captain Berry, I want you to see to this man's departure personally. Muster a squad of marines if you have to, but get this man off this ship!"

Parish didn't know what to say. He didn't know what to do. In the span of just a few minutes his world had completely collapsed around him. He had gone from hopeful pride, to abject disgrace. His head was swirling. He couldn't have been wrong; but he was. No, he was sure he was right; but, if so, then where were the French?

Parish moved like a sleepwalker as he robotically headed to the ladder leading off the quarterdeck; but Nelson could not resist one parting shot. "And Parish, when you get back under whatever rock you came from, give my regards to Sir Sidney."

*****

The *Bellerophon* rode at an easy anchor just outside of the Old Harbor, southwest of Alexandria. Owing to some bad casks she had received, she was low on water and was permitted to go in and resupply at the mouth of the New Alexandria Canal. All of the captains were aboard the *Vanguard* with Nelson, trying to decide what to do next. While this was going on, most of the crew managed to find some excuse to come on deck and look around. As with most ports of call, they knew they would never be allowed on shore, but they prided themselves in maintaining a long list of places they had "seen" in their travels.

William Parish had arrived on board as depressed and disconsolate as a man could be. Nothing that Susan, Terry, or Walker could say was of any use. He simply retired to his sleeping area and remained there. That worried Walker, but they decided to leave him be. What happened next worried Walker even more.

About an hour later, Parish emerged from his quarters as happy and chipper as he had previously been depressed. Walker had seen that kind of turnabout before. It was in a man who had decided to commit suicide. He was happy because he knew that all his problems would soon be over.

Parish wandered up to the main deck and Walker followed him.

"William, it really wasn't your fault, you know," Walker said as he joined him at the bulwark.

"Yes, I know."

"I mean, there are any number of things that could have delayed the French arrival. They could have hit a storm, or taken a longer route, or even bad navigation. We'll run them down sooner or later."

"I know, and I want to be here when they arrive."

"Right! That's the spirit. We'll run them to ground here, or in Malta, or Syracuse, or wherever they might be."

"No, I want to be *here* when they arrive, because I know they will arrive—*here*."

"William, we're aboard a ship, and we have a working arrangement with this vessel. In exchange for keeping us from drowning, we agree to go where she goes."

"That's why I am leaving the ship."

"You are leaving the ship to do what?"

"I am going to go ashore and wait for the French to arrive. When they do I'll find some way of notifying Nelson; but I need your help to do it."

"My help? In what way?"

"I have a plan. When the next watering boat leaves, I want you to tell whoever is in charge of it that I have urgent business ashore and need to go in with the boat."

"Why me? I am not an officer."

"No, but you are a warranted naval physician—not just a ship's surgeon—and that's fully the equivalent of being a senior officer."

Walker paused for a long moment, thinking. At last he sighed deeply and said, "I can't let you go into Alexandria alone."

"Don't try to stop me, Lucas. I am serious about that. Don't try to stop me because I *am* going ashore."

"I wasn't planning on stopping you. I am going with you."

An hour later the two men emerged on deck and made their way over to the boarding steps that were built into the starboard hull. Directly below was the ship's longboat, which had just completed having the empty water casks stowed aboard. The two men made their way into the boat and were greeted by a surprised Fourth Lieutenant.

"May I help you, Dr. Walker?"

"Yes, we need to go ashore with you."

"Ashore? We're not going into Alexandria, you know. We're just going to that canal over there."

"Yes, I know. We'll make our own way into Alexandria."

The lieutenant was becoming skeptical. "May I ask why you want to go there, sir?"

"You may not, as it is none of your business," Walker was doing his best to sound affronted. "But if you must know, Admiral Nelson has a message for the British consul in Alexandria and Mr. Parish is to deliver it." Parish, seeing where this was going, nodded knowingly and patted his coat pocket as if he had something in it.

"Then why would you be going with him?"

Walker hadn't anticipated that question, but Parish jumped in. "Lieutenant, it really is none of your business."

"I am sorry sir, but the captain's standing orders are that no one is to go ashore on provisioning parties in a foreign port except the people that are actually involved in the provisioning."

"The captain gave his permission," Parish replied.

"The captain is not aboard right now. He's with the Admiral, so I can't ask him about it." It was a fact that Parish knew full well.

Walker now went into his best imitation of a rage. "Lieutenant, this is absurd and I'll not have you questioning Admiral Nelson's directives. If you must know, I am going along because the Admiral is concerned with a medical matter. Several of the ships have reported cases of... of Lecznar's Disease... so if you want to be responsible for *that* spreading throughout the squadron, be my guest. But I warn you, it will go hard on you when the Admiral finds out—very hard."

That was the clincher. The lieutenant knew that Parish had recently transferred over from the *Vanguard*, so maybe the admiral *had* given him a message. Besides he certainly didn't want to be the one responsible for the spread of Lecznar's Disease—whatever that might be. He nodded acquiescence and the boat set off.

All the way in the two men thought about the notes they had written explaining their actions, William to his wife, Lucas to Susan. William knew that Terry would be upset and terribly worried about his safety. Lucas knew that Susan would be beside herself because he didn't take her with him. He also know that would be a cover for her equally deep worry for him.

When the longboat tied up, the two men got out and Walker turned to the lieutenant.

"Thank you for your cooperation, sir. If we are not back by the time you are ready to leave, just go ahead without us. We'll catch one of the later boats."

And with that the two men set off for the walls of the ancient city less than a quarter-mile away.

*****

The *Tigre* had barely furled her sails when a boat set off from the Gibraltar Navy Pier. On it was Admiral Jervis, which astonished Sidney Smith. Under any kind of normal circumstance, Admirals do not go to their captains—their captains went to them.

As they settled into Smith's cabin, Admiral Jervis was offered a drink.

"No captain, I won't be staying long—and neither will you. That's why I've come out to your ship. The moment you have finished watering, you are to be gone. No need for you to come ashore at all.

"Some time ago I received a letter from Lord Spencer regarding the duties in Constantinople he wishes you to perform; but he left it up to me to actually make the assignment. I'll be honest, captain, I immediately sent a letter back saying that, in my opinion, assigning you to that task would be a grave mistake; but my warnings have been ignored. Instead... Instead what I got back was a letter from Spencer that reads in part as follows."

He pulled out a document from the leather valise he was carrying, "'I am well aware that there may perhaps be some prejudices, derived from certain circumstances which have attended this officer's career through life, but from a long acquaintance with him personally, I think I can venture to assure your Lordship, that added to his unquestioned character for courage and enterprise, he has a great many very good points about him, which those who are less acquainted with him are not sufficiently apprised of, and I have no doubt that you will find him a very useful instrument to be employed on any hazardous or difficult service, and that he will be perfectly under your guidance, as he ought to be.'

"So there we have it. You are to proceed with all possible speed to Constantinople. On your way, however, I nevertheless have some other tasks for you. I have some dispatches I want you to take to Captain Ball who is commanding the blockade of Malta. I also have a pouch for Admiral Nelson who, I believe, is at Syracuse. I am also giving you two copies of a special code book. Give one to Nelson and keep one for yourself. Any correspondence you need to have with either him or me must be done in that code."

Smith was pleased. "Thank you, sir. Thank you for confirming the assignment."

Jervis shook his head. "As far as I am concerned, Smith, you can go to hell; but unfortunately I can not cut orders for that destination. Failing that, yes, I am bowing to the wishes of Lord Spencer."

And with no further comment, Jervis got up, walked back on deck, boarded his gig and went back to his comfortable villa on Gibraltar.

Sir Sidney Smith
1764 - 1840

Sir Sidney Smith
in the Temple Prison

The Temple Prison
Paris

Horatio Nelson

Sir John Jervis

John Wesley
Wright

George Spencer
First Lord of the Admiralty

Georges René de Pléville
Minister of Marine

Napoleon Bonaparte

Sultan Selim III

Henry Darby
Captain of the *Bellerophon*

Thomas Foley
Captain of the *Goliath*

Adm. François-Paul Brueys
Commanding the French Fleet

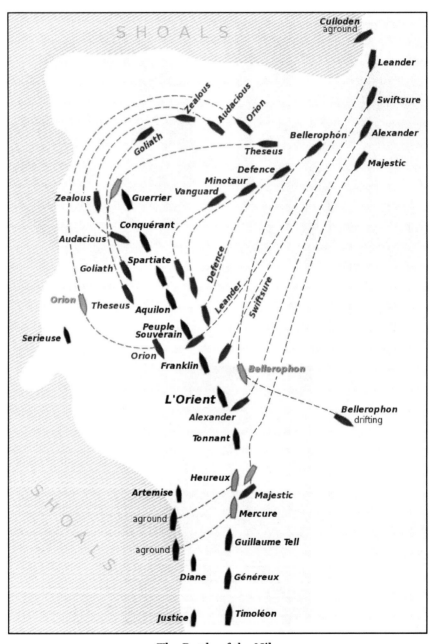

The Battle of the Nile
(From Wikipedia: Battle of the Nile)

CHAPTER SIX

The morning watch had just been relieved on the *Orient* when one of Napoleon's scouting frigates was spotted coming in under full sail on a direct course for the flagship. The captain of the 38-gun frigate came racing over in a pinnace along with a Turkish gentleman who was looking none too happy to be there.

Upon arrival, the captain asked the officer of the deck to be shown immediately to the general's quarters, where Bonaparte received them.

"My word, you seem to be in quite a rush, Capitaine... "

"Standelet, sir. Capitaine de vaisseau Pierre Standelet, at your service."

"Yes, of course. And how might you be of service, this morning, captaine?"

"Sir, my ship, the *La Junon*, was on scout duty this morning as per your orders, and we came across this gentleman in a felucca heading west along the coast. When he saw us he started to run, but we soon captured him."

"I am sure his felucca will be a vital addition to the French Navy, captain; but is there some other reason you are bothering me with this?"

The Turk could hold silence no longer. "It was not my fault, Général, I thought he was a British ship! That's why I ran."

Napoleon looked first at the Turkish captain, then at Standelet, then back at the Turk. He didn't know whether he was more astonished that the man spoke almost perfect French, or with what he had just said.

"You thought he was a British ship? Why would you think that?"

"Because two days ago the British fleet was in Alexandria."

"Damn!" Napoleon spat. He shook his head and paced to the other side of his cabin and back, muttering, "Am I finally losing my luck? A few more days. I only need a few more days." He called for the marine standing outside his door and told him to get Admiral Brueys, who had command of the French warships. When Brueys arrived he told the Turk to tell him everything he knew about the British ships.

"I don't know if I can tell you all that much, mon Général. They arrived about two days ago. I know they sent a delegation of officers to our *kashif*... our... what's the word... to our governor. I know, because I saw them land with my own eyes and proceed to his palace. They say they wanted to warn him that the French were coming to invade Egypt."

"And what did your governor do?"

"He thought it was some kind of British trick and threw them out. He refused them permission to land, or take on fresh water—even though one ship had already started to do so. He would not allow them even to remain in the harbor.

"That's all I know, Général. I swear by the prophet—that's all I know."

"Do not fear, my friend. We don't harm those who help us, and you have helped us a great deal with this information.

"Captain Standelet, you have done well in bringing this man directly to me. Now take him back to his ship and send him on his way, but say nothing to anyone about what you have just learned."

Napoleon paused for a moment, the dark pools of his eyes were sparkling with an intelligence that had just shifted into overdrive.

"Then I want you to take your ship into Alexandria and bring me the French consul there. His name is Magallon, Charles Magallon. Your visit is to be an outwardly innocent one. Keep your gun ports shut. If you are stopped by the British, say you are on a diplomatic mission and claim immunity. You are just there to confer with the consul on some matter of state; but I want an exact count of how many British ships there are, what type, and if you can find out, who is their commander."

Several hours later Standelet came back with the consul and with the good news that the British had set sail earlier that morning. Magallon confirmed the British presence and departure, and that Nelson was the commander, but had no information on where they had gone. He thought maybe they had gone toward Alexandretta on the Syrian coast.

"The problem, citizens," Napoleon began, "is not that the British are there; it's that they're not. If they are not in Alexandria, where are they; or, more specifically, when will they come back? If our ships are not completely off-loaded by then, all will be lost."

Napoleon walked over to a chart table, rummaged through one of the drawers, and pulled out a large map of Alexandria and environs. Pointing to the city, he said, "Monsieur Magallon, can we take our ships directly into one of their two harbors?"

"I do not believe so, Général. There are several forts overlooking both that will..."

"I don't fear their forts," Napoleon interrupted.

"It is not the forts alone that you should fear, sir. These harbors are spacious once you get in them, but the approaches are very narrow and treacherous with shoals. If you attempt to force your way into one or both of their harbors, the forts will certainly harass you with cannon fire, and many of your ships will surely run aground and be lost."

"So, where else can we land our troops?"

"I am neither a general nor an admiral, sir, and know nothing of military planning; but I would suggest here." Magallon pointed to Aboukir Bay, some 15 miles to the east."

Napoleon looked, thought about it for a moment, and said, "No, that's no good. First it's exactly where the Egyptians would expect us to land, and doubtless they already have manpower and firepower positioned there. Second, it's too far away from the city. It must be 14 or 15 miles if it's an inch. The objective, citizens, is to take the City of Alexandria, and you can't do that with exhausted troops."

"What about over here?" Magallon suggested. "There is a beach near a fishing village, Marabut I think it's called. It's only about 7 or 8 miles west of Alexandria."

"Excellent. That's what I am looking for. That's where we'll land; and we'll do it today."

At this, Brueys finally spoke up. "Général, that can not be done. First, we have no charts for that area. None. Who knows what rocks and shoals lurk there? We will have to take soundings of the water before we can bring the ships in close to shore. Second, the weather is turning bad. The winds are up and getting worse, and the seas will soon follow. And third, there is not enough time to do it today. It will be early afternoon before we can even start, which means the landing will take place mostly at night. Landing at night, in uncharted waters, in a gale, is a prescription for disaster."

"Admiral, we have no time to waste. Luck grants me perhaps three days, no more. If we don't take advantage of them—all of them—we are lost. No, we are landing today, near that village... What did you call it?... Marabut, that's it. We are landing at Marabut as soon as possible. See to it, Admiral."

When Brueys and Magallon left, Napoleon heaved a sigh of relief. If Nelson had not been so anxious to get away, if he had stayed for even a few more hours, he would have caught him at sea. It was the second near miss for Napoleon, and he knew that his luck had not left him after all.

✳✳✳✳✳

Parish and Walker had entered the town through a gate not far from a curious structure known as Pompey's Pillar. Standing on a small hill next to an arab cemetery, it was nearly 100 feet high, with a nine foot thick shaft made from a single piece of granite. Walker ached to explore it, but there was no time.

They emerged into the Arab quarter of the city and were shocked by what they saw. Alexandria—the pride of the Ptolemies and the Caesars—was no more. The ancient magnificence was gone and in it's place stood a squalid little town of only some 8,000 people.

It was as if Alexandria had eaten itself. Besides Pompey's Pillar and a few obelisks, nothing of it's former glory remained. The buildings that had graced the once powerful city had either crumbled into dust, or been recycled into building materials for the hovels that now seemed to be everywhere. The harbor breakwaters were a jumble of polished Aswan granite, broken hellenistic columns, and stones with ancient Greek or exquisite hieroglyphic writing on them.

The streets were nothing more than dirt tracks and filth was everywhere. Except for a few palms, there were no trees. Even the birds seemed scraggly and miserable. The people who remained tended to gravitate to the few remaining bazaars. There one could see all the usual goods on display, but the thing that caught the two men's attention were the barbers. To service their customers, the barbers sat in wooden chairs with their customer's heads between their knees. When it came time to shave them, it looked like an impending execution.

There were numerous men to be seen, but not very many women. The men seemed to specialize in doing nothing in particular, and the few women were mostly from the lower classes. Their sole garment was a thin, dirty, usually blue or black, shirt that only came down to their knees. No shoes. Given the thinness of the fabric, the only thing that was left to the imagination was their face, and that was effectively covered. The children ran around generally unsupervised, and were almost always naked.

The two spent a great deal of time wandering up and down various dead-end alleys until they came upon a Greek merchant, who spoke Italian. Parish had a smattering of that language, so they were able to get directions to the British Consulate, which was located in a newer part of town.

At last they arrived at the offices of Ernest Misset, His Majesty's representative in Alexandria. As a consul, he did not have the same diplomatic power as the British ambassador in Cairo. The ambassador's job was to represent king and country before potentates. Misset's job was the much less exalted one of simply helping out any British subjects—be they businessmen or tourists—who needed assistance of one kind or another. Walker and Parish certainly qualified in that regard.

After a cordial greeting and the obligatory glass of sherry, Walker began. "Mr. Misset, we've come to obtain your help. My assistant and I are here to conduct a scientific survey of Egyptian health issues.

"As you know, many people in England see Egypt as someday being of great importance to the empire—if we can ever find a practicable way of transshipping goods from the Mediterranean to the Red Sea. As a result, the Medical Society of London has commissioned me to conduct a preliminary survey of what medical hazards might be attendant upon that day."

Misset leaned back in his chair. "Hundreds of years ago there was a canal, you know," he replied. "But it has long since been filled in and only traces of it remain. Since then, every attempt to build another has failed."

"Yes, we are quite aware of that; but the Society feels that it's never too soon to start planning for the future, what?"

"Yes, quite, quite. So, how can I help you?"

"Our needs are quite simple. We require only food and lodging for the duration of our stay. We can pay, of course."

"And how long might that be?"

"We're not sure. The wheels of science sometimes grind slowly, you know. These things can't be rushed."

"Yes, I am sure," Misset said, although he wasn't sure at all. "Well, I can let you have lodging here in our compound, but you will need a letter of introduction that you can take with you on your rounds." He took out a sheet of paper and started writing. "If you need help, just show this to any native official.

"Do you have instruments or devices that need accommodation as well?"

"Yes, there'll be some, but they are currently aboard ship and..."

"Aboard ship? The British ships sailed hours ago. Surely you know that."

Walker had to think fast. "Yes, of course. I meant they are coming by ship—a merchantman that we hope will be here any day."

"As I think about it, Dr. Walker, how did you get ashore? My understanding is that the *kashif* had forbidden anyone from the ships from landing."

Walker had no idea how he was going to answer that question; but he was saved from having to do so by the door opening. The consul's clerical assistant came in and whispered something to Misset, who looked sharply at the man.

"Well, doctor, if you've left anything on board your ship, you're in luck. It seems the British fleet is returning."

The three men boarded the consulate's carriage for the short ride to Point Eunostos where they could watch the fleet come in.

As the ships drew nearer Misset remarked, "That's strange. I don't remember there being that many British ships in the bay this morning when they left."

Walker felt the color draining from his face as he realized the danger they were now in. Parish's face became suffused with joy.

"There is a reason, for that, sir," Parish casually remarked.

"Indeed, what's that?"

"Those aren't British ships—they're French."

*****

The wind was howling through the rigging of the French ships, and confused seas were tossing them about, making station-keeping almost impossible. Admiral Brueys tried again to postpose the landing to the following day, but Napoleon wouldn't hear of it.

The invasion began about noon. In the first phase, a number of shallow drafted launches with guns aboard were placed near the shoreline to provide defensive fire, if needed. The troops commanded by Desaix, Menou, and Reynier were to be in transports anchored about three miles out; and the troops commanded by Kléber and Bon were to be in an arc about six miles off. Getting the troops into the launches and in position in high wind and high seas, however, was only half the battle. As the day worn on, things got worse.

By 8:00 that night the sea was littered with capsized boats. If a boat went over, soldiers, weighted down with equipment and heavy uniforms, after a few brief screams, simply sank out of sight—never to be seen again. Most of those who did not drown were wretchedly seasick before they even began a ride into shore that could take up to eight hours of rowing.

By 1:00 AM Napoleon and his generals were on shore, but the drenched troops were still coming in. Napoleon took a nap.

By 3:00 AM, under a full moon, it was decided to move the men out and head toward Alexandria. No food, cavalry horses, or artillery had yet reached shore and the men had not eaten since the previous morning. Worse, there was no water. None had been brought in from the ships.

By dawn, the invaders were well on their way from the village of Marabut. There was no road so the men had to walk along the coastal sand dunes, and were beginning to truly suffer. The morning heat was beating down with an intensity that they had never before experienced; and there were no wells or cisterns available along the route of march to provide the needed water. Occasionally the silhouettes of Bedouin warriors could be seen on the adjacent hills. With ferocious screams they would charge down on the columns, but would scatter at the first musket shots from the French.

By 8:00 AM, they had reached Alexandria. Menou and his group continued along the sand dunes of the coast to the far west end of Alexandria's walls; Kléber positioned his unit at the gate near Pompey's Pillar; Bon swung his forces wide and went to the Rosetta gate on the city's east side; and the French Navy controlled the seaward side of the town. Thus, by early morning, Napoleon had the city effectively surrounded.

Inside the town all was in a state of panic; but only the town's *kashif,* Sayyid Muhammad el-Kurrayyim, knew the full extent of the trouble they were in. The city's once stout walls were crumbling in places, he had no standing army, and possessed a total of three ancient cannon that had not been fired in years. The condition of those cannon, however, was probably a moot point because he only had one barrel of gun powder. His only strength was that he had a reasonable force of Mameluke cavalry.

While the French army was trudging up the coast, el-Kurrayyim was busy firing off dispatches to Murad Bey in Cairo, who was the co-ruler of the country, along with Ibrahim Bey.

My Lord, the fleet which has just appeared is immense. One can see neither its beginning nor its end. For the love of God and His Prophet, send us fighting men.

He sent that message, or variations of it, no fewer than thirteen times during the course of the night, although he knew his pleas were hopeless. There was no way reinforcements could come all the way from Cairo before the French got to his city.

Desultory musket fire was exchanged between the townspeople and the French soldiers for an hour or two, and it seemed like Napoleon was prepared to negotiate. Then Kurrayyim decided to unleash his artillery—his three aged cannons.

As older model cannons go, these looked to be in pretty good shape. But, owning to the fact that things rust slowly, if at all, in the dry desert heat, these looks were deceiving. When the first gun fired it split its gun carriage so that it could no longer be aimed. After three rounds, the second split it's barrel. Only the third was able to continue firing until it ran out of power. But even if all three guns had remained active, the French would have considered them a joke. They replied with a storm of musketry directed at the defenders lining the walls.

By mid-morning several units of French light artillery had arrived and silenced the third gun. At this point, Napoleon called a cease fire and send a message into the town.

I am surprised to see you take hostile measures against me. You are ether extremely ignorant or extremely presumptuous, to believe you could resist me with two or three poor pieces of cannon. Moreover, my army has just vanquished one of the foremost Powers in Europe. If in ten minutes I do not see a white flag waving you will have to be held accountable before God for the blood that you will spill needlessly, and soon, you will weep at the departure of the victims that you will have sacrificed by your blindness.

Kurrayyim was not yet ready to surrender, however, for he still had an ace in the hole. In response to Napoleon's message, the main gate of the city opened and out came several hundred Mameluke cavalrymen—the pride of the Ottoman empire.

Technically the Mamelukes were slaves; in practice they were the ruling class. They first appeared in Egypt in the 13th century when they were imported—literally as slaves—by the then sultan. The first group consisted of some 1200 youths abducted from the Caucasus Mountain region, north of Turkey and between the Black and Caspian seas.

From the beginning they were trained to be an elite fighting force. As the generations rolled by, however, they never intermarried with the local Egyptian population. They remained aloof, replenishing their numbers primarily by importing new cadres of boys from the Caucasus. Over time they became an unbeatable warrior caste, which allowed them to assert power and control over the very people who had originally abducted them.

Besides having a reputation for utter fearlessness in battle, they were among the finest light cavalrymen in the world. Arrayed in their colorful, almost garish, costumes, and mounted on their superb horses, just the sight of them would strike fear into the hearts of their foes. The problem was that they had never fought a disciplined western army before.

As soon as the Mamelukes appeared, the French formed into squares. This technique consisted of massing the various units into a hollow square shape, six to ten ranks deep, with the first row kneeling, the second row standing, and all rows with their bayonets fixed. Inside the square the officers directed the battle.

What the French knew, and the Mamelukes didn't, was that horses will not charge a solid wall of bayonets; and there is nothing a rider can do that will make them do so. This came as quite a shock to the Mamelukes who had only one maneuver in their tactical arsenal—the headlong screaming charge.

The Mamelukes would charge, in an attempt to break into the squares where they could slaughter the soldiers from within. The horses would roar up to the square and suddenly stop, while the French solders fired volleys, rank by rank, picking off Mameluke cavalrymen by the droves. To add a little variation, occasionally the squares would open up, a light artillery piece would roll out and give the Mamelukes a spray of grapeshot.

After numerous failed attempts, the Mamelukes gave up and rode off in the general direction of Cairo. Alexandria fell; and Napoleon had a foothold in Egypt.

*****

"You! Out!"

Susan was cleaning her instruments after having stitched-up a sailor with a nasty cut. She looked up as if she couldn't quite believe what George Bellman had so clearly said.

She looked around. "Are you talking to me?" she asked frostily.

"Yes, I'm talking to you; and don't be putting on airs with me, woman. You're not Lady Whitney on *this* ship. You're on the books as a surgeon's mate—although God knows how *that* happened—and I am this ship's surgeon. I want you out of here, and take your useless friend with you."

Susan glared at him with a look of contempt, but said nothing. She slid her instruments into a drawer, gestured to Terry with her head, and proceeded up the ladder from the after cockpit to the gundeck above.

When they had left, a slow smile spread across Bellman's face. It was a smile that contained both satisfaction at his power over Whitney, and anticipation of what he knew was soon to come.

He went to a small solid oak cupboard, fumbled with his keys for a moment, and unlocked it. Glancing at it's contents he took out a small vial filled with a white powder and a larger container filled with a clear liquid. The vial contained almost pure opium and the container was filled with grain alcohol.

His hands trembled as he carefully measured out a small quantity of opium into a hip flask, then filled it with the alcohol. He capped it and started shaking the flask, stopped, thought for a moment, uncapped it and added some more of the opium powder. More shaking and finally he was satisfied with the results. He had created his own personal supply of laudanum.

He took a deep swig from the flask and laid down in one of the hammocks that was set aside for the use of the sick and injured. He pushed his sweaty hair up out of his eyes and took another, shorter, swig, then slumped back. His breathing was becoming labored, but he expected that and knew not to panic. He knew if he waited long enough it would pass, and in its place would come a feeling of peace and euphoria unlike anything he had ever experienced.

A part of him rebelled at his dependence on the drug. He knew it represented a weakness, a flaw in who he was. Several times he had even tried to stop, but to no avail. The craving always came back. No matter what he did—it came back. And with each relapse, along with the blessed relief, there came the knowledge that his needs had grown. The dosages that were sufficient before were no longer adequate.

Without the laudanum he was nothing. With it he... he could feel the warmth starting to spread throughout his body. He somehow felt stronger now, not physically stronger, but the kind of strength that can only be felt by someone with a superior soul—a superior spirit—a superior mind. It was as if he were a god on Mount Olympus, looking down on the petty antics of those below.

He smiled as he thought about how he had just put that jumped-up bitch Whitney in her place. Her companion Terry Parish was not worth considering—although he had to admit, she was rather good looking. He mused for a moment on how far his prerogatives as ship's surgeon might carry him with her. But before he could take that thought to an extended erotic conclusion, his mind rattled on down the road.

He was amazed at the connections he could now see between great people—people like himself—and great events. He concocted several major medical breakthroughs, but lost track of exactly what they were 30 seconds later. He thought of the last time he had spoken with that one-eyed, one-armed, twerp they called an admiral. In fact it was a conversation of no particular consequence, but he thought his remarks were witty if not hilariously funny.

After a while, the laudanum brought him toward sleep, where his maniacal mental wanderings could continue unabated, although in a less conscious form.

"Sleep! Yes, that's the ticket," he thought. "To sleep... perchance to dream."

*****

Susan stormed across the gundeck with Terry Parish in her wake, trying to keep up. She pounded her fist into the main capstan as she went by; and kicked at one of the midship pumps. When she got to the stair leading to the upper deck, she placed her hand on it as if she were going to go up, then paused. Her head dropped on to her arm for a moment, then she looked up and walked over to one of the gun ports that had been opened, hopefully to admit a cooling breeze.

"I am going to kill him, you know," she said as she gazed out the port.

"Who? Bellman?"

"Yes, him too; but I was thinking more about that jerk Walker."

"Do you miss him as much as I miss my William?"

"Terry, you don't understand." She turned to her. "Lucas and I have been through so much together. I've told you how we met, back on the old *Richmond* when we fished Walker out of the drink, half-drowned, when his merchant ship sank. Then there was our little adventure trying to get Prince William away from Yorktown and that horrid privateer we had to fight. We went through the Battle of the Saints together, then through that catastrophe at Toulon—where I nearly blew his head off by mistake. We've taken wonderful vacations together, and seen the sights of half the world; yet we were also together during that mad escape from the Temple when any minute we could have all been killed.

"Don't you see? We were always together. And now Sidney is God knows where, and Lucas is..."

"It wasn't his fault you know," Terry broke in. "He went with William to protect him. William has no business being ashore in a place like Alexandria, especially with the French likely to be landing there soon. What Lucas did was one of the most noble things I've ever seen. The man you love sacrificed himself for the man I love."

Susan's head snapped up. "I didn't say I loved him."

"No, you didn't. But... well... do you?"

"Terry, that's silly. It's simply not feasible that he and I... I mean, it's neither practical nor reasonable that..." But Susan could not complete the sentence.

*****

Meanwhile, two decks up another person was writing a letter to someone he loved, or at least at that time thought he did.

Off Syracuse, July 20th, 1798

To Lady Nelson.

I have not been able to find the French Fleet, to my great mortification, or the event I can scarcely doubt. We have been off Malta, to Alexandria in Egypt, Syria, into Asia, and are returned here without success: however, no person will say that it has been for want of activity. I yet live in hopes of meeting these fellows; but it would have been my delight to have tried Bonaparte on a wind, for he commands the Fleet, as well as the Army. Glory is my object, and that alone. God Almighty bless you.

Horatio Nelson

*****

Within four hours Alexandria had essentially been subdued. There was still a group that was holding out at the Lighthouse Fort, and they would probably not be taken until nightfall; but other than scattered sniper fire, it was relatively quiet. It was the sniper fire, however, that bothered Captain Say.

Most of the residents had barricaded themselves inside their houses, convinced that the French were about to cut off their heads. After all, that's what they would do if they had conquered a city. Others sought refuge with their God and gathered in the many mosques that were scattered about.

Napoleon had entered the city and Captain Say was a part of his entourage. Suddenly, from the roof of a nearby mosque a musket spat, and a ball landed at the foot of Napoleon, grazing his boot. He looked in disgust at General Kléber. Kléber looked over at Say and said, "Captain, for God's sake, take a detachment and go clean out that snake's nest. Catch up to us when you can."

Say annexed a sergeant and a dozen grenadiers from the 75th, and stormed into the mosque. It was filled with people—men, women and children—but no mercy was shown to anyone. In European warfare, civilians simply did not shoot at soldiers, and they certainly did not try to kill the opposing army's general. This, in French eyes, was a staggering outrage that must be severely punished.

As each squad of grenadiers burst through the doors of the mosque, they fired their muskets into the crowd, then waded into them with their bayonets. People screamed and desperately tried to get out of the way of the maddened soldiers, but that just compressed the crowd into an even smaller area. The soldiers were now simply cutting and slashing their way into what had become a solid wall of flesh.

A few men broke away from the killing ground and made a run for a far corner of the mosque. The sergeant saw their flight and went after them. He caught up with one and stabbed him in the back with his bayonet. The second man disappeared around a corner. The sergeant followed him and saw two more figures hiding behind a column. He spun around and lifted his bayonet to stab, when the smaller one raised his hand to protect himself and said: "No! Don't!" in French. The sergeant looked more closely and saw two westerners—two men, cowering in a mosque, in the middle of Alexandria, Egypt, and one of them spoke French. He decided that this situation was why God had created officers.

It took a while for order to be restored. Eventually the pleas for mercy fell on hearing ears, and the killing stopped. The sniper was found, still on the roof. It was a single man and his wife, and between them they had six loaded muskets. They were both summarily shot.

Outside the mosque the captain was forming-up his men to try to catch up with the General's party as quickly as possible. He looked up wondering what was taking the remainder of this troops so long, when two men appeared in the doorway with their hands up. His sergeant, behind them with his musket leveled, was shepherding them out of the building.

"Sergeant? What's this?"

"I don't know sir. I found them hiding behind a pillar in there."

"All right then, who are you and what are you doing here?"

Walker murmured, "William, let me handle this. I speak perfect French."

Captaine, je dois proclamer protester cette atrocité. Nous sommes des civils innocents ici sur l'affaire entreprise paisible.

[Captain, I must proclaim to protest this atrocity. We are innocent civilians here on the business undertaken peaceful.]

"Oh, Jesus," William muttered under his breath.

"What Dr. Walker means to say," William interjected in wonderful French, with a slight Languedoc accent, "is that he is a medical scientist here conducting research when we were caught up in... in your... ah, when we were caught up in this situation."

"You still haven't told me who you are."

"My apologies," William continued with a slight bow. "This is Dr. Lucas Walker and I am his assistant, William Parish. We were sent by the Medical Society of London to conduct research into a variety of diseases found here in Egypt."

"I see. Two supposed British scientists, and I am supposed to believe you are not spies?"

"Spies? Captain, how could be we spies? Who knew the French were going to suddenly arrive in Alexandria and stage an invasion?"

"That's true," Say thought. "*We* didn't even know where we were going until we got here."

"But how do I know you really are scientists?"

William was stumped by that one, then he remembered the letter. He told Walker to produce it and showed it to the officer.

"This is a letter, signed by the British consul himself, that explains who we are and what we're doing here. I can translate it for you if you'd like."

"There is no need," he said in English. "In France all cultivated gentlemen can read, write and speak several languages, unlike in some countries I could name." Say gave Walker a pointed look.

"Excuse me, Captain Say," the sergeant interrupted. "Do you want me to get the men started back?"

"Yes, that would be good; but leave me a detail to take custody of these prisoners."

Walker, knew enough French to understand the gist of that statement, and Parish knew enough to be completely alarmed.

"Captain, surely you're not going to arrest two harmless scientists," Parish began. "Our only fault was that we were in the wrong place at the wrong time. Surely, that's not a crime. You already know we're not spies, and we really are medical scientists."

"All of that is perhaps true; but I don't know what else to do with you."

Walker chimed in, mercifully in English. "Pardon me, but did that sergeant just call you Captain Say?"

"Yes. Why?"

"Are you, by any chance, from the Lyon area?"

"Yes." Say was wondering where he was going with this.

"Are you possibly related to the economist, Jean-Baptiste Say? Say's Law? Supply creates its own demand and all that?"

"Yes, he's my brother."

"Your brother? Then you must be Horace. Jean-Baptiste is a good friend of mine. I knew him when he was a clerk in Croydon, and later he stayed with me for a while when he first moved to London. How is Julie, by the way?" Turning to the astonished Parish, "That's his wife."

Horace Say was even more astonished than William Parish.

*****

At the time of Napoleon's invasion, Egypt was effectively ruled by a collection of "beys," or Lords. These beys were, in turn, vassals of the ruler of the Ottoman empire, Sultan Selim III. Control from Constantinople, however, was minimal; so the beys developed into what amounted to royalty, owning vast estates, multiple mansions, and incredible wealth.

The ruling counsel, the *beylicate,* in Cairo, was controlled by two men, Murad Bey and Ibrahim Bey. The meeting on this day was called by the former.

Murad Bey was a large man. To many people, at first glance, he appeared fat; but he was not. It was all muscle. Over six feet tall, he was capable of decapitating an ox with a single blow of his scimitar, a feat that was enormously impressive to one and all. He had received the messages from Muhammad el-Kurrayyim—all thirteen of them—and convened the divan to decide what must be done. In attendance were all of the Mameluke beys, the *kashifs,* various important political figures, and a smattering of religious clerics. He came right to the point.

"Pasha Abu Bakr, tell us how have we come to this state of affairs? The French have invaded our country; but it is inconceivable that they could have done so without the consent of the Sublime Port in Constantinople. You are his minister. You must have known this was going to happen, yet you said nothing. Why?"

"I swear to you in the name of the Prophet that I had no idea this was coming. I am as amazed as you are—as we all are.

"You say it is inconceivable that the French could have come here without the consent of the Porte? I ask you in reply, is it conceivable that the sultan would have allowed this to happen if he had known? Given our experiences with Europeans—our numerous wars with the Russians, for example—do you think he would have trusted the French for one minute?"

This brought murmurs of assent from the group. He had their attention now, so he started addressing the entire room, not just Murad Bey. He went on for several minutes, concluding with: "I tell you this is an act of infidel aggression. It is the beginning of a new Crusade. Cast aside any thoughts that the Sublime Porte knew anything about this. Be courageous and forthright. Rise up like the brave men you are and prepare to fight. The outcome will be in God's hands, but he has always favored us in the past—I am certain he will do so again. God is Great!"

The divan was now in disarray, with shouts of "Death to the Infidels!" mixing with "We shall drive them into the sea" along with assorted verses from the Koran. When Murad Bey finally restored order, Ibrahim Bey signaled that he wished to speak.

"Pasha Bakr speaks brave words; but do any of you actually know what you will be fighting against? I know these French, and I can tell you. They have fingernails one foot long, enormous mouths, and ferocious eyes. They are savages possessed by the Devil, and they go into battle linked together with chains. That is who you will be facing!"

This report subdued their enthusiasm somewhat.

There was a long period of silence until one of the *kashifs* spoke up. "Well, we must do something. I suggest we round up all the Christians in Cairo and exterminate them." This again brought general approval, until Pasha Bakir, the Sheik el-Beled, and Ibrahim Bey spoke against it. It was decided to incarcerate them instead.

But that still left the major question on the table: what to do about the French. First they decided to send a series of couriers to Constantinople to inform the sultan of what had happened. And, second, they decided that Murad Bey, with part of the army, should move south to engage the French. Ibrahim Bey would hold the rest of the army in reserve at Bulaq, a small river town just outside Cairo.

It took Murad Bey a week to assemble his army. There were a few thousand Ottoman troops in town, but they had been so marginalized by the Mamelukes that they had mostly become shopkeepers and artisans in the bazaar. Whatever money and supplies he needed, he simply took; but the population was so fearful that they mostly stayed indoors and out of sight. It became so bad that the only people who were out at night were thieves, prompting the chief of police to order all businesses to remain open all night, with lighted torches outside their stores.

Eventually Murad Bey gathered about 20,000 men—thousands of Mamelukes, all of the Cairo Militia, and some more or less useless Bedouins. He had also drawn together a flotilla of gunboats that would mirror his movement south and support him if necessary.

When Murad Bey left Cairo, the city descended into the grip of fear—and 800 miles away, in Constantinople, the sultan still knew nothing of the invasion.

*****

Smith and the *Tigre* had made good time in their Mediterranean crossing. He had stopped at Malta to deliver the dispatch pouch to Captain Ball, and was about to head to Syracuse where Nelson supposedly lay. Ball informed him, however, that Nelson was not there and had no idea where he was. So Smith, in obedience to Jervis' instructions to "proceed with all possible speed to Constantinople," left Nelson's dispatch pouch and code book with Ball for forwarding.

He rounded the Peloponnesian peninsula and entered the Aegean Sea. A quick transit of the Dardanelles, a crossing of the Sea of Marmora, and he was at the mouth of the Bosporus and the fabled City of Constantinople.

As the *Tigre* slid gracefully up the coastline, the city, off his larboard beam, seemed almost to glow with splendor. As he neared Point Seraï, Smith could see the white walls and towers of the Topkapi Palace, his ultimate destination, the home of Sultan Selim III. At that point it was up to Smith to decide how many guns to fire in salute. He decided on the full 21 guns, as if to say "I recognize your sultan as a king." The batteries on Seraglio Point replied with 17, in effect saying "we don't know who you are, but you're probably someone important, although obviously less than our sultan."

Formalities over, the *Tigre* rounded the point and anchored in the Golden Horn, just off the Customs House. Smith no sooner set foot on land than he was greeted by his brother, John Spencer Smith.

"Sidney! It's so good to see you again." The Smith family was not much for overt displays of emotion, but it was clear that the greeting was heartfelt.

"And good to see you! How've you been, little brother? Gads, I haven't seen you since... what... Spring of '93, I'll be bound."

"'93 it was, just before you decided to go galloping off like Don Quixote to rescue Sam Hood in Toulon."

"Oh yes, some rescue. I was lucky to get out of that one alive."

"Well, come along then and tell me *exactly* what happened. I've a carriage waiting, and a room all made up for you at my new house."

"Your new house?"

"The former Venetian ambassador's house—it's called the Palace of Bailes. So, you see, this Napoleon fellow is not so bad after all. If he hadn't destroyed the Venetian Republic last year—who knows where I'd be living?" Sidney just laughed and shook his head.

Spencer was five years younger than he and, even as children, they were as different as night and day. Sidney had been a hellion as a boy. Loud, talkative, he loved adventure, had a fundamental contempt for danger, and bridled under any form of subservience. His list of scrapes was endless; and it was not without a measure of relief that his father got him into the navy, at age 13, as a captain's servant. Spencer was quite the reverse. Studious, seemingly shy, it was some years before Sidney figured out that his brother, while quiet, missed absolutely nothing. Behind his placid exterior, Spencer had a mind that was every bit as intelligent and inventive as Sidney's. But for Spencer the trick wasn't to merely do the exceptional. It was to do those things and make them seem completely natural and not worth anyone's special notice. For Spencer, that kind of subtlety—especially when he was up to mischief—was true cleverness.

Spencer spent much of his early years as a page to Queen Charlotte, wife of King George III, then several years as an officer in the Guards. This, however, proved to be a much more expensive proposition than being a naval officer, and he knew that his father could not afford to help him out. His mother had been cut off from her wealthy father when she eloped with a penniless officer, Captain John Smith. As a result, he, Sidney and their older brother, Charles, grew up on the edge of genteel society, close enough to fully understand the lifestyle, but not wealthy enough to fully partake in it. If the three boys were to succeed, it would be through guts, determination and hard work—and all three succeeded.

Selling his commission in the guards, Spencer entered the diplomatic corps where his talent for subtle behavior found a home. In 1792, at the age of only 22, he was appointed to the British embassy at the court of Sultan Selim III in Constantinople. Five years later he was the ambassador.

After settling in at the Bailes, the two had a chance to sit on the veranda overlooking Spencer Smith's marvelous garden, and get caught up. Eventually, talk came around to business.

"So, my adventuresome brother, what do you think Napoleon is going to do?"

"He's going to attack Egypt," Sidney replied.

"Well, that's certainly one possibility."

"No, he's going to attack Egypt, if he hasn't already done so. I know it."

"And how have you so magically crawled inside the general's brain?"

"I didn't. I crawled inside his dispatch pouch." And Sidney told Spencer the story of William Parish and the coded message. As he did so, he could see his brother's eyes narrow as the full implications of Napoleon's move sunk home.

"We've heard nothing about that here."

"I suspected that would be the case. Nevertheless, we've got to convince the sultan that it's going to happen and to prepare his army and navy to take action."

"That might not be so easy."

"Why not? What kind of man is he, anyway?"

Spencer leaned back in his chair to think about his answer for a moment.

"The first thing you have to understand about the sultan—as well as just about everything else in the Ottoman Empire—is that nothing is ever as it seems. On one hand, the sultan could be viewed as an unbelievably cruel despot; and, in truth, by our standards, he is. If you cross the sultan and it's your lucky day, you might get off with merely being strangled by a deaf-mute eunuch.

If it's not your lucky day, you will be given over to other hands, and it might take three or four days before they finally let you die. Neither of those outcomes would raise a single eyebrow either in the sultan's court or in the city.

"On the other hand, don't let his imperious manner fool you. He's not stupid. In fact, he is something of a reformer, and very popular with his people. Within a few years after taking over the sultanate from his uncle, he had reformed the empire's administrative structure, their tax system, increased the availability of education, and opened up the empire to foreign trade. His biggest problem is that his frontiers have been almost constantly under attack by Russia and Austria; and it's hard to bring needed reforms to a country when you're constantly at war.

"As a result, he's extremely distrustful of westerners. He knows he hates Austrians and Russians; he's about to find out he hates the French; and he hasn't made up his mind yet about us Brits. That's going to make your task all the more difficult."

"Difficult but not impossible?"

"No, not impossible; but don't get your hopes up that you'll be able to convince him straight away. No matter what he tells you, he'll not be completely convinced unless and until he gets word from Egypt that it has indeed been invaded.

"And then?"

"And then prepare yourself, for it will be like trying to control a run-away horse."

*****

Sidney and Spencer rode on horseback through the hectic streets of Constantinople. They were following the Mese, the main thoroughfare of the city, and the street used by all imperial processions. Behind them were retainers in several carts carrying gifts for the sultan.

They turned at the Milion monument, a rectangular stone that marked the starting point for all distances to Constantinople; and eventually arrived at the central arch of the massive first gate, the Imperial Gate. They continued through it and up a path to the Gate of Salutation, the actual entrance to the palace grounds. At this point Spencer began his travelogue.

"We have to dismount here, Sidney, as the only person who's allow to ride through this gate is the sultan himself."

The two dismounted and Sidney had a chance to look more closely at the entranceway. On either side of the portal was an octagonal tower that soared at least twenty feet above the thirty foot high walls. The large doorway was inset into an arched alcove that was covered with the monograms of various sultans, along with numerous religious inscriptions. Sidney was examining a small fountain that was along the wall to the right while the retainers off-loaded the gifts from the cart.

"That's called the Fountain of the Executioner."

"The executioner?"

"Yes, the sultan will dispense justice on the other side of this wall, but all formal beheadings are done here, on the outside. After completing his work, traditionally, the executioner cleans off his scimitar in that fountain."

"Formal beheadings? Are there many *informal* ones?"

"Yes, plenty of them." And Spencer said no more.

The party proceeded through the gate and emerged onto a spacious grass field, perfectly groomed and manicured. Courtiers could be seen milling around in small groups under the lovely shade trees. Peacocks and even a few gazelles could be seen placidly strutting or grazing. There were four black pebbled walkways radiating out from the entranceway. One of them, the widest of the four, led to what looked like another gate at the opposite end. As they walked along, Spencer continued his narration.

"This is the second courtyard," Spencer began. To the right is the dormitory for the apprentice cooks and dishwashers, and behind that are the kitchens—one is for the harem women, one for the pages, one for the serving women, and so forth. That small mosque at the end is strictly for the use of the many confectioners.

"Confectioners?"

"Yes, it seems the sultan has a bit of a sweet tooth."

"Over on the left is the Imperial Council Hall, the scribe's room, and the rooms of the Grand Vizier. Do you see the elaborate gate leading to the Grand Vizier's rooms? When you hear the seat of the Ottoman Empire referred to as the 'Sublime Porte,' that's what they're referring to. The Grand Vizier is something like our Prime Minister, and he is the person who usually deals with foreign dignitaries. In the old days, all meetings with foreign officials took place before that gate, which became known as the Sublime Porte. Over time it became the general name for their foreign ministry.

"Next to that is the Imperial Treasury; and to the left of all that is the carriage gate to the harem."

"Now that sounds like a place I'd like to visit," Sidney quipped.

"No you wouldn't," Spencer said abruptly. "The last unauthorized person who was caught in there had a long sharpened pole hammered up his anus. The pole was then lifted up and stuck into the ground. There he sat, if you can call it that, for a day or two until the sharpened end emerged out his left shoulder. The strange thing was that it somehow emerged without hitting any vital organs, so they just left him up there. That was good for another day and a half of suffering."

Sidney swallowed hard and continued walking, all jokes about the harem had fled from his brain.

Soon they came to the third gate, the Gate of Felicity, which marked the entrance to the residential areas of the palace. No one was allowed through that gate without the specific permission of the sultan. Even the Grand Vizier was only allowed in on rare occasions. The only foreigners allowed through were full ambassadors and perhaps a handful of others if, and only if, the sultan expressly wished to see them. Here the retainers left the Sultan's gifts with a group of palace eunuchs and departed.

This gate was even more elaborate than the previous one. It consisted of a large dome supported by impossibly slender marble pillars. Like the previous gate, it was recessed into an archway, and above it were verses from the Koran. Sidney looked up and saw that the dome was painted and gold-leafed in a series of intricate designs. Hanging from the center of the dome was a large ball of solid gold.

Passing through the gate, they could see little of the third courtyard because their view was blocked by a large colonnaded building. Twenty-two columns held up an overhanging roof of a massive rectangular structure. Over the narrow doorway was the sultan's monogram.

The inside of the building was intended to make a person feel as insignificant as an ant—an objective at which it succeeded admirably. Overhead was a huge dome painted in bright blue with thousands of gold-leaf stars. Magnificent tiles ringed the walls in stunning blue, turquoise, and white—each with unbelievably intricate patterns glazed into them. Near the door was a noisy fountain, the purpose of which, Spencer explained later, was to allow people to hold conversations without being overheard.

The sultan was seated on an elevated throne, talking to one of his advisors. The throne was covered with a gold cloth into which innumerable emeralds, rubies and pearls were sewn. Above the throne was a lacquered ceiling strewn with more precious stones and painted with scenes of foliage and of a fight between a dragon and a *simurg*, a mythical Ottoman bird. Precious carpets and pillows were everywhere.

At length the sultan finished his conversation, looked up at the two men and gestured them closer. Both gave a deep bow. A translator appeared from behind a curtain and stood at the sultan's side.

"My friend, you have petitioned for an emergency audience," the sultan began, speaking directly to Spencer. "Tell me, what is the source of this emergency?"

"Your Majesty, my king has sent an envoy all the way from our humble island to warn you of a most serious problem. May I present by brother, Sir Sidney Smith. In addition to being a commodore in our Royal Navy, he has also been commissioned as Minister Plenipotentiary from the Court of St. James to the Sublime Porte."

The sultan shifted his gaze over to Sidney Smith for the first time.

"Your Highness, my king wishes to extend his greetings and his desire for long life and good health to his brother Sultan Selim III."

The sultan nodded.

"In addition, he wishes to present his brother with a few unworthy gifts, that he hopes will in some way be acceptable to you." Sidney gestured the eunuch bearers forward and displayed a perfect model of a ship, the *Royal George*, and a series of paintings of famous sea battles.

"And last, he sends you this." Sidney gestured to the doorway and twelve eunuchs came in each carrying a 3-pound field piece.

"He sends me 12 tiny cannons?" The sultan asked, unsure as to the extent to which he should feel insulted.

"Ah, but your Majesty, these cannon are made very special with the addition of these." He gestured again at the door and twelve more eunuchs appeared.

"These are specially designed gun carriages, that will allow these cannon to be carried on the backs of camels. With these weapons you will now have gun fire that can be moved about as fast as the wind. Your enemies will cringe when they hear of this, and fear even more the name of Selim III."

The sultan was delighted. He stepped down from his throne to inspect these clever devices more closely. He insisted on seeing Sidney assemble and disassemble them several times so he could see how easy it was, and to see how they might be affixed to a camel.

"These are indeed a wonder," the sultan pointed out as he eventually resumed his throne, "but your bother has informed me that you are here with alarming news."

"Indeed, sire. It is my sad duty to inform you that I believe the French, under a devilish commander named Napoleon, are about to attack Egypt."

The sultan was inspecting more closely the model of the *Royal George* that had been put on a table next to him. His head shot up.

"You believe the French are going to attack us, or they *have* attacked us?"

"It is the belief of my government, based on messages we have intercepted, that this will happen."

"And why would the the French do that?"

"We believe that this devil-spawn general wants to do two things. First, by securing Egypt, he can cut off my country's short-cut to trade with India. He will force our ships to go the long way around the cape of Africa where, doubtless, he will have his war-ships waiting."

"And second?"

"Second, I believe that once he has secured Egypt, he will come up through the Levant and attack Constantinople itself. Once he has secured this city, he will push on overland with his army and take India."

"You are describing a general with considerable ambition," the sultan declared, and his advisors started laughing.

"So, what then would you have me do?" he continued. "Would you have me declare war on the French because you have inter-cepted some messages?"

"Your highness, I have complete faith in the veracity of those messages. I know that this attack will occur. We have sent a fleet under one of our ablest commanders," Smith had to force out the words, "to try to head this demon off, but there is no guarantee he will be able to do so."

The sultan didn't say anything, but looked doubtful. Sir Sidney continued.

"Sire, may I urge you to begin preparations. My ship contains one of our best generals and 76 officers who can help to train your army to fight against a western foe. It contains a naval architect and a host of shipwrights who can help to mobilize your shipyards. At a minimum, may I urge Your Majesty to send an officer by the fastest means possible to assess the situation in Egypt."

The sultan still did not look convinced. He sat back on a cushion, thought for a moment, then replied.

"Please express my thanks to your sovereign for alerting us to this grave state of affairs. I will immediately convene an emergency meeting of my war council to discuss this situation. My thanks, also, to both of you for your concern. I will get back to you as soon as we have reached a decision."

With that, the audience was over—and absolutely nothing was done.

CHAPTER SEVEN

Even though the British fleet was not at Alexandria, that doesn't mean they were not on Napoleon's mind. He knew that to conquer Egypt he needed to conquer Cairo; but the problem was how to get his army there.

In effect, there were two possibilities. First, he could transport them by ship up the Nile River. From the army's standpoint, that would be the best way as they would arrive fresh and ready to fight. But Napoleon was worried that the British ships might return and pursue them up that same river, thus trapping him between themselves and the Egyptians. The second option was to march his army to Cairo; but on foot that was a 140 mile journey. He estimated they could make it in five or six days. He was wrong. Dead wrong. None of his men had ever experienced a desert before, all were dressed in Alpine woolen uniforms, and the supply corps had somehow managed to forget to bring canteens— although they did remember to issue each man a copy of the Koran, in French.

For Napoleon, however, the decision was simple. To travel via the Nile would mean certain defeat if the British showed up. To march overland was much more difficult, but they would get there; so the army was formed up for the march.

Along with his army, Napoleon had brought along nearly 150 artists, doctors, engineers, and scientists of all kinds. All had volunteered to go on a "voyage of discovery," to an unknown destination, under the leadership of Napoleon. That's all they knew; and yet hundreds of men, young and old, applied for admittance to the expedition.

Captain Say knew he could not turn over the two men as prisoners. Given Walker's connections to his brother, that would have been dishonorable. So, he did the next best thing; he turned them over to the scientists. He explained that Walker was an innocent British physician who had, unfortunately, been visiting Egypt when they arrived, and he introduced him to Dominique-Jean Larrey, the army's chief surgeon.

The match could not have been a better one. Larrey was born in the little village of Beaudéan, in the southwest corner of France, not far from the Spanish border. At age 13 he was orphaned and went to live with his uncle who was a physician in Toulouse. This began a six year apprenticeship which culminated in a move to Paris where he studied under Pierre-Joseph Desault, who was chief surgeon at the famous Hôtel Dieu Hospital. A few days earlier Larrey had celebrated his 32nd birthday.

Walker had been born in Boston, where his father was an apothecary. His mother died when he was 12. He was originally a college professor, but had been fired from several positions because of his alcoholism. He was on his way to Charleston, South Carolina when his ship foundered; and he was rescued by the HMS *Richmond* where he met Susan and Sidney. Because he was a college educated scientist, he was pressed into emergency service as the ship's surgeon. Left with no other choice, he emersed himself in medical textbooks and eventually performed heroic duties at the Battle of the Saintes. Later, he went to medical school at the University of Edinburgh, and had a successful practice in London for many years; but he was lured back into the navy at the prospect of teaming up again with Susan and Sidney. He was 38 when he landed in Egypt.

In short, Larrey and Walker were about the same age, both came from humble origins, both had achieved their positions via extraordinarily hard work, and both were enormously talented and creative. But that burgeoning friendship was to be tested almost immediately by hardship.

Napoleon, feeling the pressure of a possible British revisit, and not wanting to give Cairo much time to fortify themselves, decided to move immediately. He left about 2000 men in Alexandria under the command of Kléber, who had suffered a minor wound in the assault a few days earlier. He then organized his remaining army into three columns. Two were to follow the dry Alexandria canal to the Nile, and one was to proceed to Rosetta, 40 miles to the east, and then up the Nile. On paper, it looked like a good plan. In fact, it was a nightmare.

Several hours out of Alexandria the main columns encountered desert heat and sand for the first time. It was unlike anything any of them had ever experienced. The air temperature was over 115 degrees and the sun-baked sand was even hotter. Soon the heat began to penetrate their boots making every step a torment. The sun had an intensity that none would have previously thought possible; and it was literally baking their heads inside their hats. Their rough wool coats were wonderful for fighting Austrians in northern Italy, but they were a disaster in the desert. Soon men began taking them off and discarding them, not realizing that that would expose their bodies to the sun even more.

But the worst part was the lack of water. With no canteens, fluids could not be replaced; and the men were breathing air that was nothing more than superheated vapor. Soon the linings of their mouths and noses began to dry out. A thick froth formed on their lips, and their throats tightened up making breathing difficult. What began as a march, turned into a hesitant walk, which turned into a stagger.

As if all that were not bad enough, there was another phenomenon that was new to the invaders—the mirage. The men would clearly see what could only be a lake up ahead. Their pace would quicken, only to see the lake getting no closer no matter how fast or how far they walked. This added to the despair that was quickly overcoming Napoleon's men.

By mid-afternoon of the first day the men stopped hearing the moans of their comrades or even the commands of their officers. The whole army was at the point of refusing to advance; but they kept marching only because there was simply no other option. Men who fell to the ground, dying of heatstroke, were simply stepped over. Soldiers who straggled were captured by roaming Bedouin bands and mutilated—slowly cutting off the ears of one, the nose of another, and the head of a third.

Napoleon had assumed that they would be able to find water along the way. He was wrong. The Bedouins took special delight in either concealing the wells, or fouling the ones they could not hide. At one point, as they were nearing a small town, word began to circulate that there were wells outside the city. The men rushed to the water, but in less than five minutes the wells were emptied.

This didn't stop more men from pressing in, trampling those who went before; and more than 30 men died, smothered or crushed by the mob. Many others, not being able get to the water, simply placed the muzzle of their guns to their mouths and committed suicide.

It had taken them four days to travel 36 miles, but eventually they camped in Damanhur. By any standard, the town wasn't much. It consisted of some sun-baked buildings that could only be described as huts, a scattering of palm trees, and couple of mosques. Upon seeing the French advance in the distance, most of the townspeople had fled, taking with them their valuables, food, animals and even the doors off their houses. But the main thing the French wanted was water, and the town had that. Not enough to satiate an army, perhaps, but enough to keep it alive.

During the march Walker, Parish and Larrey had it slightly better than the regular troops, but that was because the expedition had a small number of horses with it. Some of them were set aside for Napoleon and his generals to ride, others were consigned to carry high priority supplies—mostly ammunition and, in one case, medical stores. This latter fact allowed the three to walk alongside the "medical horse," and he indirectly kept them alive. What water the army had was strictly rationed for the animals. Being European bred, they would never make it to Cairo without it. Despite the injunction against drinking water that was set aside for their horse, the three were able to share what was left at the bottom of his drinking bag whenever he was done.

The majority of the troops were bivouacked outside the town, and soon men began to fan out looking for anything that could be used for firewood. A few minutes later one of the men came running over to where Larrey had dropped onto the sand.

"Doctor, come quick. There's... there's a woman who... just come with me, quickly."

The three got up and followed the soldier over a rise. On the other side was a woman on the ground amid some scrub brush. She was about 16 years old, nearly naked except for a tattered shift, and emaciated to the point of death. Larrey and Walker bent down to see if she was still alive. She was, but when they looked at her face a chill went through them, and they almost wished she weren't. Her lips were blackened from the heat, her face was scarred, and both of her eyes had been gouged out. The eye sockets were still bloody, and flies were swarming in them. With one hand she was clinging to a long dead infant the way a child would clutch a rag-doll. With the other, she had a stick with which she was clawing the desert sand near a bush in hopes of finding part of a root to eat or a drop of water for her throat.

The two physicians stared at each other for a moment. Walker kept repeating "Oh, my God!" over and over as Larrey ordered Parish to go get a cup of water from the horse's supply.

"Tell them you are there at my order and that it is a medical emergency. And get a biscuit out of my kit when you go past."

Parish quickly returned to where Walker was bent over the woman to hear what she was trying to say; but words would not come out of her mouth—only an inarticulate gurgle.

Larrey offered her the water and biscuit. She would not take the biscuit, but eagerly drank the water.

"You men," Larrey said to a group of soldiers who were standing around gawking. "Carry her back to my camp site. And be gentle with her. She's in really bad shape."

The men did as ordered, but she died literally as she was being picked up. They carried her back anyway. As soon as they had returned to the camp, Larrey sent for one of the expedition interpreters that they had picked up in Alexandria.

"Nazir, I want you to go into the town and find out if they know anything about this woman."

"There is no need. Several villagers are here in our camp and I have already asked them."

"What did they say?"

"It seems the woman was found guilty of adultery, and the child is the product of her filthy sin. She was punished and cast out of the camp."

"Punished? Her eyes were gouged out and she was cast into the desert heat nearly naked. That's what you call punishment?"

The man was completely unmoved. "It is traditional," he said with a shrug of his shoulders.

"And what happened to the man involved?"

Nazir thought he had heard every stupid question he could possibly hear from these Franks, but this one surprised even him.

"Why... nothing."

Larrey stared at him for a long moment, and then gave up trying to understand this tragedy. "I want you to see if you can locate someone from the girl's family to give her a proper burial."

"But, monsieur, her family is almost as disgraced as she is."

"I don't care! Just find someone to bury her."

A little while later Nazir returned with a mounted horseman. "This is her brother," he said simply.

The man dismounted, tied a rope to her ankle, got back on his horse, and rode off into the desert, dragging her along the rough rock-filled ground. When he got about 200 yards out, he dropped the rope, threw the baby down on top of her and rode off.

The burial of his disgraced sister was complete.

*****

The citizens of Syracuse were gathered in the hundreds along the waterfront, witnessing a sight they would tell their grandchildren about. Arrayed before them was a sample of the might of the British Royal Navy—thirteen 74-gun warships—each precisely anchored, with their sails neatly furled and their masts soaring proudly into the air. The water of the bay was alive with small boats going to and from the shore, taking on provisions. Some boats were loaded with 100 gallon barrels of water; other boats had fresh vegetables; still others had sides of beef.

During the previous few weeks the ships had been all over the eastern Mediterranean. From Alexandria they had gone northward along the coastline of the Levant and Asia Minor. Periodically they would capture some hapless merchantman, or Nelson would detach a ship to go into a port and ask for information; but no one had seen the French.

At one point the master of a Genoese brig said he thought the French had gone to Sicily. This struck real fear into the heart of Nelson. If Napoleon had landed there, if he was attacking the Kingdom of the Two Sicilies, then Nelson's career was over. His stock in Admiralty circles was still high following his actions at the Battle of Cape St. Vincent; but if the Two Sicilies was lost, it would be because of a failure of judgement on his part. He knew that no amount of valor in battle would overcome that mistake. He would not be court-martialed. In fact, he would not even be overtly punished in any way; but he would also never again be given a substantive command. It would be a terrible fate to a person for whom "Glory is my object and that alone." Nelson's relief at finding that the French were not in Syracuse knew no bounds.

He was in his cabin alternately watching the re-provisioning of his fleet through his gallery windows, and getting caught up on correspondence. His first letter was to St. Vincent blaming his failure, yet again, on his lack of frigates.

Yesterday, I arrived here; where I can learn no more than conjecture, that the French are gone to the eastward. Every moment, I have to regret the frigates having left me; to which must be attributed my ignorance of the movements of the enemy. Your lordship deprived yourself of frigates, to make mine, certainly, the first squadron in the world; and I feel that I have zeal and activity to do credit to your appointment: and yet, to be unsuccessful, hurts me most sensibly.

"There. That should hold St. Vincent," he thought.

His second letter was to the British Ambassador in Naples, Sir William Hamilton, thanking him for arranging permission for his fleet to re-provision in Syracuse.

Thanks to your exertions, we have victualed and watered: and, surely, watering at the Fountain of Arethusa, we must have victory! We shall sail with the first breeze; and, be assured, I will return either crowned with laurel, or covered with cypress.

At this point he paused. He knew that the victualing arrangements had not been made by Sir William at all; they had been made by his lovely young wife, Emma.

Emma Hamilton and her good friend Queen Maria Carolina had nothing but distain for formal treaties—especially those that sought to keep the Kingdom of the Two Sicilies neutral in Britain's war against France. When Emma heard that there was a movement afoot to keep Nelson's fleet from re-provisioning anywhere in the Kingdom, she immediately rushed to see her friend, who was still in bed. She told the Queen that "all would be lost" if Nelson was not freely resupplied, and begged her not to hesitate but to act on her own. She should issue an order, in her own name, to all the governors of the Two Sicilies to receive the British fleet with hospitality—to water, victual and aid them.

Maria Carolina, whose sister, Marie Antoinette, had been guillotined a few years earlier by the French revolutionaries, needed no convincing and issued the order. Her husband, King Ferdinand IV had little option but to go along with his headstrong wife.

But Nelson's thoughts also came back to a curious letter he had received from Emma Hamilton a few months earlier, the first time he was in Neapolitan waters. He had written her saying: "As soon as I have fought the French Fleet, I shall do myself the honor of paying my respects to your Ladyship at Naples and I hope to be congratulated on a victory."

He fumbled around for her reply in a mahogany chest where he kept his personal correspondence.

My Dear Admiral,

I write in a hurry as Captain T. Carrol stays on Monarch. God bless you, and send you victorious, and that I may see you bring back Buonaparte with you. Pray send Captain Hardy out to us, for I shall have a fever with anxiety. The Queen desires me to say everything that's kind, and bids me say with her whole heart and soul she wishes you victory.

God bless you, my dear Sir. I will not say how glad I shall be to see you. Indeed I cannot describe to you my feelings on your being so near us.

Ever, Ever, dear Sir,
Your affte. and grateful
Emma Hamilton

"Interesting," he thought. He had never met Emma Hamilton, but her reputation for beauty was was very well known in London circles. "Very interesting."

A few days later, the fleet got underway again, and Nelson headed for Greece. He still had no idea where Napoleon was located, other than he believed he was somewhere in the eastern Mediterranean; and Greece was as good a place to look as any. He continued his tactic of directing ships to go into ports to get information and of stopping any merchantmen they could find. Eventually the tactic paid off.

On July 28th he signaled Thomas Troubridge in the *Culloden* to go into a small port called Koroni. A few hours later he was seen coming back to the fleet with all sails set, towing a French brig. He scrambled aboard the *Vanguard* with the brig captain and breathlessly announced to Nelson that the man had seen the French Fleet.

"When? Where?" Nelson anxiously asked.

"About four weeks ago, Amiral. About 20 warships and hundreds of transports sailed past here. Anyone in town can tell you, because we were all so glad they didn't stop."

"In which direction were they headed?"

"To the southeast."

If they were headed to the southeast, there was only one reasonable destination—Egypt. Nelson didn't know whether he should be elated at finally getting some definite news, or depressed because Parish had been right. It was a question he would think about later, however. Right now he had a fleet to get underway.

*****

There was nothing they could do to stop them, although Walker, Larrey and even poor confused William Parish tried.

There was no rest for the western branch of Napoleon's army at Damanhur. The following morning Napoleon had them up at dawn and on the move. Their goal was to reach the town of Rahmaniya, only 12 miles away on the banks of the Nile. There they would rendezvous with the column of troops under General Dugua that had been sent to Rosetta and from there up the Nile. The army, mildly revived by the water they found at Damanhur, was in Rahmaniya by the afternoon and dehydrated all over again. It was then that the trouble began.

As they approached the town, all discipline ended. Before them was a massive source of fresh water—the Nile. On both sides of the town were acres of lush watermelon patches. This was no mirage and there was no holding back the parched, sun-addled, troops. It started with a few men, then hundreds, then the whole army broke ranks to run to the river or to the melon patches. In both locations they gorged themselves and there was nothing the medics could do to stop them.

"Men! Men, stop!" Walker and Larrey were trying to get in front of the mob, waving their hands.

"Don't drink that water! We don't know what's in it. We don't know if..."

The two physicians were brushed aside by hundreds of soldiers trying to quench the fires of thirst that had been tormenting them for days. When the first troops got to the river bank they simply jumped in. Those coming behind did the same, pushing the first group into ever deeper water. Before long they were over their heads and their soaked woolen uniforms pulled them under.

Hearing the commotion, every crocodile within a mile in either direction headed to the scene. Some of them were as big as a canoe; but all of them, large or small, feasted. The worst fate, however, was reserved for those who simply drank water from the wrong spot.

Rahmaniya was not directly on the main body of the river. It was set back several hundred yards and was fed by a channel coming off the Nile. In that channel there flourished a very small species of leech—easy to miss in the muddy water, and especially easy to miss when your only thought was to get as much water into you as possible. The men who drank from that channel, hundreds of them, ingested dozens of those tiny leeches, which over the next few days attempted to eat their way out.

Failing at the river, the three men walked dispiritedly over to one of the large melon patches. Larrey did his best.

"Men, don't eat those melons without cooking them first." His message fell on deaf ears as the troops stuffed themselves on the luscious fruit.

Finally, one of the men looked up and said: "Doc, why are you going on like that? In France we never cooked watermelon."

"In France your watermelon was never fertilized with camel dung either," Larrey replied.

Walker finally got Larrey's attention and addressed him in the "perfect French" he was so proud of. "*Jean, je ne m'inquiéterais pas de la pastèque tout de suite. Nous allons avoir beaucoup d'autre travail au cours des prochains jours.*" [Jean, I would not worry about the watermelon at once. We are going to have many of the other work during the next days.]

"Do you mean the crocodile bites, or all those live leeches the men are probably swallowing."

"*Aucun. Regard là-bas*" [Nobody. Look over there.]

Larrey looked in the direction Walker was pointing and saw a thousand Mameluke cavalrymen lined up on a ridge about a quarter mile away.

*****

It was two days before the battle took place. That was time for the French to become rehydrated and fed, time for the column to arrive from Rosetta, and time for the Mamelukes to get reinforced.

The first day Napoleon sent out a scouting column under General Boyer to locate the enemy. That afternoon he sent word back that they were in the vicinity of Chobrakit, a small town further up the Nile. The following day the rest of the army made their way the seven miles to the town.

The battle was in many ways a repeat of Alexandria. The Mamelukes believed they were invincible on land; but they had never faced a disciplined western army. They charged on their magnificent horses. The French formed bayonet-studded squares and the horses balked. The Mamelukes circled the squares looking for weak spots. The French sharpshooters picked them off. The Mamelukes massed to regroup, and the French light artillery sent cannon balls into them like they were bowling.

If the Mamelukes charged, they died. If they circled, they died. If they massed, they died. They had never seen anything like it. Finally, they broke off and fled. It was the first direct contact between Napoleon and the forces under Murad Bey; but it would not be the last. Between the battles at Alexandria and this one at Chobrakit, however, Napoleon now knew what he was facing—and he knew he could beat them. It was time to move on to Cairo

*****

"Sidney, can I speak to you for a moment?" Smith was sitting on the veranda of his brother's palatial embassy, equally enjoying a delicious Turkish sherbet and the cool morning breeze off of the wide inlet known as the Golden Horn.

"Certainly, John. Have a seat. Would you like one of these drinks? It is truly a marvel. I am not sure exactly what's in it, but there's nothing like it in England, I can tell you that."

John Wesley Wright coiled his lean athletic frame into a spacious padded chair next to Sir Sidney. "No thank you, Sidney. I've got other things on my mind."

"Such as?"

"Slaves."

"What about them?"

"Western slaves—being held here in Constantinople."

That got Sir Sidney's attention. "Western slaves? Do you mean white slaves?"

"Just so."

"Who are they; and how on earth did they get here?"

"I don't have all the details, but they are French. Yesterday I was in one of the bath-houses meeting with... ah... meeting with someone I needed to see. I asked him the whereabouts of another contact, and he said I was in luck. I could meet with him immediately if I wanted, and that he was right behind me.

"I turned around but could see nothing except the city's prison, which was right across the street. Then I saw a string of prisoners being lead back to the main gate. They were galley-slaves. Forty Frenchmen linked together by neck shackles and being returned to the dungeon for the night.

"They looked awful, Sidney. Simply awful. We have to do something to get them out of there."

"I didn't know you had a soft spot for Frenchmen."

Wright stiffened. "I don't. You of all people know me better than that. I told you that there was a contact amongst those prisoners I need to see."

"You're right. I do know you better than that, and there is more to this than meeting with a contact."

Wright finally surrendered his tough-as-nails professional facade. "Sidney, killing a Frenchman on the field of battle, or in the performance of a mission, is one thing. I've done that often enough. But to see them suffer the slow death of a galley-slave is quite another."

Smith nodded gravely. He knew what Wright meant. There really were things that were "a fate worse than death" and being a galley-slave was one of them.

"But what can I do about it?" Smith asked.

"I don't know. I was thinking maybe sometime if you're with the sultan and he seems in a particularly good mood…"

Wright was not able to finish his sentence. A small detachment of Turkish cavalry was riding hard up the semi-circular road in front of the embassy. Behind them was an empty western-style carriage with a team of two black horses. An officer quickly dismounted.

"I am seeking Commodore Sir Sidney Smith and Ambassador John Spencer Smith," he said in passable English.

"I am Commodore Smith."

"You must come with me immediately, sir, along with your brother."

"I'll see if he's available."

"This is not a matter of being available or not."

"May I ask what this is about?"

"The sultan wishes to see you both, as fast as you can get to the palace. My job is to see that that happens."

The officer was not exaggerating about the speed of their journey. The Palace of Bailes, Spencer's residence, was located along "embassy row" on the opposite side of the Golden Horn from the sultan's palace, but rapid transportation had indeed been arranged. A quick carriage ride to the Turkish naval shipyard, was followed by a small boat being rowed across at top speed, and another carriage ride on the other side—at breakneck speed—to the middle gate of the palace.

As the two approached the Gate of Felicity at the opposite end of the Second Courtyard, they were startled to see two male slaves emerge from the colonnaded building in which the sultan received visitors. Both were bloody, and had obviously been beaten.

As they entered the building they could hear shouts coming from the throne room. They looked through the door and could see the room was in a state of chaos. Priceless Iznik vases had been smashed against incredibly valuable Bergama rugs. Exquisite hand-decorated pillows had been torn apart. A large chunk had been gouged out of a delicately inlayed tile wall panel. Even the canope over the sultan's throne had been torn off. And at the center of it all was Sultan Selim III.

"There you are!" the sultan exclaimed as he was about to kick a chair. "There are the two ass tulips who have betrayed me."

"Your majesty," Spencer began, "I am afraid I am at a loss. What has happened?"

"What has happened? You dare ask what has happened?" The sultan's voice was rising at each iteration. "The bastard Franks have invaded Egypt, that's what's happened. They have invaded one of *my* provinces, and your government could have stopped it."

"Sire, I can assure you..."

"You can assure me of nothing!" The sultan screamed. "The French landed within days after your Royal Navy came, saw, and left Alexandria."

"Oh, nice work, Horatio," Smith said under his breath.

"And yet, even though you must have known it was going to happen, you said *nothing* to me."

Sidney couldn't believe his ears. "But your highness, we *did*..."

Spencer elbowed him and stepped in front of his brother. "Your majesty, the fault is completely mine. There had perhaps been some rumors to that effect, but I had no way of knowing whether they were true. You are the greatest ruler in the world. You are called upon daily—even hourly—to make decisions that shape the destiny of all mankind. I could not possibly have troubled your serene highness with mere rumors—mere gossip. I am ashamed that I have failed in my duties, and in so doing, failed my country and my king." Spencer looked suitably stricken, which mollified the sultan somewhat.

The sultan sat down heavily in what was left of his throne. "What you say is quite true. I can't tell you the weight of the responsibility that hangs on my shoulders; but..." And suddenly the sultan looked more like a lost little boy than an all-powerful ruler. "But what do we do now?" He said plaintively. Then, realizing that he had momentarily showed vulnerability and weakness—something he had been trained from childhood to *never* do—he gathered himself and went on.

"My information indicates that the British fleet—the one that *failed* to catch the French on the high seas," he said with caustic emphasis, "is still in the eastern Mediterranean. I want you to order them immediately to Constantinople. I want as much naval support as possible from your government."

Sidney knew this was off to a bad start. A part of his secret instructions from Lord Spencer was that he could not promise more than four ships to the Turks.

"Your majesty, on behalf of our navy, I can promise you our full support." Sidney began. We can offer you two of our finest ships of the line, and two frigates."

"Four ships? I lose my favorite provence because of your fleet's incompetence, and you can only promise four ships?" In fact, Selim knew little and cared less about Egypt, other than whether their tax payments were up-to-date.

"Ah, but what ships they are!" Smith continued. "The two ships of the line will both be glorious 80-gun vessels—my ship, the *Tigre*, and one other. Plus we will send two of our best frigates." Smith had no idea where he was going to get those ships, but he could work out the minor details later.

"But so much else needs to be done," the sultan interrupted. "My army needs to be prepared to fight the Franks. My navy needs to be built-up."

Things were now back on an even keel; and they spent the next several hours making plans. Smith explained (again) that his ship "just happened" to be carrying a large cadre of British army officers who could serve as trainers; and he "just happened" to have a cadre of shipwrights who could modernize his shipyards and train his workers.

The sultan was so delighted at this good fortune that he appointed Smith to be a member of his Divan, his state council, for the duration of the war. He also gave him command of the Turkish Army and Navy as they would need to work cooperatively against this foe.

As negotiations were ending, Spencer decided the time was right to propose a Treaty of Friendship, the first such treaty ever between Great Britain and Turkey. The sultan, who was by now feeling much better about things, agreed.

"I can not wait until I get the first French prisoners in my hands," the sultan said ominously. "They will understand the folly of invading the glorious Ottoman Empire, and they will pay dearly for their foolishness."

Sidney Smith thought about that remark for a moment, and saw an opportunity. He said, "Sire, may I ask that you not do that."

"That I not wreak vengeance upon my enemies? What nonsense is this?"

"It's not nonsense at all, sire. In fact, I want you to give orders to all your troops to treat any and all French prisoners very well."

"Why should I do that?"

"Because Egypt is a long way from France, and I can't believe the average French soldier is very happy about being there. I want to encourage as many French soldiers as possible to defect. In fact, with your permission, I want to circulate a proclamation in your name to as many French troops as possible. It will say that a vast army is on it's way to free Egypt, but anyone who wishes to save himself may do so. Any soldier, of any rank, who wants to avoid the coming catastrophe, need only present themselves to an allied army or navy unit. They will be treated well, as other French prisoners have been, and guaranteed safe passage back to France or anywhere else they want to go."

The sultan reacted with a slow smile. In the course of the last few hours he had learned to respect Sidney Smith's military mind, but here was something new. Here was a mind that was as devious as his own.

"As a first step, your highness, I would beg that you release a small group of French prisoners you already have in the Bagnio Prison."

"Release them?"

"Yes, release them to me. I will personally charter a vessel to take them back to France as an example of your mercy. All I require is your permission and a letter guaranteeing safe passage in case the vessel should meet with pirates along the way. No pirate would dare harm or even delay anyone traveling under the direct protection of Sultan Selim III."

"And you say, this will undermine French morale?"

"Yes, sire. That and the other measures I mentioned."

The sultan shrugged and said, "I care nothing about these prisoners. Let it be so."

After they left the throne room, Smith smiled at how well the meeting had gone; and he was especially proud of his getting the prisoners released. He didn't know it, but that act was the opening shot in a personal battle that he and Napoleon would wage for the next seventeen years.

*****

Saying that the French won the battle at Chobrakit was not the same thing as saying that they had no casualties. Dr. Lucas Walker and Dr. Dominique Jean Larrey were well aware of this fact as they had been up to their elbows in blood all day and well into the night.

It was after midnight when Walker finished sewing up his last patient and joined Larrey outside the tent where, having finished his own last patient a few minutes earlier, he was seated around a fire with William Parish. Larrey looked tired but satisfied with his day's work. Parish was looking into the fire with a thousand yard stare. He had wanted some adventure in his life, but in his wildest dreams he never envisioned himself in the Egyptian desert applying tourniquets, holding down screaming, thrashing patients, and carrying away limbs that had been sawed off with machine-like effectiveness by two surgeons.

Walker sat down heavily. He had been on his feet for 14 hours and the rest provided by a simple camp chair seemed like heaven. The three were silent for several minutes, then Larrey spoke.

"Lucas, I want to thank you for your work today."

Lucas nodded, too tired to speak.

"You went to Edinburgh for your training, didn't you?"

"Yes, but how did you know?"

"I could tell by the linked stitch you used to close wounds. In France we call that an Edinburgh seam, but we don't use it. I can't think why. Probably because it's British."

"Yes, I went to Edinburgh, but I feel like I should be paying you tuition for all that I learned today."

"How so? You certainly seemed to know your way around a operating table well enough."

"It wasn't the surgical part that amazed me. It was how the wounded got here and what happened after they arrived. For example, what were those... carts, I guess you'd call them... in which the wounded arrived?"

"Ah those. I call them *ambulance volantes*—flying ambulances. I designed them myself, you know."

"How on earth did *that* come about?"

"I suppose it all started about six years ago. In '92 I was at the Battle of Spires and we had a different system then. We had ambulances, but they were large cumbersome wagons. Moreover, Napoleon required that they stay several miles away from the battle, and not show themselves until the fighting was completely over. The wounded would then be carried or dragged to some central location that the wagons could access, and they would pick them up and haul them back to the aid stations.

"You know as well as I, that's no good. The men would often lay out there in torment for 24 to 36 hours or more before they saw any treatment. And that's assuming the looters didn't get to them first and kill them to make the process of stealing their valuables easier.

"But during the battle I noticed something. We had an artillery corps called the "flying artillery." This consisted of small two-wheel carriages, with light cannon mounted, and pulled by two horses. They were like water-bugs; and could get to almost any point on the battlefield with amazing speed over almost any kind of terrain. They would get to a desired location, quickly unlimber, fire a few rounds at the enemy, and be gone before the enemy artillery could return fire. I thought about those carriages and realized that if they could carry a cannon, they could carry a couple of wounded soldiers.

"So, I got ahold of one of them and redesigned it. I put open-windowed sides and a roof on it, and folding doors in the front and back for easy access. The floor had a hair mattress on it, covered in leather; and the floor was removable. It would slide out on four small rollers so it could also serve as a litter. Then I trained some orderlies on how to apply tourniquets and simple bandages, and told them to go anywhere on the battlefield any time the fighting died down. It no longer had to be completely over before they could go in.

"Napoleon was so impressed with the speed and efficiency of these devices that he ordered their use throughout all of his armies."

"Amazing," Walker said with genuine admiration. "But that brings me to the second mystery. How on earth did you organize the patients so beautifully? When we first started, I was seeing nothing but amputations and serious wounds. Then for the past several hours, I've seen nothing but relatively minor cuts. How did that happen? They couldn't have come in that way."

"No, they didn't," Larrey began. "That was the product of another little idea of mine. I call it *"triage."* It comes from our verb *trier*, meaning to separate, or sort."

"How does it work?"

"Well, again, I have some specially trained orderlies. When a wounded man comes in he is placed in one of three categories. First are those who are wounded so badly they are going to die no matter what we do. Second are those whose wounds are so minor that they will live no matter what we do—or when we do it. And third are those for whom immediate care might save their life. They are the ones we see first, followed by the more minor wounds. The first group..." Larrey just shrugged his shoulders.

"But what about officers? Don't they mess up your system? Surely they're seen first no matter what their wound status might be."

"No."

"No?"

"That's right. Officers are seen in their turn based on the same criteria as private soldiers. In fact when I presented the system to Napoleon he announced that no officer would be treated ahead of anyone with more serious injuries—even if *he* were the wounded officer. I doubt if he really meant it; but, then again, I doubt if he will ever be wounded. I am convinced he does not have blood running through his veins, he has some kind of magic fluid."

Walker shook his head at the simplicity, the elegance, and the overwhelming common sense of Larrey's system. "If I ever get back to my side of the lines, I hope you don't mind if I recommend that system to our people."

"Be my guest," said Larrey. "While I can't get you all the way back home, maybe I can at least get you part way."

"How's that?"

"Tomorrow a special detachment is heading back to Alexandria with our wounded. They will need a physician to go with them, and I can't spare any of my regulars. Thus, you're elected; and take William with you in case you need an assistant."

William Parish's head popped up at this announcement, and life seemed to come back into his eyes. Walker was less excited. "I will be glad to get back to my research, Jean; but sad to be losing your company. You are an incredible man, as well as an incredible surgeon."

"And I will be sorry to lose your company as well, my friend. I just hope when next we meet it won't be on a battlefield."

"Well, that's fairly unlikely. I am just a simple medical researcher and will be going back to..."

"Lucas, spare me. I saw the speed with which you amputate limbs. I saw the ease with which you extract musket balls; and your ability to seal and cauterize open blood vessels is something to behold. You didn't learn all that by treating wealthy dyspeptics in London. You, sir, are a military surgeon to your very fingertips; but your secret is safe with me. I wish you well, Lucas. I truly do."

And, with that, the two men rose and shook hands; knowing that each would be the other's special friend until their dying day— even if they never saw each other again.

*****

It had been nearly a week since Nelson's fleet left Koroni and progress had been slow. In addition to contrary winds, there were the ongoing headaches of keeping the squadron together and in some kind of order.

Sailing in formation wasn't nearly as easy as it might appear to a landsman. To begin with, no two ships—even if they were identical twins when built—ever sailed at the same speed. Invariably other factors such as the amount of weed they had growing on their hull, the condition of their hull's protective copper sheets, even the age of the canvas they were using—all conspired to force some ships to add sail, some to remove it, and some even to back smaller sails into the wind to act as a kind of air brake.

Second, if they wanted to stay together, the fleet could travel no faster than the slowest ship. This alone was the source of major frustration to Nelson who wanted to get to Alexandria as soon as he possibly could.

But the biggest headache was caused by the problem of station keeping.

Throughout most of his journey Nelson didn't have fast frigates he could send out to scout around and report back; but he had to cast his existing net as wide as possible. As a result, most of the time, he had his ships in a line abreast, each with another ship to their left and right instead of in front and behind; but this brought it's own set of problems.

In a line abreast, each ship had to make its own decision as to when to tack, to take advantage of wind conditions. This maneuver could involve a movement as relatively simple as altering course so they were taking the wind on a different part of the ship—from the larboard, to the starboard bow, for example—or achieving the same result by swinging the ship into a large sweeping turn, winding up on the new course. Either way, the ships needed room to maneuver, which meant they had to be spaced wide apart.

Nelson's line stretched for almost three and a half miles, allowing a quarter-mile between ships for maneuvering. This was great for searching for the French, as the eyes of the fleet were spread over a much greater distance; but it made station-keeping a nightmare. The down side was that, if the French were found, it could easy take a half-day to get the ships from a line abreast to a line ahead fighting formation.

On this day he had no such concerns as his ships were traveling in a line-ahead, one following immediately behind the other. All a helmsman needed to do was to keep their ship in the wake of the ship ahead of it, by visually keeping the other ship's three masts lined up as one. Keeping the proper distance interval was a bit more difficult. The officer of the watch knew how tall the masts were on the ship in front of him, and what distance interval he needed to keep. Those two datum were applied to a table that told him what the angle should be from his ship to the top of the other's tallest mast. He could then dial that angle into his sextant, look through it, and know whether he needed to speed up or slow down. The endless tweaking of the sails. however, was a tremendous burden on the crew. If the wind changed and the ships needed to tack in a new direction, it would be done by the lead ship, and the others would simply follow him, one at a time.

Nelson was well aware of all these problems as he paced his quarterdeck, frequently glancing up at his lookouts, and trying not to show the frustration he had felt up to this point. On the gun deck, frustration levels were equally high.

Susan found Terry Parish folding bandages near an open gun port. "Where's Bellman," she demanded.

"I am not sure, but the last time I saw him he was taking another one of his 'laudanum naps.'"

"Damn it! It's almost time for sick call. I suppose I am going to have to do it for him... again."

"That's probably true, Susan; but you know, you're a lot more knowledgeable than he is. I know it, the men know it, the other surgeon's mates know it; and I think even Bellman knows it. If I were a seaman, I would *much* rather be seen by you than him."

"That might be, but it's still his job. What is it about these naval surgeons? It's like every one of them is either an alcoholic or an opium addict."

"Wasn't Lucas once an alcoholic?" Terry innocently asked. Susan just nodded and silently continued gathering up the materials she would need at sick call.

After a moment Terry looked up. "What do you think has happened to them?"

"Lucas and William?"

"Yes."

"I don't know, but I am sure they'll be all right. Lucas is very resourceful, you know, and William is no slacker in that regard either." Susan was not at all convinced they were all right; but she could not say that to Terry. She seemed to be coming more unstrung by the situation with each passing day, so Susan decided to change the topic.

"How did you meet William, anyway?"

Terry visibly brightened as she pulled together her memories.

"We met at a music festival in Oldenburg, Germany."

"Really? William was performing there?"

Terry laughed, "Oh no, he was an usher. I was from a little village not far away called Elsfleth." She paused for a moment. "I was so young then," she dreamily recalled "but then so was William. Anyway, I badly needed a job and, as head usher, William was responsible for hiring."

"Love at first sight?" Susan coaxed.

"By no means. At the end of each night's performance he would invariably say, 'I'll see you tomorrow, young lady—and wear a clean shirt!', which I thought was an outrageous thing to say—as if I would come in a dirty one. But after a while I began to realize that it was simply his form of humor. Then I began to notice his smile, and his laugh, and I even began to think his jokes were funny, even though I was probably the only one.

"At the and of the summer, as the festival was ending, he asked me to take a walk with him in a grove of aspen trees; and he asked me to marry him. I just looked at him for a moment and quietly said 'yes.' I knew immediately it was the right decision."

"Any regrets?"

"No. Oh, I won't tell you that being married to a musician is the easiest life in the world; but we always found a way to get by and, in many ways, do quite well."

Susan was now the one who became thoughtful. Terry couldn't have known it, but her words had landed very close to home. She envied Terry. She wondered if she would ever experience a love like that. Then her thoughts turned to Lucas. What if he were in trouble right now? What if he were seriously hurt? What if he were to die without her ever telling him...

"Land Ho!" The lookout cried; and the ship turned into a beehive of activity.

*****

On the quarterdeck of the *Bellerophon* the sighting of land was not news, it was a confirmation.

Earlier that morning Nelson had sent the *Alexander* and the *Swiftsure* ahead to make a land sighting. About 10:00 in the morning the *Alexander* signaled back that she had sighted land. Nelson then headed the fleet in a more easterly direction, to feel along the coast until they could find Alexandria.

A few hours later the *Bellerophon* could see land herself, and the lookouts vied with each other, each wanting to be the first to spot Alexandria. It was not long in coming, but the news was a blow to the fleet and especially to Nelson.

The lookouts could now clearly see the bright white minarets and spires of the city, contrasted against the brown hills in the background. By noon they could make out French flags flying from those spires, and hope rose. The French *were* there! But where was Napoleon's army and, more importantly, where were his ships?

The main harbor at Alexandria was guarded by a hook of low sandy ground with a lighthouse at the tip. As Nelson's ships rounded this point they could see the anchorage filled with vessels. There were the lateen rigged local craft with their rakish triangular sails. There were hundreds of transports. There were even a couple French ships of the line and several frigates. But, there was no battle fleet!

Nelson was bitterly disappointed. He had missed them again. He might have been able to dismiss his earlier failure to find the French as bad luck, or bad timing, or even on the hapless William Parish. But the bottom line was that his mission was to find them. The line from his commissioning document kept running through his head: "Hereof nor you nor any of you may fail as you will answer the contrary at your peril."

He looked at the tricolor flags that were proudly waving from towers and rooftops across the city—taunting him, accusing him of failure. He knew an entire country had fallen to the French because of his mistakes, and he could only hope that future historians would somehow forget that fact. But the worst part for him was the sheer ignominy of it all. Countries come and go. The French own Egypt now, maybe the British would own it in the future. He knew that that fool Jervis would protect him from the worst of the criticism; but history would forever record that he—Horatio Nelson—had failed to find the French.

The quarterdeck of the *Vanguard* was deathly silent. Edward Berry, his flag captain, could read the devastation in Nelson's face; but didn't know what, if anything, he could say. No other officer would have dared to speak.

Nelson sighed heavily and slowly walked to the back of the quarterdeck and the door that would take him to his quarters. He was just reaching for the door handle when the signal midshipman called out from the foretop: "On deck, there. The *Goliath* is signaling."

Nelson turned. He might as well see what this was. Earlier he had sent the *Zealous* and the *Goliath* to scout to the east, but he held no hopes that they would find anything. Still...

"The *Goliath's* signal flags are tangled, sir," the midshipman continued. "Wait, there's the *Zealous*. She's signaling: 'Strange fleet in anchor.'" Then a few minutes later: "'*Zealous* to Flag - Sixteen sail of the line at anchor bearing East by South.'"

The crews of the British ships started cheering, each in turn, as their signalmen decoded *Zealous'* message. Nelson, however, had one thought and one thought only—get to a chart and find out exactly what on earth was East by South of *Zealous'* current position.

CHAPTER EIGHT

For Lucas and William, the trip back to Alexandria was not nearly as taxing as the outbound trek; but then, it would be hard to imagine any journey that could have been worse than that. For one thing, this time it was being done in a shaded wagon, instead of walking under the blistering sun. For another, there was plenty of water in the wagons both for the wounded and for the caretakers of the wounded. No more stealing what the horses didn't want.

The first part of the journey consisted of retracing their steps from Chobrakit, to Rahmaniya, and from Rahmaniya to Damanhour. There they stayed the night, which allowed them to obtain some additional wagons. This allowed them to transfer more men from Larrey's flying ambulances to more comfortable vehicles.

The following morning they started as soon as it was light enough to see their way. They would be following an old caravan trail that led from Damanhour to El Akrich, a small city not far from Alexandria. It was a demanding stretch. In distance it was only about 25 miles; but most of it was across sand dune covered wasteland, making progress slow; but it was a lot faster than following the Nile to Rosetta and then following the coast back to Alexandria.

They had passed through the village of El Kérioun and were nearing the town of Le Iohâ, on the outskirts of El Akrich, where it had been decided they would stay for the night and press on to Alexandria in the morning. As they got closer to their destination, William and Lucas found themselves talking about the future.

"I am assuming you have a plan, William. Tell me you have a plan," Walker implored.

"A plan?"

"Yes. When we started this merry adventure the idea was to wait until the French arrive, then somehow notify Nelson of that fact. I think it is safe to conclude that the French are here; so, now what?"

William stared out the back of the wagon for a moment. "Well, in fact Lucas, I happen to have a carefully thought out, well conceived, plan."

"Which is?"

"First we get to Alexandria. Then we buy a ship..."

"I have £20 on me, and you have nothing."

"Then we rent a sailing ship for a month or so..."

"Twenty pounds, William!"

"Then we steal a fishing boat, go find Nelson, and report in.

"Go find Nelson, where?"

William was silent for another long moment. "All right, perhaps I don't have every last detail worked out. But we'll find him. I am sure he's somewhere in the eastern Mediterranean."

"Oh, that narrows it down." Walker checked himself, marveling at how much he was starting to sound like Susan.

The two continued in silence for another mile, when William finally spoke up.

"Lucas, what do you plan to do once we get back?"

"If we get back!"

"We'll be all right. Trust me."

Walker rolled his eyes.

"But what do you plan to do *when* we get back?"

"I am not sure what you mean. I'll link up again with Susan, and together we'll try to figure out how to rejoin Sidney. That's the way it's always been. When we're together we're a team. When we're apart, we find a way to get back together."

"I envy you."

"Envy me? Why on earth?"

"Yes, the life you lead. Look at all the adventures you've had with Sidney and Susan... it's just... I don't know; but I want that life. I want the excitement, the risks, the dangers, the stimulation, the..."

Walker started laughing. "William, that's not going to happen."

"Why? You think I am not man enough? You think I can't handle it?" It was the first time Walker had seen Parish genuinely agitated.

"No, William, not at all. You've more than proved yourself in my eyes, and in the eyes of everyone around you; but that's precisely the problem. You've shown yourself to be resilient, resourceful, and courageous. But, believe it or not, our military is littered with resilient, resourceful, and courageous men. You, however, went one step further—you cracked one of France's best ciphers. Do you think that's the last code that will need to be broken before this war is over?"

"Alright, so that one was a little tough, but it was not that big a deal."

"Not that big a deal? How many people in the world... in the *world*, mind you... do you think could have broken it? Three? Maybe four? Believe me, when you get back aboard a British ship, you are headed straight to London via the fastest means available."

"But I want to..."

"No, William. Stop. Think about it. If Nelson had not botched the intelligence you gave him, he would have caught Napoleon at sea. He would have never made it to Egypt; and how many people would still be alive today if that had happened? What about the next 'unbreakable' message that needs decoding? What might that contain? Might it save a life? A hundred lives? Ten thousand lives?"

William looked deeply thoughtful. He turned to Walker with the most curious questioning look on his face. "So, you're saying I am... that in some way by sitting in that miserable office I am still a fighter, just like you and Sidney and Susan?"

"You are among the finest weapons in the king's arsenal, William. The only difference is that you do not strike with a sword, you strike with your mind—and that can be far, *far*, more devastating to the enemy than any sword blow or cannon shot.

"And then, don't forget, there's Terry. You have to think about her too. What is she supposed to do while you're galloping off on some exotic mission or another?"

"Yes, I have to admit, I do miss her. I really do. But, what about you and Susan—and please don't tell me that you are just friends."

"Well, to be sure, I have a certain fondness for Susan. But she and I..."

"Lucas!" Parish admonished.

"All right, I'll admit it. I do miss her. I miss her terribly."

Lucas became quiet as his thoughts turned to Susan. What if she were in trouble right now? What if she were seriously hurt? What if she were to die without him ever telling her...

"Riders approaching," the picket shouted as he rode at top speed back into the caravan.

*****

Nelson looked through his telescope for what seemed like the 20th time as they approached the French fleet; and each time he looked, he liked less of what he saw.

Aboukir Bay is shaped roughly like a fish-hook laid horizontally. At the curved end was a peninsula with an ancient castle at it's tip—ancient but still containing dangerous cannon. About 2.5 miles northeast of the tip was a small island on which the French had installed several batteries. Shoal water lay around this island extending out for about a half-mile.

The French fleet was deployed at anchor in a line running from about two miles off the barb of the fish-hook, in a south-easterly direction, across the curved end of the bay. Nelson had nine 74's and one 50-gun ship in a ragged formation some nine miles away. Admiral Brueys had nine 74s and three 80-gun ships, with the 120-gun monster—the *Orient*—occupying the center. All of the French ships were anchored by the bow.

"Captain Berry," Nelson said as he paced back and forth along the forward edge of the quarterdeck, "I would be obliged if you would see what information we have about that bay over there. Aboukir, I believe it's called."

A few minutes later Berry reappeared, studying a book.

"I have some information right here admiral," Berry announced as he showed the open book to Nelson. There was no way Nelson was going to be able to read the book's small print, with his one functioning eye, on the deck of a swaying ship. He turned away and said, "Excellent. Please read it."

"'South of Rosetti is a great Bay called Mady, or Medy Bay.'" Berry stopped to point out, "Rosetti is, of course, Rosetta, and Medy Bay is the bay before us, now called Aboukir. He continued, "'...Medy Bay, where there runneth also a great stream from another arm of the River Nile, into this Bay.

"'Before this Bay lies an island, behind which is good riding, and good ground; and if you are forced to remove from Rosetti, then you may run into the Bay of Mady, behind the aforesaid island, and come to anchor in six or seven fathom water.

"'Four leagues to the southward of Rosetti, lies Cape Becur, between these two lies the aforesaid island before the Bay of Mady.

"'Between Cape Becur and that island, you can not sail with great ships, except you are very well acquainted, for the ground is very foul, some rocks lie above, and some under water; the Turks sometimes with small ships sail through, but to the northward of the island is a broad and good passage.

"'Upon Cape Becur standeth a castle, called Apokera, which when you first get sight of, is like a sail.

"'From Apokera, or Cape Becur, to Alexandria, the coast reacheth southwest by south, about four leagues; this land is high and full of trees.'

"There you have it sir."

"Captain, why are there all those 'standeths' and 'reacheths' in there? From what are you reading?"

"From *The English Pilot*, sir."

"No, I mean, from what year is that book?"

Berry flipped to the front, "Ah, I'm afraid it's not terribly current."

"How 'not terribly current'?"

"1677, sir."

Nelson blinked in astonishment. "So, I am to attack a French fleet, which is anchored in a bay; and the most recent information I have about that bay is 121 years old."

Berry was trying to decide whether that statement required an affirmation or not. He decided it didn't.

"That will be all, captain. Thank you." Nelson needed to be alone to think this problem through. The issue was not *whether* to attack the French—that was a foregone conclusion—it was *when* that attack would be made. Should it be done immediately, or should he wait until morning?

There were a number of reason whys he should wait until morning. It was nearly 3:00 in the afternoon and, in the moderate breeze he was in, it would be several hours before his ships could reach the French. By the time the last of his ships could be brought to bear, it would be dark, and that posed all manner of hazards.

To begin with, he would be navigating in the blind. He had no accurate idea of the depth of the water, or whether there were special navigation hazards in the vicinity of the French ships. This situation would have been bad enough in daylight; but at night it bordered on reckless. But the biggest fear he had was the utter confusion that is inherent in any night attack. It was almost impossible, in the heat of a mobile night action, for captains to keep track of where all the other ships in his squadron were located. Flashes of gunfire would be shattering the darkness in all directions, and British gun flashes look exactly like French. It was more than merely likely that, at some point, one British ship would start firing on another—it was expected. The French had no such problem. They were at anchor. They knew full well where their ships were at.

But counter-balancing these dangers, was the wind. It was perfect. It was coming out of the north-northwest, and would be almost directly behind the British ships as they began their attack run. If he waited until morning, who knew where the wind would be? Maybe it would be coming from the opposite direction, and he would have to tack his ships for hours, back and forth against the wind, to even reach the enemy. The other factor was the element of surprise. If he waited, it would give the French all night to think things over and get ready.

No, it had to be now.

Over the next two hours, a series of signals flashed from the flagship.

Signal flag #9 (to the *Alexander* and *Swiftsure*) Leave off chase and rejoin.

No. 53 (to all ships) Prepare for battle.

No. 54 (to all ships) Prepare for battle, when it might be necessary to anchor by the stern with springs.

No. 45 and No. 46 [hoisted together] (to all ships) Engage the enemy's center. Engage the enemy's van.

No. 31 (to all ships) Form line of battle ahead and astern of the Admiral as most convenient.

There was a pause for over an hour. Then flew:

No. 34 (to all ships) Alter course one point to starboard in succession.

No. 66 (to all ships) Make all sail, the leading ship first.

Then came the signal that every captain in Nelson's squadron was awaiting: No. 5 [with red pendent] (to all ships) Engage the enemy closer. It would remain flying on Nelson's flagship for the next 14 hours.

*****

Going to battle stations, on any ship, in any navy, was an exercise in controlled chaos. Every person aboard ship, from the captain to the cook, had a designated place to go and specific tasks to be done once he got there. It was no different on the *Bellerophon*.

The moment the flags for the numbers 5-3 appeared on Nelson's main mast, the order was given for the ship's drummer boy to begin his tattoo. Driven by the urgency of the rapid drum beat, over 500 men tumbled from every corner of the ship to convert it from a stately, placid, sailing vessel into a killing machine.

Two groups scrambled up the ratlines of the fore and main masts. Their job was to take in the huge mainsails that hung from the lowest yard arms, leaving the topsails in place to drive the ship. This reduced the vessel's speed somewhat, but it gave the officers on the quarterdeck an unobstructed view forward. Nets were rigged above the upper deck and quarterdeck to keep men from being injured by falling debris if the rigging or masts should be shot away. Tightly rolled hammocks were brought up and stowed in special storage nets around the rails of the ship, and covered with a canvas tarp. Some of them were also taken to the fore and maintops where marines would be stationed to deliver musket fire down upon the enemy. The function of these rolled hammocks was the same in both places, to provide at least some protection from enemy return musket fire.

Below deck a complete transformation was in progress. Under normal circumstances the various decks would contain screened off "cabins" where officers and petty officers could take their ease. Each cubicle would contain a hanging bed, a small table and chair, a washstand, and perhaps a few mementos of a wife or sweetheart. A set of working clothes and maybe a hat would be found hanging on a hook; but everything else would be neatly placed in the person's sea chest. All would be swept away in minutes by the carpenter and his mates. The screens would be taken down, the beds unhooked, the mementos pushed into the chest, and everything would be carried below into the hold. No one was exempt from this clearing process—not even the captain. Within moments a splendid cabin that was complete with as many amenities as was feasible on a warship at sea, was reduced to an empty room with four guns in it.

On the gundeck, the change was even more dramatic. With no enemy in sight, this deck was a combination sleeping area, mess hall, and recreation area for the men. Under its low slung ceiling could be found hammocks, sea chests, hanging dining tables, benches, pets, and even some chicken coops and a few head of cattle or pigs. The tables would be swung up into the ceiling and lashed down. Everything else would be carried to the hold, if not pushed overboard, until nothing remained except two rows of very deadly guns.

The guns were what the ship was all about; for, in the final analysis, the *Bellerophon* was nothing more than a floating 74-gun wooden fortress. Weighing over 3000 pounds, each was mounted on a heavy wooden carriage and lashed up tight to the ship's bulkhead. This was absolutely necessary to keep them from crashing around as the ship worked it's way through the seas. Each piece was now surrounded by it's respective crew—a crew that would work the gun until either the battle was over, or they were all dead.

The captains of each of the guns made their way to the gunner's storeroom. There each would pick up a leather case filled with hollow quills. These quills were filled with a very light, fast burning form of gunpowder and were used to ignite the main powder charge inside the weapon. To ignite the quills, they checked out oversized flintlocks, like those found on muskets, to be bolted on to the top of the gun.

The gun crews were also getting ready. After the guns had been cast loose from their lashings, they were rolled back, the protective tampions were removed from the guns' mouths, and the protective lead apron was removed from the touch-hole. A thick circle of rope was placed on the deck by each piece containing a pyramid of cannon balls. Stacks of wadding were placed next to the shot pile, and the various crowbars, handspikes, sponges, and ramrods were made handy. Next to the gun also was placed a tub of water over which a slow-match was burning. This was considered insurance in case the flintlock failed.

When the gun was finally made ready, and only then, the men were allowed to get themselves prepared. Shirts would come off and, if they had a neck handkerchief, it would be bound around their ears to try to stave off permanent deafness from the roar of the guns. When the gun-captains were satisfied, and when the "powder monkeys," boys usually around 12 years old, had returned with their initial powder charges, the gun crews could relax until the battle started. But this was not so in other parts of the ship.

The marines were mustered in front of the quarterdeck. Most of them would be placed high up in the rigging to try to pick off enemy officers with their muskets. Each group of sharpshooters would be assigned some "ship's boys," boys even younger than the powder monkeys, to bring them ammunition. Other marines would be helping to pass out pistols and cutlasses to men who might be called upon to form boarding parties.

Because the battle was expected to be fought in whole or in part in the dark, the purser was passing out "purser's glims," candles mounted in heavy battle lanterns to provide some measure of light. These would be securely tied to the bulkhead next to each gun.

Bucket brigades were formed to wet the sails, to reduce the possibility of fire. For the same reason, pumps were rigged and fire hoses laid along each deck. The ship's boats were lowered overboard and towed behind. No one wanted those boats on deck during the battle. If an enemy shot were to hit one, the resulting shower of splinters would be deadly to anyone in the general vicinity.

But this battle was to be fought differently than most others; and the men knew it when the order "5-4" was sent. It meant they would be anchoring by the stern when engaging the French. This technique, while not unknown, was unusual and added an additional burden to the ship's preparation.

A massive anchor cable was hauled out of the cable locker and wrestled back to the stern. One end of it was secured to the most rearward of the three masts, the mizzenmast. The other was fed out through one of the stern windows and the loose end was walked forward on the outside of the ship. There it would be secured to the anchor in the bow. By this means, when the captain gave the order to let go the anchor, it would splash into the sea and the cable would pay out down the side of the ship. When it reached the limits of its length, it would snap taut, the ship's forward progress would be checked, and it would be anchored by the stern.

But the signal contained an additional requirement—it demanded that "springs" be set. A second, much smaller line, with plenty of slack, was attached to the anchor cable and run through the ships' hawse pipe, the opening in the bow where the anchor cable would normally have run. The opposite end of this smaller line was attached to the ships' capstan. When the anchor was let go, this line would pay out and remain slack as the anchor, the stern anchor cable, and the ship itself assumed a straight line. But suppose during the battle the captain wanted to turn the ship's direction so he could level gunfire at a different target. Getting underway to turn the ship was utterly impractical, and that's where the spring came in. By turning the capstan, the smaller line was reeled in; and by reeling it in, the ships bow would be forced to turn like a horses' head with a bridle. This meant either the port or starboard guns could be brought to bear against a target in almost any direction.

But as the bosun and his mates were wrestling with anchor cables and springs, other people, in other parts of the ship, were also busy.

Under the forecastle, the cook was extinguishing the galley fire and dumping the hot coals overboard. While he was doing that, each deck was being covered with a wet sand mixture to provide extra traction, dampen any fires, and reduce the possibility of bare feet slipping on pools of blood. But there was another place where blood was very much on the minds of sailors.

Below the weather deck, and below the gun deck, lay the orlop deck. The only thing below that was the hold and the ship's keel. Forward on the orlop were the carpenter's, bosun's, and gunner's storerooms. Behind that was the sail storage room, and behind that was the cockpit, where the midshipmen normally slept and where a makeshift surgery was now being set up.

There was no light and very little air on that deck, as it was below the waterline. This also meant that it was one of the safest places on the ship, because direct enemy fire could not reach it. That was good. Men who found themselves in the cockpit during the battle were there for one reason—because they had been seriously wounded. For them, the battle with the French was over; and their personal battle to stay alive had just begun.

The same kind of organized chaos could be seen in the cockpit as everywhere else on ship. The loblolly boys, boys who served as assistants to the surgeon's mates, were gathering armloads of tourniquets and compresses to be distributed around the ship. These would be used by the men to staunch bleeding as they carried wounded comrades to surgery. Two of the surgeon's mates were pushing together a couple of the midshipmen's sea chests to form a makeshift operating table. Buckets were placed near at hand to catch blood and to hold amputated limbs. Tables were set up containing gags, tie-down ropes, bottles of laudanum, containers of rum and, most importantly, the surgical instruments—forceps, probes, picks, tweezers, knives, scalpels, lancets, several types of saws, two chisels, a hammer, and a drill.

Susan was directing the set-up when someone brought in a large wooden chest and put it on the table with the surgical instruments. It was gorgeous. It was made of solid oak, beautifully finished, with solid brass carrying handles on the ends, and protective brass fixtures on each corner. Three seashells were carved on top. The ones on the left and right were raised, and the one in the middle was recessed.

For a moment, Susan's world came to a halt. This was Lucas' medical chest. As she ran her hand across the seashells she thought about how they had acquired it, in Toulon, just before the city fell to the French army. She thought about how proud Walker was when he discovered that the chest and the superb instruments it contained had been made in America, his native country. She thought about how she and Lucas and her friend, Lady Inge Fuhrmann, had barely escaped Toulon with their lives. And she thought, yet again, about Lucas.

"Susan, where do yer want these tourniquets?" asked Old Eddie Mass, a superannuated surgeon's mate who wisely deferred to Susan's experience.

"Put one group at the foot and one at the head of the operating table," she replied. "That way they'll be handy whether we're cuttin' off arms or legs."

"And where the hell is our princely surgeon," she continued. "That son of a bitch should be here setting this theater up, not me!"

"Yer mustn't be so 'ard on 'im," Eddie said.

"Oh? And why not? Have you seen him do anything around here except walk about in a laudanum haze?"

"They's a bit yer don't know about mista Bellman, Susan."

"Like what?"

"Well, yer probably know 'e were a surgeon back in '94 aboard th' frigate *Latona* at the Glorious First of June."

"Yes, I know that. He's talked about it enough. I assume he was sober at least part of the time back then."

"Oh, right, he were indeed. I served wiv 'im. But did yer know shortly after that th' *Latona* were captured in the West Indies and Guvnor Bellman spent over three years at 'ard labor in a French prison camp?

Susan did not know that, and it showed in her expression.

"And I'm not goin' on about some rest 'ome in Paris. This were a prison camp in the chuffin' West Indies... the *West Indies*, Susan... 'ard labor on some God-forsaken, disease-ridden, hell-hole island. And 'e were never quite right after that... never quite right."

Susan said nothing and turned away to hide the surprise on her face and the shame she felt at the way she had talked about Bellman. She didn't know he had been a prisoner, and that would explain a lot. But does it excuse his current incompetence as a surgeon—a man with hundreds of people depending on him? Why does he stay on? Doesn't that responsibility require that he at least step down if he can't perform?

"Damn this war!" she muttered under her breath. "Damn and double-damn! And where the hell is that fool Walker when you need him?" And she continued to set out the gruesome instruments that she knew would soon be called into use.

*****

The captain in charge of the caravan had his telescope out and was studying the dust trail left by two horsemen in the distance. Snapping the device closed he said, "It's all right. It's two of ours. Hussars from the 2nd, I believe. But why on earth are they in such a hurry?"

The answer was not long in coming. The two riders barged into camp and immediately drew a crowd—including Lucas and William.

"The British are here," one man breathlessly exclaimed while the other took a deep swing from a water flask that was offered him. "Their fleet is bearing down on our warships in Aboukir Bay."

"Slow down," the captain ordered. "Tell me what happened."

The second man, his thirst quenched for the moment, replied. "Yes, sir. We're part of the detachment at the caravansary at Maison Carrée, overlooking Aboukir Bay. A few hours ago we spotted two ships out beyond Canope Point. They saw our fleet anchored in the bay, then turned 'round and fled with all sails set. A bit later we see numerous other sails come up over the horizon. A whole war fleet, sir, making for our ships in Aboukir."

"Numerous sails? Exactly what does that mean?"

"We counted 13 ships of the line, sir. British."

"Listen carefully. This is a very important question. Did you see any transport ships? Are the British landing an army?"

"No, sir. No transports. Just 13 warships. Big ones. Unless there are still transports out there beyond the horizon."

"Who is your officer?"

"No officer. Just a sergeant. He sent us here to El Akrich to find an officer to tell us what to do."

"All right. I want you to continue on to Alexandria to inform the authorities there—although surely they must have spotted the British fleet too. But go there anyway, just in case. I don't know if there's anything else we can do other than that."

Parish and Walker looked at each other. The French officer might have been at a loss as to what to do, but they weren't. They quietly walked away from the crowd surrounding the two messengers.

"Lucas, we've got to get to Aboukir Bay."

"I know, but we need horses. If those two messengers can come down that road over there, then we can go up it."

"But how do we get the horses?"

"Leave that to me. I suddenly remembered there's a medical emergency in town that we need to get to."

Twenty minutes later the two were on horseback trotting into El Ekrich. A few minutes after that, they were headed north out of town at a full gallop.

*****

"Yes, I *know* you know how to fire a gun when the ship is heeling; but that's not what I'm talking about." Midshipman Richard Janverin waited patiently for his sentence to be translated. "I am talking about what to do when the ship is rolling, not heeling."

He was aboard a Turkish warship off Constantinople firing guns at a raft of barrels floating in the Sea of Marmara. Surrounding him was a group of newly minted gunner's and gunner's mates from the Turkish Navy. His friend, Midshipman Charles Beecroft, was two guns over conducting the same class.

191

"When a ship is heeling, tilted over by the wind, you can lower the gun's muzzle by placing a wooden wedge, a quoin, underneath the breech of the gun. That raises the aft end, and lowers the mouth, equalizing for the tilt of the ship.

"What I am talking about is when the ship is in heavier seas, when it's rolling back and forth, starboard to larboard. You can't adjust the aim by using a quoin, because by the time you get it in place, the ship will have rolled past the target.

"So what then are we to do?" one of them asked.

"Point the gun level, and wait for the target to come to you. Get it all ready to fire and watch through your gun port. When the ship is recovering from a roll to one side, and heading in the other direction, wait until just before the target is dead level relative to your ship, then fire.

"It's all a matter of timing. If you fire too soon, your shot will go over the enemy. If you wait too long, it will hit the water in front of them and do no damage."

"But which should we aim for, captain? The hull or the sails?" The Turkish sailors had taken to calling all British naval officers "captain." If they were actually a captain it was fine. If they weren't, it would be flattering; and who knew whose ear these pasty-skinned Englishmen had in higher quarters.

"That's a good question. In general, we in the British Navy tend to shoot at the hull of our opponent. That's not always true, but it's true enough most of the time. The idea is that if you blast away at the enemy's hull, you will be killing or wounding the sailors on the other side. And a ship that has no crew can not fight.

"The French, on the other hand, tend to aim for the sails and rigging. Again, that's not *always* true, but it is most of the time. Their theory is that if you destroy the sails or the masts, the ship can't go anywhere, and is thus at your mercy."

"So then, we should always aim level for the hull?"

"No."

The Turkish gunners were now showing signs of exasperation.

"It depends on which gun you're using, and when you're using it. If you are shooting from a distance, just aim for the hull anywhere. Any hit you can get will be excellent. If you're close aboard the other ship, depress your muzzles as much as you can when firing. The exception is if you're firing a carronade."

"Captain, you have me confused," an older petty officer said. "Aim level on the roll. Shoot downward if you are close; but don't shoot downward if you have a carronade." He shrugged his shoulders.

"It's quite simple. Let me explain.

"Naval guns must be built to fire at long distances—up to a mile or more. As a result, their powder charges have to be made quite powerful. If you're close aboard the enemy, the guns are so powerful, and the balls are traveling so fast, they will enter one side of the hull and exit out the other, leaving little damage in between. By depressing the muzzles as much as possible, the balls will pierce the hull, travel downward, pierce a deck or two, and hopefully exit out the bottom of the ship. This creates leaks that the enemy will have to deal with, in addition to whatever other annoyance you're causing him."

"Then what about these carronades?"

"A carronade is different. We call them 'smashers.' It's a special gun with a much shorter barrel; and it uses a much smaller charge. This means the ball isn't traveling as fast. It will penetrate the hull, but stop short of going out the other side. This creates a shower of wooden splinters, which will kill or maim anyone who's anywhere near it's point of entry."

The Turks seemed duly impressed with "Captain" Janverin's reasoning, but another question remained.

"Why not just use less of a charge to slow the speed of the shot in a standard gun?" the petty officer asked. "Wouldn't that have the same effect as a carronade?"

"In theory, yes; but, in battle, that's easier said than done. Remember, the bags you receive from the powder room were made up long before the battle ever started. At that time, the gunner and his mates had no idea what the ship's needs would be; and, when the battle starts, they will be too busy handing out bags as fast as they can to the powder monkeys to create custom loads.

"Besides, what happens if the ship changes her position? Let's say the captain is able to maneuver the ship so that his broadside is pointing directly at the bow or the stern of the enemy. That's called 'raking,' and it's the most devastating blow a ship can deliver.

"The guns will be loaded with double or even triple shot. When the broadside goes off, all of those balls will be concentrated within the width of the enemy ship, and traveling down her full length. They will be taking out groups of sailors like bowling pins, overturning hot guns, ricocheting in all directions, and showering splinters every time a ball touches wood. But to rake another ship, you need maximum power in all guns; and the likelihood that the gunners filling the bags can change over that quickly, for all guns, is remote indeed.

"Trust me, almost all of the bags you get will carry maximum charges."

He pulled out his pocket watch and said, "That will be all for today. We'll need to head in soon; but tomorrow I want to review the loading and firing procedure that was developed by our Sir Charles Douglas, and you *will* learn how to fire on the roll."

As the Turkish gunners dispersed, Janverin looked over and saw that Beecroft had dismissed his men as well, and was walking over. They left the confining environment of the gundeck and went up to the weather deck to get some air.

"So, this was your last class," Janverin began. "Tomorrow you'll be off as captain of your own ship and master of all you survey."

"I will be in charge of an aging, leaky, xebec, hauling some prisoners back to France."

"Ah, yes, but how does that old saying go: 'Tis better to be the king of the smallest kingdom, than a prince in the largest?'"

"Maybe that's true. I don't know. I guess I'll find out."

The two spent a moment looking out over the glistening ocean. Janverin was looking more thoughtful than usual, however. Beecroft finally broke the silence.

"Why are you looking so serious? Where is the chipper Richard Janverin on my last day in this eastern paradise?"

"A few minutes ago I looked at my pocket watch." He pulled it out to show to Beecroft. "It was a gift from my uncle, Ralph Miller, who's the captain of the *Theseus*. The last I heard, he was assigned to Nelson's squadron; and I was just wondering where they were and what they were doing right now."

Beecroft laughed. "You aren't the only one. I overheard Sir Sidney talking to his brother the other day, and he was asking the very same question—only his way of putting it wasn't quite as polite."

"Do you think we'll ever get a chance, Charles?"

"A chance?"

"Yes, a chance to fight—a chance to distinguish ourselves."

"I hope so; but not real soon. I am about to take an overgrown fishing smack through several hundred miles of pirate-infested waters, and into Toulon—an enemy port. I've got one 3-pound gun, and I can carry the entire ship's supply of shot in the pockets of my greatcoat."

Janverin smiled and turned back to gazing over the rail. "Yes, but I still wonder what they're doing."

*****

The *Orient* was the pride of the French fleet. Indeed, she would have been the pride of anyone's fleet, as few nations had anything that could match her size and firepower. No ship, except perhaps another 100+ gun vessel, could possibly stand against her.

For the past hour captains from the other 12 French ships of the line and the four frigates had been assembling in the *Orient's* wardroom. Shortly after 3:00, Luc Casabianca, the flag captain of the *Orient* entered the room and snapped, *"Attention sur le pont!"* The assemblage stood up at attention, and through the door appeared Admiral Brueys.

Brueys was 45 years old, only a few years older than Nelson and, by all rights, shouldn't be alive.

He was thin, almost willowy, with shoulder-length silver hair, long sideburns, and a handsome patrician face. He was in full dress uniform, complete with a large red sash tied around the gold embroidered leaf designs running down the front of his blue coat. His massive epaulettes with their heavy bullion fringe glistened even in the dim light of the cabin. He was a man who inspired confidence just by the way he looked at you, much as did Horatio Nelson.

That he wasn't dead by now had more to do with luck than anything else, for he was born the Comte de Brueys, of an old and distinguished aristocratic family. He had joined the French Royal Navy at age 13 as a boy volunteer. Rising steadily through the ranks, he had shown surprising competence in numerous battles, including the Battle of the Chesapeake which sealed Cornwallis' fate at Yorktown.

With the coming of the French Revolution, he managed to hide away long enough for the Reign of Terror to burn itself out. When he emerged, he found he was in great demand, as most of the old royalist admirals and senior captains had been lead, in wholesale lots, to the guillotine. The Revolutionary Navy was now in desperate need of trained and skilled leaders, and Brueys was more than adequate to the task. He was regarded in most circles as France's finest admiral.

"Citizens, please be seated," he said as he strode to the front of the room.

"As you know, about an hour ago, the British fleet was seen on the horizon, headed toward Alexandria. We expect them to be here in the next two or three hours. Therefore I have called you all here to outline my battle plan and to personally give you your orders.

"Now, I am not sure which ships these are, but I believe this is the same squadron that had been trying to blockade us in Toulon before we left on this journey. If so, it's commanded by an Admiral Nelson. He is a young man, not without merit, I suppose, but completely untried in fleet action. As a result, I believe he will be cautious in his approach.

"We obviously don't know exactly what the enemy is going to do; but we can surmise a great deal. To begin with, the only sensible way to attack us in our present position is for them to swing wide and come up upon our line from the rear. This will keep them from being exposed to our fire as he is positioning his ships for the attack. Fortunately I had foreseen this possibility when we anchored here, which is why our largest and most powerful ships are in the rear and middle of our line.

"I believe the British will attack on the seaward side, therefore I want each ship to run a heavy cable to the next ship astern. They will be on the outside of us and I mean to keep them there. I do not want any British ships getting between us, or between us and the land.

"Next, I want each ship to attach a spring to their anchor cable. I want you to be able to easily turn your ship and redirect your fire at a moments notice. This will allow you to keep your fire on your targets with maximum effectiveness.

"Finally, I want all ships to fly the recall signal. We have too many sailors ashore at the moment. They need to get back as fast as they can.

"That's the general outline. Are there any questions?"

After a long pause, one of the younger captains spoke up. "Admiral, why are we waiting for them to attack us? Why not get underway and meet them at sea?"

"I thought of that but decided against it. For one thing we would be sailing short handed. Every ship here has large numbers of crewmen ashore getting water, provisions, or any one of a hundred other tasks. Second, the wind is against us. We would have to form up into battle order while trying to tack against the wind. That's a prescription for both chaos and, more than likely, collisions."

"When do you think the British will attack, admiral?"

"Not until morning.

"The same wind that keeps us from getting underway, will keep them from coming up on us from our rear. They will have to tack against it, while trying to maintain battle order and, at the same time, fight us. Besides, it's already past 3:00. They won't be here until 5:00 or 6:00 and the sun goes down at 7:00. By 8:00 it will be pitch dark. For them to fight a night action, in unknown waters, against an anchored foe, would be madness.

"So that's it, gentlemen. Please get back to your ships and make ready for tomorrow's battle. And don't forget to run those cables between your ships, and set your springs."

Unfortunately, they didn't set the cables. They didn't set the springs. And Nelson didn't do anything the way Brueys thought he would.

*****

In one respect Brueys was right. Wind direction would indeed affect the outcome of the battle, but not in the way he expected. While the wind might keep Nelson from coming up from the rear, it assisted him in attacking from the front. Which is precisely what he did.

The squadron swung, in a ragged formation, around Aboukir island. The French battery on the island did their best to fire on the fleet, but it had little effect. The ships kept coming.

It was the first time they had a view of the French that was not partially obstructed by Cape Becur. But, at the moment, it was not the 500 French guns staring them in the face that worried them; it was the shoal that extended out from the island. They knew it was there, but they had no idea how far out it extended.

Captain Samuel Hood in the *Zealous* became the first to cautiously make his way through the passage, taking soundings as he went. Nelson in the *Vanguard* stationed himself to direct the following ships along Hood's path. Even with all this caution, however, the *Culloden*, astern of the fleet because she was towing a prize, found the shoal and ran aground. They eventually managed to get afloat; but, to her captain's mortification, it was only after the battle was over.

At 5:00 Nelson sent the signal "Attack the enemy's van and center." At 5:30 he sent "Form line of battle as convenient." This became, in effect, a signal for all ships to begin a sprint to the French. There was no time to wait for the slower ships to catch up; so the line became well strung out.

The first ship to arrive was the *Goliath,* and her captain, Thomas Foley, made the decision that would ultimately win the battle for Nelson. He was able to make it, however, because he had a secret weapon—an accurate map of Aboukir Bay.

The map was a part of the *Petite Atlas Maritime.* He had picked up the five volume set years ago in a small London bookstore, and had almost forgotten that he had it on board. It wasn't as detailed as he would have liked, but it was only about 35 years old and a lot better than the 121 year old *English Pilot,* which is what the other ships were using.

It told him, first of all, where the limit of the shoal water was around Aboukir Island. This allowed him to run out his studding sails, charge past the *Zealous,* and have the honor of being the first one to engage the French. But, most importantly, it told him that between the line of French ships and the shore, the water was four to seven fathoms deep, 24 to 42 feet. He knew his ship drew 23 feet, so there was room—just barely in places—to get on the other side of their line.

To confirm the chart he called up to a midshipman, George Elliot, who he had stationed in the maintop with a telescope. He told him to look for anchor buoys on the French ships. After a minute, Elliot reported back that there were, and they were about 200 yards out from the bow of each ship. There were no stern anchors, or cables linking the ships together.

That cinched it for Foley. He knew the wind could theoretically come from any direction and swing the ships around. That meant there had to be at least 200 yards of deep water around each ship; and if there was room for a French ship to swing, there was room for an English ship to pass.

His only hesitation was that he had no orders from Nelson to do it. On one hand, he remembered the tactical order that Nelson had issued several weeks earlier stating that "...the commanders of divisions are strictly enjoined to keep their ships in the closest order possible, and on no account whatever to risk the separation of one of their ships." And later in the same order, "The commanders of divisions are to observe that no consideration is to induce them to separate in pursuing the enemy, unless by signal from me... and the ships are to be kept in that order that the whole squadron may act as a single ship."

On the other hand, Nelson was not there. He was miles away shepherding the other ships around the shoal. Foley had to make the call on his own. He remembered the almost daily meetings into which Nelson had called his captains during the chase to discuss tactics, if and when they found the French. He knew that Nelson was generally orthodox when it came to battle tactics; but he also encouraged his captains to make independent decisions if the situation called for it. Then he remembered something that Nelson had once said, "The boldest measures are the safest, gentlemen. The boldest measures are the safest," and that decided things for him.

At 6:15 PM Foley threw the *Goliath* across the bow of the *Guerrier,* the first ship in the French line, raked her as she went past, and turned to go up her inshore side. The next ship in the British line, the *Zealous,* followed Foley's lead, as did the *Audacious,* the *Orion* and the *Theseus.* Each ship poured a broadside into the hapless *Guerrier* as they went past.

In line-ahead situations like this, standard procedure for the previous 40 years was for the first British ship to engage the first enemy ship. The second British ship was to pass on the disengaged side of the first, and engage the second enemy ship. The third British ship, would then take on the third enemy, and so on. This was not to be at the Nile.

The *Goliath* wanted to drop her anchor so she would wind up next to the *Guerrier,* but she overshot her mark. Instead she wound up between the *Conquérant* and the *Spartiate,* the second and third French ships. Hood, seeing this, anchored the *Zealous* next to the *Guerrier,* whose captain refused to surrender, and opened fire. In short order the *Audacious* came up to help the *Goliath* to pound away at the *Conquérant.*

The *Orion* swung wide of all the engaged ships, and parked next to the *Peuple Souverain;* and the last ship of the first group, Robert Miller's *Theseus,* came up to take on the *Spartiate.* It wasn't done by the book; it didn't look pretty; but the first five British ships found a way to start hammering the first five French ships—on the opposite side from where they were expected.

Nelson saw what Foley had done and knew he had to keep his group of ships on the seaward side of the French so as to get them in a crossfire. The *Vanguard* accordingly pulled up on the outside of the *Spartiate*, the *Minotaur* next to the *Aquilon*, and the *Defence* found itself across from the *Peuple Souverain*. Every ship in the French van was now under attack.

At this point, the battle was all going in favor of the British. This was not to last, however. The next ship to come up was the *Bellerophon*, and she was to be nearly destroyed by a case of simple bad luck.

*****

"I'll have only topsails, Mr. Daniel," Captain Henry Darby snapped to his first lieutenant.

"Mr. Kirby, place us alongside the sixth ship in the French line, if you please. Head directly for her. Don't bother with following the line ahead."

"Aye, sir," the two men answered. The first lieutenant, Robert Daniel, began barking orders to the bosun; and Edward Kirby, the ship's Master, proceeded over to the helm. When all sails had been taken in except the fore and main topsails, Kirby broke the *Bellerophon* out of the British line. It was Captain Darby's intention to place his 74-gun ship next to the *Franklin*, an 80-gun French vessel. It would be a fair fight, and he was anxious to get it started.

The *Bellerophon* reached a position off the bow of the *Franklin* and turned so that the two ships would eventually be facing each other, starboard-to-starboard.

"Take in all sail," the captain called. "Mr. Daniel, release the anchor."

At a signal from the first lieutenant, a bosun's mate pulled on a knot, releasing the one remaining restraining line on the anchor. The massive iron hook splashed into the water and line began paying out down the ship's side as the she bled off her remaining forward momentum. At length the cable went ramrod straight, from the anchor, through a stern window, to the mizzen mast. The Bridport hemp of the anchor line squealed as it tightened to slow down the ship. The mizzenmast groaned as it took the strain of stopping the 1600 ton vessel.

But the *Bellerophon* did not stop.

"Mr. Daniel, what the devil is going on!" the captain shouted, the concern evident in his voice.

Daniel raced to the stern rail to look out at the anchor. "Sir, she's not holding! The anchor's dragging!"

At this point, there was nothing anyone could do to stop the impending disaster. The *Bellerophon* continued to slide down the side of the *Franklin*—past her midship, past her stern, passed the gap between ships, until she came to rest almost off the starboard beam of the next ship in the French line.

Anyone who was on deck, officers and men, stopped what they were doing and stared in open-mouthed astonishment. Towering over the *Bellerophon* was the massive 120-gun *Orient*. They were so close, Captain Darby could have thrown a rock from his quarterdeck to that of the opposing ship—if he could have thrown one that high. Unfortunately, rocks were not the missiles of choice that day, and the *Orient* immediately poured a 60-gun broadside into the *Bellerophon* as a way of welcoming her unexpected visit.

The shock to the British ship was so great that it literally moved her several feet sideways in the water. The gundeck was a scene of carnage and chaos. Breeching ropes snapped and guns were torn from their carriages as if a child had thrown a box of toy cannons across a narrow room. The low-ceilinged deck quickly filled with acrid smoke; and the only light came from the few battle lanterns that had not been extinguished by the French blast. Gun crews frantically picked themselves up and sought to pour a return volley into the enemy.

A second broadside came from the *Orient* disabling even more men with wood splinters and fragments. But order was starting to be restored. Sweating, smoke stained, men were heaving guns back into position, loading and firing. Years of training and discipline were now taking over as each man went into a well-rehearsed dance with their deadly weapons.

The gun fires and recoils backwards until its travel is halted by a series of breeching ropes. Immediately the gun crew descends on it. One man runs a "worm" down the length of the barrel—a pole with a corkscrew-like device at the end. This cleans out any hot embers left over from the previous firing. Next a wet sponge—a piece of padded sheepskin on the end of a pole—is run down the barrel. This extinguishes anything burning that might still be left.

Another man places a cylindrical flannel bag filled with gun powder in the mouth of the muzzle, and the first man runs it home with a plunger. After this, a circular wad is run down the barrel, followed by the shot, followed by another wad; and a group of men pull on a series of ropes and pulleys to run the gun's muzzle back out the gunport.

As soon as the powder is in place, the gun captain slides a hollow quill down the touchhole until the tip breaks the bag and enters it. This quill is filled with a special fast burning powder mixed with spirits of wine.

On this day little time is spent aiming the gun. The two ships are so close together, neither could possibly miss. The gunner simply runs his quoin under the breech of his gun to depress the muzzle as much as possible—and half the time he doesn't bother doing even that.

When the gun captain is satisfied with everything, he pulls on a lanyard. This releases a hammer on a mechanism that looks like the flintlock of a musket. The flint causes a spark, which ignites the powder in the hollow quill, which travels into the powder bag, which explodes, and sends the shot out the muzzle. This causes the gun to recoil back and the process begins all over again.

It was dirty, backbreaking work, punctuated by the possibility of death or dismemberment at any second. The world view of the sailors shrunk to the space of a few feet around them. They were no longer in the eastern Mediterranean. They were not even aboard a ship called the *Bellerophon*. Their entire world now consisted of whatever task lay immediately before them; and no thought was given to anything other than that task.

Guns fired with deafening regularity. Carriages rolled back. British smoke mixed with French until the mere act of breathing became an exercise in pain. Small boys raced about taking bags of powder to their gun crews. The wounded shrieked and the silent dead were dragged out of the way.

On it went, for over an hour, the 74-gun *Bellerophon* standing by herself, toe-to-toe, with the mighty *Orient*.

*****

The situation in the cockpit was not much better; but it was chaos of a different kind.

Laying in front of the operating theater, in all sorts of grotesque positions, were dozens of wounded men. In one corner was a man screaming with a long splinter sticking out of his eye. In another was a man desperately holding a tourniquet taut where once his right hand had been. Next to him was a huge burly man, whimpering like a child from burns that covered his chest, face, and arms. And next to him was a small almost effeminate-looking man who was bearing his wounds in complete silence. He was dead.

Susan had seen the horrors of battle before. But nothing had ever unnerved her quite like the high-pitched nasal sound that was drifting over the cries of the injured. It was George Bellman, at the operating table, amputating someone's leg... and singing.

> Oh they calls me hanging Johnny.
>   Away, boys, away.
> They say I hangs for money.
>   Oh hang, boys, hang.
>
> And first I hanged me father.
>   Away, boys, away.
> And first I hanged me father.
>   Oh hang, boys, hang.

Susan had no idea what to do. She was trying her best to work with the patients who were waiting, perhaps to give them water, or apply bandages, or stop a serious bleeding. Sometimes the only help she could give was a kind word or a smile; but, to the men, those simple acts meant everything.

Terry was in a state of complete shock. She was over to one side, folding and unfolding a bandage. Her brain simply could not process what her eyes were seeing. That fact had placed her in a state of stunned disbelief that caused her to be unable to do anything useful at all.

Susan's attention shifted back to Bellman.

> And then I hanged me mother.
>   Away, boys, away.
> My sister and my brother.
>   Oh hang, boys, hang.

The man's leg dropped off into a bucket placed at the end of the operating table.

"Next!" Bellman called. He didn't bother to cauterize and stitch up the man's stump. It had taken him over five minutes to perform the amputation, an unconscionable length of time in the days before anesthesia, and the patient had died about a minute into the operation. Nevertheless, Bellman proceeded to finish cutting his leg off.

"I say... N-e-x-t!" He called again. No one moved. The men desperately wanted treatment, but not from *him*.

Bellman wiped the blood from his cutting knife onto his apron, tipped his head back, and took a long pull from the laudanum flask he had in his pocket. At just that moment the *Bellerophon* was rocked by another blast from the *Orient*, which caused the mirrored lanterns above the operating table to sway.

"I am sorry," he said to no one in particular, "but this is simply unacceptable!" He threw his knife down on the deck. "How can a man work under these conditions? All that infernal racket. I am going on deck this very moment and demand they cease and desist."

He got as far as the ladder leading to the gundeck and stopped.

"No. As they say: if you want something done right, it's best you do it yourself. I shall personally lead a boarding party on to that other ship and end this disturbance myself."

He started making fencing motions. "Avast, you lubbers! Splice the main-mizzen, and shiver the poop deck!" And he disappeared up the ladder. He got to the gundeck, stepped over several dead bodies and proceeded up another latter to the wardroom. From there it was a quick walk to the quarterdeck.

The sun was setting as he emerged, but there was still enough light, compared to the near darkness below deck, to cause him to blink. When his day vision returned, he walked over to the starboard quarterdeck rail and began shaking his fist and swearing at the *Orient*.

Lieutenant Daniel was the first person to notice him. "Bellman! What the blazes do you think you are about? For God's sake—don't stand there!"

The next two people to see him were two marine sharpshooters stationed in the *Orient's* foretop. The first musket ball took away Bellman's lower jaw. He was quick enough to catch a part of it as it was swept away, and was curiously examining what had formerly been his teeth when the second musket ball hit. With a sound like a rock being thrown into wet mud, the ball entered his brain.

*****

Parish and Walker were sitting on a sharply rising hill overlooking Aboukir Bay. They were trying to sort out the scene before them.

"My God," Parish exclaimed. "That first French ship has been raked again."

"But look at where the British are firing from," Walker added. "How did those ships get between the French and the shore? How did they know the water was deep enough there?"

"There's a second group bearing down on the outside. What ship is that? The one leading the second group?"

"That's the *Vanguard*," Walker replied. See that thin streamer at the top of the mainmast? That's Nelson's pennant."

"Then where is the *Bellerophon*?"

"I don't know. Wait. See the ship that has sheered off from the back of Nelson's group?"

"Yes."

"That's the *Bellerophon*."

"How do you know? They all look the same to me."

"Look at her fore topsail. See how the right one-third of it is so much whiter than the rest?"

"Yes."

"That's the replacement panel they put in just before we left when the old one tore out."

And from then on their eyes were glued on that one ship.

They saw her make her approach on the *Franklin*, and slide past into the jaws of the *Orient*. They visibly winced when the first broadside went into the side of the *Bellerophon,* and became progressively more concerned with each passing minute of the unequal battle.

"William, we've got to get back on board. They're being pounded. God knows what the casualties must be."

"I agree, but how... wait a minute... look there." William was pointing down toward the beach.

"What?"

"Over there." And Walker finally made out a small ship's boat grounded against a rock outcropping. They didn't know whether it belonged to French sailors who were ashore when the battle started, and decided that ashore was a good place to stay, or whether it was cast adrift by one of the combatant ships. It also didn't matter. It was a way to get on board the *Bellerophon* again.

*****

Word quickly spread to the cockpit that Surgeon Bellman had been killed. It was received with a mixture of relief and dismay by the wounded. Part of each man was relieved that he would not have to undergo treatment at his hands; but another part asked the question: Who *was* going to treat them?

It was the same question that Susan was asking herself, until the answer suddenly became obvious. It had to be her.

She felt a weight descend that she had never known before. She had served for years as a surgeon's mate, but she had never been a surgeon. She had assisted in countless operations, but had never herself held the knife.

She recoiled at the thought. She wouldn't. She couldn't.

Then she thought about a conversation she had once had with Lucas Walker. It was back when they were on the old *Richmond*, and Lucas found himself summarily appointed the ship's surgeon, against his will. He refused to do it, until Susan finally leveled with him. Her mind flashed through the conversation as if it was yesterday.

The armorer had just finished sharpening the ship's surgical instruments and she came over to Walker who was standing by the larboard rail. "Mr. Walker, may I have a word with you," she said rather sternly.

"Sure Susan. How's it going?"

She ignored his question. "Do you know what's in this chest?"

"Yes, I saw the armorer sharpening them. They're surgical instruments... some rather nasty-looking saws and knives."

Susan nodded. "And do you know what they're for?"

Walker was getting a bit disturbed. Why was she talking to me like I was a child, he thought. "Yes, I do. If we get into a battle, men are going to be hurt, some very seriously. Some will have to be operated on, legs removed and such."

"Uh-huh. And precisely who do you think will be wielding these instruments if and when that comes to pass?"

It was at that point that the enormity of Captain Hudson's words came back to him: "...and you will also be the Ship's Surgeon."

"Holy Mother of God," he muttered. "Susan, you're not suggesting that I... I mean, look, I have no training, no experience at all in... I couldn't possibly..." Walker was unable to get a coherent sentence out.

"Mr. Walker, like it or not, you are the ship's surgeon. Now, I've been doing the sick calls and all the other work ever since you were appointed. I don't mind that, but you're going to have to start pulling your weight."

"No, you don't understand, Susan. You see I am *not* a physician. All right, I know a little about anatomy, sure, but that doesn't qualify me to take care of the sick and wounded, and it certainly doesn't qualify me to perform operations."

Susan looked at Walker for a long moment, cocked her head and said: "Do I somehow look like I went to Oxford?"

"No, but..."

"But nothing. I was made assistant to a surgeon who hasn't had two back-to-back days of sobriety since I've known him. Men were suffering, and in some cases dying, because of his incompetence. So, do you know what I did?"

Walker shook his head dumbly.

"I learned, Mr. Walker. I learned." And, with that, she spun on her heels and proceeded below to the infirmary.

She sighed as she thought about how young they both were back then; and she proceeded to the corner where Terry Parish was sitting on the floor.

"Terry! Terry, look at me." Susan said as she knelt beside the still stricken woman. "George Bellman is dead."

That seemed to penetrate her brain somewhat. "Dead? Why is he dead?"

"I don't know the details, but you've got to help me."

"Help you do what?" Her voice still seemed far away.

"I've got to take over the surgery; and you've got to take over my job."

Her head pivoted around. "Do your job? I can't do your job. Those men are..." Just as she began the sentence a man a few feet away started vomiting blood. Terry shrieked and scuttled quickly away. Susan caught up to her.

"Yes, do my job, or at least part of it. Terry, I am not asking you to do anything you can't do."

"But I..."

"Can you give a man a drink of water?"

"Well, yes."

"Can you adjust a bandage, or help a man lie a little more comfortably?"

"Yes."

"Good. Then do it." She handed her a water bucket with a ladle sticking out of it. "If you do nothing more than say a kind word or two, you'll be helping enormously."

She looked at he water bucket in her hands as if she were still undecided.

"Terry, suppose William were one of those men..."

The look of doubt disappeared from her eyes.

*****

The two men slid down the steep embankment and half-walked, half-trotted, over to the rock formation. Parish was the first to get there; but instead of proceeding to work the boat free from its grounding, he stood silent, looking down into it.

"Well, how is it?" Walker said as he caught up.

"It's not," Parish said in disgust as he turned away. He looked out to sea at the *Bellerophon* being hammered only a short distance away and his face mirrored his frustration.

Walker looked at the boat. It was a small two-man rowboat. Of the four oars, one was shattered, one was missing, but two seemed to be in workable condition. One of the rower's benches was broken, the other intact. But the biggest problem was that there was an eight-inch hole in it's bottom. The fact that it had been beached kept it from filling with more than about six inches of water; but, still, it was unusable.

"I can't believe it," William said. "I simply can't believe it. We've come all this way. There's the *Bellerophon* in sight; and we can't do a damn thing to get to her." In his exasperation he picked up a stone and threw it down inside the boat. It made a splash.

Walker stood looking at the boat for a long moment. "Maybe not. I have an idea. Wait here."

He turned and retraced his steps back up the hill to where the horses were trying to decided if the sawgrass at their feet was worth eating. He got something from the saddle bag of his horse and returned to where Parish was still standing.

"All right. Let's go. Get in the boat and sit down." Parish looked at Walker quizzically, but did as he was asked. He started to sit on the one remaining rowing bench when Walker said: "No, not there."

Parish looked around him, confused. "There's no where else to sit."

"Yes, there is. On the hole."

"On the hole?"

"You'd rather row?"

Parish did as directed. "Oh! This is cold"

"Sometimes you have to make sacrifices for king and country," Walker said unsympathetically. He then gave him the drinking gourd he had retrieved from his saddle bag. "Now, start bailing while I push off."

And in this manner a proud new addition to His Majesty's Royal Navy set forth to rendezvous with the *Bellerophon*.

*****

Captain Darby had been hit. A musket ball had grazed his head knocking him unconscious. He was taken below. Lieutenant Daniel, the first lieutenant, assumed command.

Lieutenant Daniel took a flesh wound to his left arm, but refused to leave his post. As he was about to give an order to one of the midshipmen, a cannon ball took off his right leg. As he was being carried below, a spray of grapeshot killed both him and the man who was assisting him. Philip Lander, the second lieutenant, assumed command.

About 8:00 PM a lucky shot from the *Orient* shattered the mizzenmast. It came down slowly, almost gracefully, and crashed across the stern. As men worked frantically to cut this mast away, another ball hit the mainmast. It too started a graceful descent, but this time the consequences were greater. It fell forward and to the right, landing on the starboard side of the forecastle. In so doing, it crashed through the rigging of the foremast, taking it's yards down. The sky suddenly started to rain blocks, tackle, canvas, and ropes. One spar landed on Lieutenant Lander, killing him. Robert Cathcart, the third lieutenant, now took command.

Lieutenant Cathcart looked around him in horror. The captain and the two officers above him had been killed or wounded. The fourth lieutenant, John Hadaway, had been wounded and taken to the cockpit, along with Edward Kirby the Master. The fifth lieutenant, George Jolliffe, had been killed, but he didn't know how. He was now the only officer above the rank of midshipman who was still standing, and even one of the midshipmen had been wounded.

The only thing he knew for sure was that when Captain Darby had found the *Bellerophon* next to the *Orient*, he fought her. And if that's what the captain intended, that's what he would do... at least for as long as he too remained alive.

But the effect of the *Bellerophon's* mauling was being felt in places other than the quarterdeck. Susan had organized Terry, the surgeon's mates, the loblolly boys, and even the purser and the cook, both of whom had innocently wandered into the cockpit, into an effective unit. But, despite this organization, the unit was being overwhelmed.

Susan interspersed amputations with treating bullet wounds, with removing huge splinters, with treating concussions. Sometimes the men lived, sometimes they were dead by the time she got to them, and sometimes they died under her care. Either way, she had to keep going. She had to do her best—no matter what. It would be what Lucas would have... no, she thought... no time to think about that.

She looked up and saw that Terry had been transformed. She went from abject fear, to tentatively offering water to a few men, to aggressively managing the patients. She seemed to be everywhere at once, bandaging a patient here, staunching the bleeding there, offering a word of encouragement somewhere else. She directed the flow of men to Susan by assessing which ones needed her attention the most. She was right far more often than not. She had found a reservoir of strength inside her that she never knew was there—and she would never be the same as a result of having found it.

Susan heard a squeal come from Terry and saw her rush over to the gun deck ladder. She couldn't imagine what could have caused her to do that after she had been doing so well. Then she saw William Parish come down the stairway. She held her breath... and Lucas Walker came down as well.

Terry had William in her arms. Susan rushed over to Lucas and, before she had a chance to think about it, threw her arms around his neck and kissed him. Lucas responded with a passion that he had forgotten he possessed. The two of them quickly became lost in a world of their own. Then, as if the thought "what are we doing" occurred to them both at the same time, Susan pulled away. Unexpectedly, she delivered a blow to his chest that would leave a bruise for the next three days.

"You bastard! What do you think you're doing—going off like that without telling me! Don't you ever... and I mean *ever*... do that again!!"

"Good to see you too, Susan." Walker smiled while rubbing his chest. "Did ya miss me?"

She kissed him again.

*****

By 9:00 it was reported that the *Orient* was on fire; and that scared Lieutenant Cathcart even more than the enemy guns.

The ships of that period were little more than floating fire traps. They were made almost entirely of wood. The ropes were coated with flammable tar as a preservative. Even the seams of the deck planks were caulked with tarred oakum. The paint used on the hull and masts was flammable, as was the canvas that was used in her sails. To make matters worse, several months in the hot Mediterranean sun had dried out the wood and the sails, and the tar had become soft and runny.

But the worst part—the part that truly caused the fear—was that all of the above was wrapped around several tons of gun powder stored below deck.

Saying that a ship close aboard your own was on fire was tantamount to saying that your ship was *about* to catch fire. Cathcart therefore knew he had to get away from the *Orient* before it was too late; but that would not be an easy task.

His mainmast and mizzenmast were gone. The foremast was still standing, but just barely. It would never handle the stress of a sail. So Cathcart ordered a spritsail to be placed on the bowsprit. This was a small sail that hung from a yardarm and attached to the bow of the ship. He then ordered that the anchor cable be cut.

For a while, it worked. The spritsail filled and, in obedience to the northwest wind, the ship slowly started to gather speed, moving away from her endangered foe. But the boom to which the spritsail was connected was itself linked to the foremast for support. When the sail filled, it put a strain on the *Bellerophon's* one remaining mast and soon brought it down with a sickening crash. She was now completely dismasted.

But the movement of the ship had begun and enough momentum was built up so that she would continue to drift slowly away from the *Orient*. This, however, only brought a fresh danger.

The *Swiftsure* and the *Alexander* were 74-gun ships just like the *Bellerophon*. They were in the third attack group and their task was to get the *Orient* in a cross-fire between them, the *Alexander* on the inside and the *Swiftsure* on the outside.

The sun had set several hours previously and, except for the flashes of gunfire, the night was pitch black. When the *Swiftsure* arrived on station, she didn't know that she was occupying the position formerly held by the *Bellerophon*. What she did know was that she could see a dismasted ship a short distance away and assumed it was French.

The order was given to load her larboard guns to give the *coup de grâce* to this French wreck and put her out of her misery. But something caused her captain, Ben Hallowell, to hold his fire. He couldn't quite put his finger on why, but he just wasn't sure about things. Suddenly the voice of one of his junior lieutenants cut through the night. "Sir, don't fire! Don't fire! She's British! I know her; she's the *Bellerophon*."

And the *Bellerophon* dodged yet another potentially deadly bullet.

*****

While the *Bellerophon* was officially out of the fight, Walker's job was hardly over. With a sigh of resignation he assumed his position at the operating table. He briefly looked over at Susan and Terry, and smiled. They had quickly joined forces to bring at least some relief to those who were waiting. It was as if the two women had worked together their whole lives, the strengths of one supporting the weaknesses of the other.

Walker began his gruesome work.

The first patient was Sergeant Maxey. His legs were broken in so many places that when he was lifted on to the table, they hung down like tentacles. He did not live long enough for Walker to set them. One of the jagged bones had severed an artery and he bled to death internally.

Robert Reardon was next. He had been shot in the chest. Walker was able to extract the bullet as well as the bits of clothing that had gone in with the ball. Reardon was young. Walker thought he would live.

Next came a series of head wounds and fractured skulls, followed by a shattered knee, two people with broken ribs, and a man who had lost three fingers on his right hand.

That last patient seemed to trigger a wave of amputations, and Walker did four in a row—an arm, two legs, and a man who had to lose both legs and one arm. Two of the first three died. The man with only one limb left, Seaman Nieley, lived. Walker almost wished he hadn't because he knew what was in store for him for the rest of his life.

The next patient was a man he knew well. It was Lawrence Curren, a sailor with whom he used to play an occasional game of chess. Curran was both amazingly intelligent, and completely uneducated; a combination that Walker always thought was tragic. He was clutching his stomach as Parish helped him on to the table.

"Lawrence, what brings you to my thriving practice?"

"Well, doc, I don't mean ter be no shirker—yer know ahm not that sort'a lad—but I got a 'urt in me belly and ever'body said I should 'ave ya take a look."

"I am sure it's not too bad; but let me see anyway."

Curren removed his hands and about a third of his intestines fell out.

Walker had no sooner tucked the man's innards back and sewn him up, when something happened that defied description. You couldn't really say that you heard an explosion, because it was so powerful it was felt more than heard. The *Bellerophon* rocked heavily from side to side. Almost everyone standing was knocked off their feet, and the air seemed to be sucked out of the room.

Walker picked himself up. He knew that they had not blown up, but only because the *Bellerophon's* powder room was only one deck below where he was standing. But, what was it?

"William, go topside and find out what the hell is going on."

William Parish scurried up several ladders and reached the weather deck. There he stopped and stared along with every other man from both fleets. The *Orient* had literally disintegrated.

After the *Bellerophon* had been dispatched, the crew of the *Orient* began fighting their fire in earnest. It was an uphill struggle. Some people say the fire was fed by the paint that the crew had recently been using to freshen up the ship. Others say it was fed by flammable chemicals that Napoleon's academicians had stored on board. Whatever was the cause, it was raging out of control; and matters were made worse by the *Alexander* and the *Swiftsure* who were pouring shot into the *Orient* as fast as they could load their guns. In addition, the Marine sharpshooters in the *Alexander's* tops were placing a withering fire down on the *Orient's* deck, keeping the firefighters from reaching the blaze.

Admiral Brueys might have been able to solve the problem, but he was dead. He had been standing on his quarterdeck when a round shot almost cut him in half. He refused to be carried below, ordering instead to be placed in a chair, saying: "*Un amiral français doit mourir sur son banc de quart.*" [A French admiral is duty bound to die at his post.] A minute later a second round shot took off his head.

As the flames grew higher and higher, the ships in the vicinity began to close their gunports and move all powder charges deep into their hulls. Those who could haul their anchor and move away, did so. They knew what was about to happen, and happen it did.

About 10:00 the fire reached the *Orient's* fore magazine and it blew. That, in turn, touched off the main magazine. Tons of gunpowder erupted, throwing whole sections of the *Orient* into the air. Pieces of wood—and pieces of human beings—rained down on the surrounding ships. Four thousand pound guns were thrown over a quarter-mile away. For a moment the blast had turned night into day, and the subsequent burning hulk cast an eerie glow over the proceedings for the rest of the night.

For a span of 10 minutes not a shot was fired by either side. Officers and men, French and British, stood in mute amazement at the enormity of what they had just seen. Of the more than 1000 men on the *Orient*, all but 70 of them had been vaporized in an instant.

As the shock wore off, firing began again; but, for all practical purposes, the battle was over. The French ships in the van were so badly mauled they were barely able to get off a shot anymore; and they started to surrender. Nelson ordered his ships to move down the line and find new quarry. The ships did so, but when they arrived at their stations the French did not fire. Of the thirteen French ships of the line, two escaped, and the rest either surrendered or were sunk.

When the sun rose the following morning, Aboukir Bay was the scene of a carnage such as few had ever witnessed. As one observer put it: "The whole Bay was covered with dead bodies, mangled, wounded and scorched, not a bit of clothes on them except their trousers."

Nelson quickly organized his ships to mount what rescue efforts he could. He eventually landed almost 1000 wounded Frenchmen in Alexandria so they could be treated by their own physicians. But in mounting this effort he noticed that one of his ships was missing—the *Bellerophon.*

He sent Captain Miller in the *Theseus* to find her. He did. Six miles away. There was not a single mast standing, she could barely keep afloat; but the British flag had been nailed to the stump of the mainmast and was waving in the fresh morning breeze.

CHAPTER NINE

The following day was more than a little hectic for Horatio Nelson. He had a thousand details concerning the battle to wrap up; and he had a splitting headache.

The headache was understandable. During the battle his flagship had taken on the *Spartiate*, but was also receiving fire from the *Aquilon*. At one point a piece of shrapnel caught him in the forehead, opening up a serious gash. Nelson fell, a piece of skin covering his one remaining eye. When Captain Berry went to him, he dramatically cried, "Berry, I am killed. Remember me to my wife." They took him below to the surgeon, Michael Jefferson, who took one look, pushed the skin back, declared it a superficial wound, and applied a bandage. But Nelson would not believe the wound was superficial and sent for his chaplain, Stephen Comyn. As the battle raged on outside, Nelson conferred with his pastor in the breadroom of the ship where they would not be disturbed.

That's not to say that the wound had no effect. It really did hurt, and he really did have a blinding headache. Nevertheless, he sat down to write a report to his superior, Sir John Jervis.

Vanguard, off the Mouth of the Nile,
August 3, 1798

My Lord,

ALMIGHTY GOD has blessed His Majesty's Arms in the late Battle, by a great Victory over the Fleet of the Enemy, whom I attacked at sun-set on the 1st of August off the Mouth of the Nile.

The Enemy were moored in a strong line of battle, for defending the entrance of the Bay (of Shoals), flanked by numerous Gunboats, four Frigates, and a battery of guns and mortars on an Island in their Van; but nothing could withstand the Squadron your Lordship did me the honour to place under my Command. Their high state of discipline is well known to you, and with the judgment of the Captains, together with their Valour, and that of the Officers and Men of every description, it was absolutely irresistible.

Could any thing from my pen add to the characters of the Captains, I would write it with pleasure; but that is impossible.

I have to regret the loss of Captain Westcott of the Majestic, who was killed early in the Action; but the Ship was continued to be so well fought by her First Lieutenant, Mr. Cuthbert, that I have given him an order to command her, till your Lordship's pleasure is known.

The Ships of the Enemy, all but their two rear Ships, are nearly dismasted; and those two, with two Frigates, I am sorry to say, made their escape: nor was it, I assure you, in my power to prevent them. Captain Hood most handsomely endeavoured to do it; but I had no Ship in a condition to support the Zealous, and I was obliged to call her in.

The support and assistance I have received from Captain Berry cannot be sufficiently expressed. I was wounded in the Head, and obliged to be carried off the Deck, but the Service suffered no loss by that event. Captain Berry was fully equal to the important service then going on, and to him I must beg leave to refer you for every information relative to this Victory. He will present you with the Flag of the Second in Command, that of the Commander in Chief being burnt in the L'Orient.

Herewith I transmit you Lists of the Killed and Wounded, and the Lines of Battle of ourselves and the French.

I have the Honour to be, &c.
HORATIO NELSON.

To Admiral the Earl of St. Vincent,
Commander in Chief, &c. &c. &c.
Off Cadiz.

Line of Battle

1	Culloden	T. Troubridge, Captain	74 Guns	590 Men
2	Theseus	R.W. Miller, Captain	74 Guns	590 Men
3	Alexander	Alex. John Ball, Captain	74 Guns	590 Men
4	Vanguard	Rear-Admiral Sir Horatio Nelson, K.B., Edward Berry, Captain	74 Guns	696 Men
5	Minotaur	Thomas Louis, Captain	74 Guns	640 Men
6	Leander	Thomas B. Thompson, Captain	50 Guns	343 Men
7	Swiftsure	B. Hallowell, Captain	74 Guns	590 Men
8	Audacious	Davidge Gould, Captain	74 Guns	590 Men
9	Defence	John Peyton, Captain	74 Guns	590 Men
10	Zealous	Samuel Hood, Captain	74 Guns	590 Men
11	Orion	Sir James Saumarez, Captain	74 Guns	590 Men
12	Goliath	Thomas Foley, Captain	74 Guns	590 Men
13	Majestic	George B. Westcott, Captain	74 Guns	590 Men
14	Bellero-phon	Henry D'E. Darby, Captain	74 Guns	590 Men
	La Mutine		Brig	

French Line of Battle

1	Le Guerrier	74 Guns	700 Men	Taken
2	Le Conquérant	74 Guns	700 Men	Taken
3	Le Spartiate	74 Guns	700 Men	Taken

4	L'Aquilon	74 Guns	700 Men	Taken
5	Le Souverain Peuple	74 Guns	700 Men	Taken
6	Le Franklin, Blanquet, First Contre Amiral	80 Guns	800 Men	Taken
7	L'Orient, Brueys, Admiral and Commander-in-Chief	120 Guns	1010 Men	Burnt
8	Le Tonnant	80 Guns	800 Men	Taken
9	L'Heureux	74 Guns	700 Men	Taken
10	Le Timoleon	74 Guns	700 Men	Burnt
11	Le Mercure	74 Guns	700 Men	Taken
12	Le Guillaume Tell, Villeneuve, Second Contre Amiral	80 Guns	800 Men	Escaped
13	Le Généreux	74 Guns	700 Men	Escaped
14	La Diane	48 Guns	300 Men	Escaped
15	La Justice	44 Guns	300 men	Escaped
16	L'Artemise	36 Guns	250 Men	Burnt
17	La Sèrieuse	36 Guns	250 Men	Dismasted and Sunk

A RETURN OF THE KILLED AND WOUNDED IN HIS MAJESTY'S SHIPS, UNDER THE COMMAND OF SIR HORATIO NELSON, K.B., REAR-ADMIRAL OF THE BLUE, ETC. IN ACTION WITH THE FRENCH, AT ANCHOR, ON THE 1ST OF AUGUST, 1798, OFF THE MOUTH OF THE NILE.

Theseus.—5 Seamen killed; 1 Officer, 24 Seamen, 5 Marines wounded. —Total 35.

Alexander.—1 Officer, 13 Seamen killed; 5 Officers, 48 Seamen, 5 Marines , wounded.—Total 72.

Vanguard.—3 Officers, 20 Seamen, 7 Marines, killed; 7 Officers, 60 Seamen, 8 Marines, wounded.—Total 105.

Minotaur.—2 Officers, 18 Seamen, 3 Marines, killed, 4 Officers, 54 Seamen, 6 Marines, wounded.—Total 87.

Swiftsure.—7 Seamen killed; 1 Officer, 1 9 Seamen, 2 Marines, wounded.—Total 29.

Audacious.—1 Seaman killed; 2 Officers, 31 Seamen, 2 Marines, wounded.—Total 36.

Defence.—3 Seamen, 1 Marine, killed; 9 Seamen, 2 Marines, wounded.—Total 15.

Zealous.—1 Seaman killed; 7 Seamen wounded.—Total 8.

Orion.—1 Officer, 11 Seamen, 1 Marine killed; 5 Officers, 18 Seamen, 6 Marines, wounded.—Total 42.

Goliath.—2 Officers, 12 Seamen, 7 Marines, killed; 4 Officers, 28 Seamen, 9 Marines, wounded.—Total 62.

Majestic.—3 Officers, 33 Seamen, 14 Marines, killed; 3 Officers, 124 Seamen, 16 Marines, wounded.—Total 193.

Bellerophon.—4 Officers, 32 Seamen, 13 Marines, killed; 5 Officers, 126 Seamen, 17 Marines, wounded.—Total 197.

Leander.—14 Seamen wounded.

Total.—16 Officers, 156 Seamen, 46 Marines, killed; 37 Officers, 562 Seamen, 78 Marines wounded.—Total, 895.

OFFICERS KILLED.

Vanguard.—Captain William Faddy, Marines; Mr. Thomas Seymour, Mr. John G. Taylor, Midshipmen.

Alexander.—Mr. John Collins, Lieutenant.

Orion.—Mr. Baird, Captain's Clerk.

Goliath.—Mr. William Davies, Master's Mate; Mr. Andrew Brown, Midshipman.

Majestic.—George B. Westcott, Esq. Captain; Mr. Zebedee Ford, Midshipman; Mr. Andrew Gilmour, Boatswain.

Bellerophon.—Mr. Robert Savage Daniel, Mr. Philip Watson Launder, Mr. George Joliffe, Lieutenants; Mr. Thomas Ellison, Master's Mate.

Minotaur.—Lieutenant John S. Kirchner, Marines; Mr. Peter Walters, Master's Mate.

OFFICERS WOUNDED.

Vanguard.—Mr. Nathaniel Vassal, Mr. John M. Adye, Lieutenants; Mr. John Campbell, Admiral's Secretary; Mr. Michael Austin, Boatswain; Mr. John Weatherstone, Mr. George Antrim, Midshipmen.

Theseus.—Lieutenant Hawkins.

Alexander.—Alexander J. Ball, Esq., Captain; Captain J. Cresswell, Marines; Mr. William Lawson, Master; Mr. George Bulley, Mr. Luke Anderson, Midshipmen.

Audacious.—Mr. John Jeans, Lieutenant; Mr. Christopher Font, Gunner.

Orion.—Sir James Saumarez, Captain; Mr. Peter Sadler, Boatswain; Mr. Philip Richardson, Mr. Charles Miell, Mr. Lanfesty, Midshipmen.

Goliath—Mr. William Wilkinson, Lieutenant; Mr. Lawrence Graves, Midshipman; Mr. Peter Strachan, Schoolmaster; Mr. James Payne, Midshipman.

Majestic.—Mr. Charles Seward, Mr. Charles Royle, Midshipmen; Mr. Robert Overton, Captain's Clerk.

Bellerophon.—H. D'E. Darby, Esq., Captain; Mr. Edward Kirby, Master; Captain John Hopkins, Marines; Mr. Chapman, Boatswain; Mr. Nicholas Bettson, Midshipman.

Minotaur.—Mr. Thomas Irwin, Lieutenant; Mr. John Jewell, Lieutenant Marines; Mr. Thomas Foxten, 2nd Master; Mr. Martin Wills, Midshipman.

Swiftsure.—Mr. William Smith, Midshipman.

*****

The *Tigre* was a picture of organized confusion. Several days earlier all hands had been recalled from shore and were busy storing the hundreds of items that a ship needed to get underway. The heaviest items, food and water in particular, had to be carefully stowed. Where that weight was carried effected the ship's trim, and Smith was very particular about that.

The speed of a ship was not necessarily determined solely by how much sail she was carrying. The condition of her hull— whether it was encrusted with barnacles, for example—was a major factor, as was the ship's trim. Smith couldn't do much about the barnacles, but trim was another matter.

A ship that was badly balanced would yaw excessively when the seas got high. If the trim were biased toward the stern, she would tend to fall off the wind. If it were biased toward the bow, it would pitch heavily into oncoming waves. In short, a ship that was out of trim would sail like an unruly pig—almost impossible to control or maneuver.

A few minutes earlier Smith had left the ship's purser and the first lieutenant to continue the task of stowage. The purser was there to make sure they were getting all the supplies they had paid for; and the first lieutenant was there to make sure it was put away properly.

Wandering back to his cabin, he resolved to get some of the endless paperwork done. He sat at his desk, looking for a while at the harbor through his gallery windows.

Durbin was fussing in the background, putting Smith's personal effects away. He would put something into a drawer, then take it out, put it on a shelf, and place something new into the drawer. Then he would take that item out, replace the item from the shelf back into the drawer, and put the new item into a chest. This process would go on for hours until, through some mystical insight or another, he had determined that "everthin' was Bristol fashion."

Smith sighed, convinced that he would never understand his servant, but that didn't matter. He genuinely liked Durbin. He liked his openness, and honesty, and sense of duty. Smith had been born into the minor gentry, Durbin to a day laborer, yet in many ways, he admired—even envied—him.

He dipped a quill into the inkwell and, at his brother's suggestion, wrote a letter to the British ambassador at the court of Naples, Sir William Hamilton. It read in part:

I hope to be off Alexandria soon with time enough to burn a little of the Tigre's powder. I look forward to seeing again my friend the zealous Hood, who, as my junior, naturally falls under my orders when we meet. You can no doubt see the advantages of a policy which provides diplomatic rank to the naval officer who will have to act in concert with the Russians and Turks.

Sir William did not see the advantages of Smith having those powers, nor did Admiral Jervis, nor did Rear-Admiral Nelson, and later it was nearly to cost Sidney Smith his life.

*****

Just after the Battle of the Pyramids, Napoleon held out an olive branch to the Mamelukes. He sent the Austrian consul in Cairo, Carlo Rosetti, as an envoy to meet with the Mameluke leader, Murad Bey. Rosetti was to convey an offer. If Murad Bey would lay down his arms, Napoleon would give him Girga province in Upper Egypt as his personal fiefdom. Murad Bey sent the following reply: "Tell the commander-in-chief to assemble all his troops and go back to Alexandria. I shall pay him 10,000 gold purses to cover his army's expenses. In doing so, he will spare his soldiers' lives and save me the trouble of fighting him."

Napoleon was outraged. After hearing this he sent one of his best generals, Louis Desaix, after Murad Bey with orders to hunt him down at all costs.

But what could have caused such an arrogant reply? What Murad Bey knew, and Napoleon didn't, was that the French fleet had been destroyed at Aboukir Bay. To him, it was now just a matter of time before the French army would be defeated.

Napoleon received the news of the naval defeat on August 13th at Es Saliya, a small town near the edge of the Sinai Desert. What happened next is perhaps best described by a letter written by Dominique Larrey, the chief surgeon with Napoleon's army. It was to his wife in Paris, and read in part:

> The news that the fleet had been lost was shattering. We could see that all communication with France was now at an end, and many started to give up hope of ever going home. I had never seen morale so low; but, strangely, Napoleon did not seem to be affected.

> He called together his officers, myself included, into a large meeting. I will never forget his opening words:

> "Well, gentlemen, now we are obliged to accomplish great things; and we shall accomplish them. We must found a great empire, and we shall found it. The sea, of which we are no longer master, separates us from our

homeland, but no sea separates us from either Africa or Asia."

His fleet might have been destroyed, but Napoleon and his army was still alive, and well, and living in Egypt.

HISTORICAL POSTSCRIPT

Historical novels are, by definition, based on historical events. But, after completing one, most readers are left with the question: How much of what I just read actually happened, and how much was created, or at least modified, to fit the author's story line? For that reason, all of my novels contain a "Historical Postscript" where I can separate fact from fiction for you. I thought that that might be an interesting feature, but I had no idea how popular it would be until reader response to the first two books started to come in.

As you will see, most of the major events in this book, as well as the others, are based on actual occurrences. Simply put, Sir Sidney Smith led an extraordinary life; and it's a good thing he did. There's no way I could have made up this stuff on my own.

CHAPTER ONE

The first two paragraphs of the letter that opens the book were actually written by Sir Sidney to his mother from the Abbaye Prison, on April 28, 1796. This is the prison in which he was held prior to being transferred to the Temple; and the paragraphs contain only minor editing by me. The rest of the letter I made up to get you oriented to time, place and circumstance.

I should point out first that Sir Sidney was indeed held in the very same rooms that once held Louis XVI prior to his execution. I managed to locate an item-by-item description of those rooms (I am rather proud of that, by the way), and there is no reason to believe that they would have substantively changed between Louis XVI death in 1793 and Smith's arrival in 1796.

I know it sounds farfetched to have Sir Sidney operating a spy ring (of all things) from inside a maximum security prison in the middle of Paris, but... I didn't make that up, folks. That's exactly what he did. Sir Sidney was heavily involved in espionage throughout his career (as you will see in these books). Indeed, many of the misunderstandings and hard feelings that occurred later in his career between Smith and some of his superiors happened because he simply could not tell them what he was actually doing.

The same thing, I believe, was true of Smith's reported idiosyncrasies such as his alleged large ego, constant boasting about his accomplishments, occasionally strange manner of dress, etc. I believe these were part of a well thought-out campaign of misdirection on his part. You see, most people don't bother to dig deeper into a person once they have written him off as a fool or a blowhard; and I believe that was exactly what Sir Sidney wanted. I can guarantee you this, however. Sir Sidney was many things during his life, but a fool was not among them.

I made up Smith's conversation with the gardener on the question of the dauphin's death. However, the controversy it represents is real and has been raging for over 200 years. Did the dauphin really die in the Temple Prison in 1795, or was he spirited away by Royalist sympathizers? And, if he made good his escape, where did he go? Dozens of people later claimed that they were the real dauphin; and others made claims on behalf of still more. In the latter category was John James Audubon, the famous American naturalist and painter. Many people have argued that he was, in fact, the missing dauphin, although as far as I know he never claimed it himself.

Smith's servant when in prison was in fact the Chouan officer François de Tromelin. He was given the hastily constructed persona of John Bromley, a French-Canadian, only minutes before they were captured on April 19, 1796. John Wesley Wright was also a real person, a master spy, and incarcerated with Sir Sidney. The little that is known about Wright is utterly fascinating. The problem is that, as a spy, his job was to *not* leave any traces. As a result, reconstructing anything like a biography of him is nearly impossible. Nevertheless, both he and de Tromelin will appear many times in these books, just as they did in Sir Sidney's life.

Lucas Walker is, of course, a fictional character; but an attempt was indeed made to exchange Captain Jacques Bergeret for Sir Sidney. The deal eventually fell apart, but only after Bergeret had actually been delivered on French soil. His sense of honor, however, required him to return to England and resume his life as a prisoner. Later, after Smith made his escape to England, the British government ordered Bergeret released and returned to France with no exchange required.

The *coup d'état* of 18 Fructidor (September 4, 1797) actually occurred as described and was the event that established Napoleon (and his army) as the true power in France.

Richard Etches and Antoine Viscovitch were real people, as described, and were involved in arranging for Sir Sidney's escape. In all likelihood Etches was the financier of the plot, and spent at least £10,000 in getting Smith and Wright free. Viscovitch was probably the one who obtained the signed blank sheet of paper from de Pléville's office, although whether that was done by theft or bribery is unclear.

Georges de Pléville was also a real person, and in fact did the things described. He really did lose his leg to British privateers; he really did rescue John Jervis in 1770; and he really did have a signed blank page stolen from his office. As you know, this blank sheet, appropriately filled in, plays a major role in Chapter Two.

The signaling system with the "magic lantern" projecting letters on a sheet and Sir Sidney signaling back by grabbing bars, was *not* made up. That is exactly how communication from his prison cell was done. (I told you, I couldn't make up this stuff if I tried.)

The head jailor at the Temple was indeed Antoine Boniface who succeeded Mutius Lasne the previous September. The specific dinner described here and the walk outside the prison was fictional. However, Sir Sidney did occasionally have "parole" privileges; and there were even instances where Smith and the warden would go out together and get so drunk that they had trouble getting back in to the prison. But, as Walker explained to Whitney that evening, giving one's word (in this case not to escape) was taken *very* seriously. Once that word was given, neither Smith nor Walker would have ever thought of escaping—under any circumstances.

The message warning of a possible escape attempt within ten days was—word-for-word—real; and the escape, in fact, occurred ten days later.

CHAPTER TWO

Writing with accuracy about any historical person is difficult. It is made even more so in the case of Sir Sidney Smith because, first, in order to cover his espionage activities, often even *he* did not reveal the full story; and second, because the writers of the day were not particularly conscientious about declaring whether what they were writing was fact or fiction. I have found, for example, three different "authoritative" dates for Sir Sidney's escape from the Temple. Then one authority says it happened in the morning, another in the evening; and other writers add incidents like biblical apocrypha that are preposterous on their face, yet are presented as fact. Even Sir Sidney's own account, written when he got back to England, is questionable in many respects. Nevertheless, one must press on.

I have used, wherever possible, accounts written at the time or at least within Sir Sidney's lifetime. From these I've tried to look for patterns of agreement, and things that could have at least plausibly happened. The fact versus fiction in this chapter breaks out as follows.

The message that Smith wrote to Napoleon on his prison wall was real—word for word. It was later reported in the French newspapers and became known as "Smith's Prophecy." It is the reason, many believe, that in 1808 Napoleon ordered most of the Temple torn down in order to make sure the prophecy did not come true. Napoleon III tore down the remainder of the Temple about 1860, and the site survives today as a park near a Paris Metro stop called "The Temple."

The safe house they used to stage his escape was indeed located on the Rue de l'Université, but I could not determine its exact location. I placed it near the Hotel d'Auvergne for no particular reason other than it was a well-known landmark.

The planning meeting with Susan Whitney did not happen (How could it, as Susan is a fictional character—almost forgot, didn't ya?), but the people involved in the rescue plot were real and as described. They include: Jacques Tromelin, Louis Boisgirard, Le Grand de Palluau, Hyde de Neuville, and Picard de Phélippeaux.

The escape from the Temple took place as described and is considered one of the most daring prison breaks of all time. In fact, to this day you will see the basic outline popping up in the plot lines of modern fiction books.

While Phélippeaux waited in the carriage with Tromelin on top, Boisgirard and Le Grand appeared as officers and presented an officially signed, but otherwise forged, document, stolen from the Minister of Marine's office. Hyde de Neuville, Viscovitch, Laban and Sourdat milled around inconspicuously in the vicinity of the carriage in case anything should go wrong. The wording of the release order is exact, as are their stories, as is Smith's cleverly worded statement: "...I give you my word... that I will accompany you wherever you choose to take me." In wording it in just that way he avoided the horrific dishonor of breaking a parole agreement.

The driver started off as described but soon crashed the carriage, injuring a pedestrian, drawing a hostile crowd, and forcing the passengers to scatter and flee on foot. The streets they followed to the safe house are based on an 1834 map of Paris and represents their probable route.

The meeting between First Lord Spencer and Admiral of the Fleet Gambier with Parish is fictional, although both men occupied those posts at the time. Throughout this book any resemblance between William Parish, a fictional character, and my cousin and his wife—both talented musicians—is purely coincidental (right!); but the information concerning the use of cyphers is accurate.

Now, I know what you're going to say. "What's up with having them have a carriage breakdown twice in two days? Can't you think up anything besides crashing carriages?" And you'd be right. I'd never put two such occurrences back-to-back in a plot line—except that's what actually happened.

The specific route they took out of Paris and to Le Havre is fictional, but it is probable and is based on a series of 1790 maps.

When the escape was discovered the proverbial excrement hit the fan, but no real attempt was made to look for the negligent officials, as it would make too many high-ranking persons look bad. The only person to suffer was the most innocent of all, the jailer, Boniface. He was fired from his job and arrested for being a Royalist sympathizer. He wasn't, of course, but the experience so soured him on the Republic that he became an anarchist. This also did him no good, and he was eventually exiled to the Seychelles Islands. He died in poverty in Besançon, France in 1803.

The incident with the fisherman during their escape is fictional, or at least I think it is. It's based on a tale that I found in an 1865 document, but whether that document was intended to be fact or fiction is unclear. Nevertheless, it was a good story and a good story is a terrible thing to waste, so I decided to go with it.

CHAPTER THREE

The hoopla surrounding Sir Sidney's return to England after his escape actually occurred—including the writing of songs and plays. He was not at all comfortable with the attention, and retired to Bath to get away from it. That didn't help as the attention just followed him there.

The scene where Sir Sidney is visited by the student delegation from Bath Grammar School actually happened. And, yes, the Thomas De Quincey mentioned in that scene was the same Thomas De Quincey who later became the famous author (*Confessions of an English Opium-Eater*, etc.). De Quincey relates the incident in his *Autobiographic Sketches*, which is where I got it.

As a side note, it might be asked: if Sir Sidney were really the self-promoting egotist that historians tend to paint—why did he hide behind a delegation of schoolboys when confronted with adulation? As De Quincy writes in later life in his *Sketches*, "...to this hour it remains a mystery with me, why and how it came about, that in every distribution of honors [throughout his career] Sir Sidney was overlooked."

I think I know why this "oversight" took place; but I am afraid you'll have to read the remainder of these novels to find out. (I know... I am being mean.)

The interaction between Admiral Gambier and Parish is fictional, but Gambier was real and the information about early ciphers is accurate.

From here until Sir Sidney takes command of the *Tigre*, the plot becomes largely fictional with regard to Sir Sidney's activities. However, as you will see, most of the incidents, events, locations and people I describe were quite real. But, to get you to those events and locations, I somehow had to get the characters there.

The *Mutine* was a real ship, and was captained by Lt. Thomas Hardy, who had captured her about a year earlier. The ship was a small brig-sloop and was as described—or at least as close as I can make it by studying other ships like her. She played an important role in Nelson's cornering of the French fleet at the Battle of the Nile; but was *not* in England at the time described here. Like I said, I've got to get you to the action and the *Mutine* was as good a vehicle as any.

The French officers, Joseph-Marie Moiret and Jean-Honoré Horace Say, were real; and most of the French side of the story in this book and the next will be told through their eyes. Why? Because they both wrote journals of their experiences in Egypt under Napoleon, and that's where I got most of the information. Believe me, I would never have given a character the last name of "Say," if only to avoid ever having to write: "Say said."

And before you ask... Yes, Horatio Nelson really did hate the name "Horatio" and preferred to be called "Horace." His mother, Catherine Nelson was the great-niece of Sir Robert Walpole, the famous prime minister; but her first five children all bore traditional Nelson family names. When her sixth child was born on September 29, 1758, she drew the line. This child would have a Walpole name: Horatio.

Admiral Jervis gave Nelson the squadron, as described, and ran into a lot of hot water as a result. More senior officers, notably Sir William Parker and Sir John Orde, were extremely miffed that so junior an admiral should get such a plum command. And Orde really did challenge Jervis to a dual as a result.

CHAPTER FOUR

The information about the storm that caught the *Vanguard*, and the damage she suffered, is mostly accurate. It was taken from a letter Captain Berry wrote to his father-in-law a week or so later.

After the storm was over, the *Vanguard* had to be towed by the *Alexander,* who refused to cast-off and "shift for herself" when they were later becalmed. Nelson and Captain Ball of the Alexander had not previously been very close. After this incident, however, Nelson and he become fast friends.

Nelson's belief that the storm was sent by God to check his vanity is true. Afterwards, to his wife he wrote: "I ought not to call what has happened to the *Vanguard* by the cold name of accident: I believe firmly it was the Almighty's goodness, to check my consummate vanity. I hope it has made me a better officer, as I feel confident it has made me a better man."

Nelson's sojourn to St. Pierre for repairs happened, as did the loss of the frigates. The four ships decided to return to Gibraltar, without orders, assuming that Nelson and the other 74's would do the same thing. Bad decision. This lack of frigate scouts was to severely hamper Nelson's later efforts to locate the French fleet—although why he couldn't have used the *Leander* (50), the *Mutine* (brig) and a few of his 74's in this capacity, I've never been able to understand.

The *Mutine's* journey to Gibraltar is fictional, but the description of the town and of Lucas and Susan's trip up "the rock" is not. I based much of it on a travelogue written in 1889 and there is no reason to suppose it would have looked a whole lot different ninety years earlier.

The history of the development of the 74-gun ship is accurate, as was the mystery of where Napoleon had gone. Everyone had an opinion, but no one actually knew.

The contentious meeting between Smith and Jervis never happened; but it easily could have, or at least something like it. I believe Jervis saw Smith as a dangerous rival to his protege, Horatio Nelson. Smith saw Jervis as a fraud, and Nelson as pretentious and overestimated. No, I can not e-mail anyone a specific citation backing up that statement; but after reading as much of the primary source material as I have, that conclusion, to me, is inescapable.

Parish's explanation of the French code is accurate. It's called a Vigenère cipher after the French diplomat and cryptographer, Blaise de Vigenère, and at the time was considered unbreakable.

CHAPTER FIVE

The fall of Malta was a bit more involved than portrayed here, but the essential elements are covered. The Knights of St. John of Jerusalem—the Hospitallers—after a glorious 700 year history, were basically sold out by their own leaders. Matthius Poussielgue was indeed Napoleon's friend and confidant, and was sent to Malta specifically to prepare the way for him. Napoleon later remarked, "I took Malta when I was in Mantua," which was the city in Italy from which he dispatched Poussielgue.

Smiths interview with Spencer, as with his confrontation with Jervis in the previous chapter, never happened; but his opinion of Smith is accurate as is his assessment of John Wesley Wright. As Nelson was a protege of Jervis, Smith was a protege of Spencer. He saw something in Smith that many others did not, and he believed in his abilities. As mentioned earlier, Smith was heavily involved in espionage, which might account for some of his behavior. Spencer would have known about Smith's duties in that regard, Jervis and Nelson would not.

The sighting of the ships, outlying scouts for the French fleet that Nelson was seeking, actually happened. In his haste to get to Egypt, Nelson sailed right by the fleet he was so desperately trying to find. One might speculate as to how history might have changed if Nelson had said something obvious like: "What? Strange Sail? They can't be ours, so maybe I should send someone to investigate."

The letter of appointment that Smith read to his crew is accurate, as is his assessment of what it meant and the hordes of officers who would be more than willing to accept them. Spencer's orders were exactly as presented.

Upon arrival, Nelson indeed did not find the French in Alexandria—he had passed them a few days earlier, remember?

Jervis' second meeting with Smith in Gibraltar is fictional as described. They did meet, but it was in Rosia House, not aboard ship. I have no idea what they said at that meeting. It is true, however, that Jervis did raise formal objection to Smith's appointment, and the quotation from the letter from Lord Spencer trying to smooth things over is accurate.

CHAPTER SIX

The opening sections of this chapter are mostly based on fact. The incident where the Egyptian governor (*kashif*), threw out the British delegation that was trying to warn him that the French were coming actually happened. The French consul in Alexandria was Charles Magallon and Napoleon sent for him as described. His local knowledge was invaluable to the invasion planning.

The invasion actually occurred near the village of Marabut; and Admiral Brueys was dead set against it. As I have him say: "Landing at night, in uncharted waters, in a gale, is a prescription for disaster," but Napoleon overruled him. And many French soldiers died as a result.

The description of Alexandria as a semi-ruin is accurate and is taken from contemporary travel accounts; and Ernest Misset was indeed the British consul in Alexandria at the time of Napoleon's invasion.

The French landing and attack on Alexandria was difficult to write, but not because I lacked information. I had several accounts to draw from. The problem was that they were all contradictory. So, I wound up describing those events in which I found a consensus, and choosing from the others those that made for a good plot development. Among the things that apparently did occur...

The landing was indeed a mess with boats overturning and soldiers drowning in great numbers.

The wording of el-Kurrayyim's message is accurate and he really did send it to Cairo thirteen times that night. Napoleon's message demanding surrender is also accurate.

The French practice of forming into squares to defend themselves against cavalry was a well established technique in western warfare; but it was completely new to the Mamelukes. The only way a square can be broken is with cannon fire. Unfortunately for the Mamelukes, the sum total of their tactical playbook consisted of "scream and charge." This was the all the edge Napoleon needed, and the technique was used time after time to defeat them.

George Bellman is a fictional character. In the first draft of this book I had named him George Bellamy who was the actual surgeon aboard the *Bellerophon*; but then I chickened out. The real George Bellamy was *not* the laudanum addict and general all-around creep portrayed here. In fact, in my reading of the source documents, he performed admirably—even heroically—throughout the Battle of the Nile. I decided I couldn't tarnish the man's good name; but I still needed a "heavy" to ratchet-up the tension on Susan and Terry. So I changed it to Bellman.

Nelson's letter to his wife, written off Syracuse, is accurate. "Glory is my object, and that alone."

Napoleon was in fact shot at by a sniper in Alexandria and the ball came close enough to clip a part of his boot. While Captain Say was a real person, the episode at the mosque did not occur. It was just my way of getting Lucas and William back into the plot.

As Horace Say was real, so was his brother Jean-Baptiste Say. He was a famous economist, created "Say's Law" which is studied even today, was a clerk in Croydon, England, and lived in London for a while.

Murad Bey was as described, and the meeting of the Cairo Beys took place as described. At that meeting the French were reported to be other-worldly monsters; and, for lack of anything better to do, it was proposed that all the Christian's in Cairo be killed. Fortunately cooler heads prevailed and they were only thrown into jails.

Sidney Smith's meeting with his brother, Spencer Smith, took place as described, although I had to time-shift events somewhat. The *Tigre* did go to Constantinople, and Sidney and Spencer did team up, but it was several months after the Battle of the Nile—not before it. Spencer Smith's biography is accurate. For being a diplomat, he was a rather interesting person, but quite overshadowed by his brother.

The description of Sultan Selim III's palace and grounds is very accurate. Fortunately, the Topkapi Palace still exists and is a major tourist attraction in Istanbul, which means pictures and maps abound. I took special care in setting that scene because we will be coming back to it in this book and especially in the next (*Acre* - which I hope will be out in 2010).

CHAPTER SEVEN

Napoleon's fears with regard to the British fleet coming back, going up the Nile and trapping him, were very real. That was the main reason he chose to march his troops overland—a rather bad decision.

Dominique-Jean Larrey was indeed the chief surgeon of the French Army and his biographical information is accurate. Not mentioned however was that Larrey had a boss with whom he did not get along at all. This was René Desgenettes, who was the army's physician-in-chief. Perhaps I'll explore this tension in the next book. It would have been too much of a digression in this one.

The march to Cairo in the August heat was not as bad as I depicted it. It was worse. I only had room to touch on the torment they went through. The incident at the wells, for example, where men were trampled to death trying to get water, actually happened. And the incident with the woman who had been cast out of her village for adultery... yup, that happened too. As with so much in these Sidney Smith novels, I couldn't make this stuff up if I tried.

When Nelson got to Syracuse, he knew he was in trouble. He had not found the French and he knew that if they were off conquering some country or another the blame would be laid squarely at his doorstep. The letter he wrote to St. Vincent is accurate and I believe was intended to lay the basis for a "lack of frigates" defense in case he needed to use it later on. His letter to Sir William Hamilton is also accurate, even though the victualing arrangements were more the work of Emma Hamilton than Sir William. The gushing letter he had received earlier from Lady Hamilton is quoted in its entirety.

The French Army's rush to the Nile and to the melon patches happened as described. So did the men drowning, the crocodiles eating, the tiny leeches burrowing, and the massive dysentery that resulted from eating the melons.

The Battle of Chobrakit took place as described and was the point that Napoleon knew he had little to fear from the Mamelukes. He knew he could beat them. I did not go into the Battle of the Pyramids because it would have just been more of the same. Besides, everyone's heard of the Battle of the Pyramids—have you ever heard of the Battle of Chobrakit before now?

The French galley-slaves being held in Constantinople were real, although they came first to the notice of Spencer Smith via a letter that had been smuggled out of the prison. Nevertheless, Sidney Smith did appeal to the sultan for their release and rented a small ship out of his own pocket to take them safely back to France. That ship was commanded by Midshipman Beecroft. We will see more of Midshipmen Charles Beecroft and Richard Janverin in the next book. Neither are fictional characters, and played important roles in the defense of Acre.

The meeting with Selim III concerning what to do about the French invasion of Egypt was my invention, but Smith's plan for offering an immediate return to France to anyone who would turn themselves in was real. This kind of psychological warfare was to become a common occurrence. You will see Smith and Napoleon playing mind games with each other throughout the remainder of these books, just as they did in real life.

Dominique-Jean Larrey was a really interesting person. He in fact invented the "flying ambulance" which permanently changed the way wounded were evacuated from the field of battle. He really did invent the process of "triaging" injured people, a policy that is a routine part of any disaster response, military or otherwise, up to the present day. Not mentioned was the fact that he also invented the forerunner of today's MASH (Mobile Army Surgical Hospital) units. At the Battle of Waterloo, the Duke of Wellington actually gave orders to not fire in his direction. But I am getting ahead of my story (Yes, Sidney Smith was in fact also at Waterloo, and therefore so eventually will you.).

Nelson was indeed devastated when he thought that he had again missed the French battle fleet. Couple that with the fact that the French had obviously landed their troops and taken Alexandria, and Nelson knew his career was over. One can only imagine his relief when the *Zealous* reported that the French fleet had been found in Aboukir Bay.

CHAPTER EIGHT

The description that I had Berry read to Nelson is a quote from *The English Pilot*. Printed in 1677, it was all the information they had on Aboukir Bay. Foley was able to perform his maneuver of getting behind the French because, as described, he had a much more recent copy of the *Petite Atlas Maritime*.

The issue of whether to attack immediately or wait until morning was a very real one for Nelson, with the pros and cons as stated. When he did decide to go immediately, the flag sequence he sent is accurate, as is the description of how a ship prepares for battle.

The description of how a ship anchors by the stern, and how a "spring" worked, is also accurate. Nelson's orders in this regard was one of the key elements in his victory.

The descriptions of gunnery and the firing of the guns throughout this chapter is accurate.

The Flag Captain on board the *Orient* was indeed Luc Casabianca. With him he had his 10 year old son, who died when the *Orient* blew up. It was this boy who later became immortalized in the poem "Casabianca" by Felicia Hemans which starts out:

> The boy stood on the burning deck
> Whence all but he had fled;
> The flame that lit the battle's wreck
> Shone round him o'er the dead.

The description of Admiral Brueys is accurate, as well as his analysis of what Nelson was going to do and why he would do it. He (obviously) guessed wrong. But there are a whole lot of unanswered questions concerning this battle.

For example, why was Brueys at anchor in Aboukir Bay at all? Many have speculated that it was because Napoleon ordered it, and then shifted the blame to Brueys to cover his mistake. That Brueys had died in the battle made this conveniently possible. Why did Brueys not have frigates out as scouts to give him ample warning that the British fleet was coming? He had the frigates and certainly knew that the British were out looking for him. No one knows the answer to that. Chalk-up a mistake in Brueys' column.

Why didn't the French captains run the cables between the ships that would have hindered the British from getting behind them? No one knows. Why didn't Brueys move his ships closer to shore where the shallow water would have kept the British from doubling them, whether the cables had been run or not? No one knows. And the biggie: Why did the rear of the French line sit there, fat, dumb and happy, while the front was being chewed up by the British? The excuses range from "the wind was against them" to "they had no orders;" but none of the excuses make any sense to me. The British won the battle because they doubled the French line and started eating it up a piece at a time. If the French rear had gotten underway, they could have doubled the British.

It was a fascinating battle with many twists, turns, and interesting details—only a portion of which could be presented here. (Hey, it's a novel, not a history book.)

The details of how the battle unfolded are accurate, or as accurate as it can be given the multiple, often conflicting, accounts.

The fate of the *Bellerophon* is accurate, up to and including the names of the officers involved and what happened to them. Lieutenant Cathcart, the 24 year old third lieutenant, indeed suddenly found himself as the only officer remaining alive on his ship and performed heroically under very difficult circumstances. After the battle, he was promoted to captain.

The names and descriptions of the patients treated by Walker are accurate. They are taken from an account written by the actual ship's surgeon, George Bellamy. And, no, a ship the size of the *Bellerophon* would *not* have had more than one surgeon. A 60- to 80-gun ship would typically have one surgeon and three to five surgeon's mates; and that is probably just as well. Where would the drama have come from if I had described the *Bellerophon* as a floating Mayo Clinic?

The explosion of the *Orient*, around 10:00, took place as described. It effectively ended the battle, although some fighting went on until 3:00 AM. Brueys died as described.

And the *Bellerophon*... They did indeed find her the following morning, six miles away, flying the British flag from the stump of a mast.

CHAPTER NINE

Nelson's injury happened. He was hit on the forehead by a piece of langridge shot and the events transpired as described. As a result of this injury, Nelson was to suffer from severe headaches for the rest of his life. Indeed, many historians have speculated that it resulted in a frontal lobe brain injury, which would explain some of his more erratic behavior in later years.

His actual letter to Admiral John Jervis is quoted in it's entirety. It's interesting to note, however, that no specific captain's name was mentioned in the dispatch other than Captain Berry. This must have frosted-off his second-in-command, James Saumarez, as well as many others, as this kind of important recognition would traditionally have come in the initial dispatch.

The quote from Sir Sidney's letter to Sir William Hamilton is substantively correct. I edited it a bit (it was originally one long sentence) to make it easier for the modern reader to follow.

Napoleon did indeed make that offer to Murad Bey through the Austrian consul. Ironically, the consul was dispatched to the Mamelukes on August 1, 1798—the day that the Battle of the Nile was fought. Murad Bey's reply is a direct quote; and historians assume he made it because he knew of the French naval defeat.

Although the letter from Dominique Larrey to his wife was fictional, the quote from Napoleon about their new-found opportunities is reportedly accurate.

What happens next to Napoleon, Sir Sidney, Nelson, Susan, and Lucas will require your reading the next volume in this series.

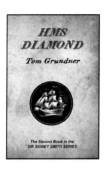

Lightning Source UK Ltd.
Milton Keynes UK
28 January 2011

166546UK00009B/85/P